NEAR MISS

A cozy British mystery

TRAUDE AILINGER

THE
BOOK
FOLKS

Published by The Book Folks

London, 2022

© Traude Ailinger

ISBN 978-1-80462-007-6

www.thebookfolks.com

NEAR MISS is the first book in a series of amateur sleuth mystery titles set in Edinburgh. For details about subsequent books, head to the back of this one.

Prologue

Fabian was disappointed. Fifteen minutes, Danny had said, and you'll be blown away. Really blown away, not like last time. Danny had carefully wiped the tiny specks of white powder off the desk and, with a wink at him, disappeared to speed up the party for the others. He looked at his phone again. Seventeen minutes and, apart from a tingling in his nose, he felt nothing.

Last time. He still cringed with the humiliation of it all. Danny had organised some weed for everybody and soon the first joint had been handed round. He had puffed and puffed but couldn't inhale without coughing his heart out, and all the others had laughed at him and told him not to waste the good stuff. Soon they all sat there staring into some sort of Nirvana with a dumb smile on their lips, while he had tried to get drunk on a bottle of Baileys and thrown up in the toilet. He was so useless, he couldn't even get drunk, let alone high. No wonder Connie never looked at him. He was just another posh bore, and two years younger to boot, and they said she liked a big, bad boy.

When he had slipped Connie's name into the conversation at home, Tristan had frowned and told him to stay away from her. She was bad news, he had muttered. Easy for him to say. He was in the cool crowd, full back in the 1st XV rugby team, and he? Rubbish at sport and pretty rubbish at everything else. He imagined his father's disappointed face when he would have to show him his GCSE certificates. Thank God the results didn't come out until August, so he'd get some peace at least until then.

Pricking up his ears at the mention of a potentially unsuitable girlfriend, his father had looked up from his newspaper to pass on his usual piece of wisdom. Work hard, get a good job and then find yourself a nice girl, he had said. What did he know, eh? He was old and would never do anything exciting in his life again. If he ever had done anything exciting at all. The only thing that got him going were old trains. Trains! And not even the fast ones, like the Japanese bullet train, no, choo-choo trains. Choo-choo! Choo-choo! He repeated the sound a few times and couldn't stop laughing. Then suddenly everything became clear. Why did he listen to the old fart anyway? Or to anybody, for that matter? He was clever, he was strong, he could do anything he wanted, and what he wanted more than anything was Connie. He looked down at his crotch. He'd never had an erection like that before, ever. This was his night, and tonight he would show Connie what he was made of.

He burst open the door of his room. He was almost propelled back by the wall of noise that hit him. Jungle drums beat in the rhythm of his heart, faster and faster. He ran downstairs, no, he flew, his legs barely touching the carpet. The living room was a riot of colours, everybody seemed to be wearing huge exotic flowers instead of clothes, and the brightest flower of all was Connie's dress, red, blood-red, undulating around her body. It was that body he needed to possess, right now.

He grabbed her arm and dragged her into the next room telling her how he had always, always, always loved her. She giggled and protested, but he knew it was only to tease him. He threw himself on top of her. She screamed. That was good, he knew people were noisy when they had great sex. He would give her the best time ever, he was just going to smash it, and Connie would never look at another boy again. But what was this? A gang of gorillas grabbed him and pulled him off her, and the one with the face of Connie's boyfriend punched him so hard on the chin that he fell backwards onto the floor. Open jaws were roaring at him, threatening to kill him!

He jumped up and ran, ran out of the room, across the hall, up the stairs. They came after him, but he was faster, as fast as lightning up the ladder to the loft. He banged the trapdoor shut and stood on it. He heard the creaking of the rungs under their weight, their fists banging against the trapdoor. How dark it was here, the black enclosing him, tighter and tighter. It smelled of decay. He was trapped, he was suffocating! He looked around in a panic. A pale moonbeam pointed him to the skylight. He ran across, pushed it open and pulled himself out onto the roof. The cold night air chilled the sweat that was running down his face and back and, looking up in wonder, he took a deep, deep breath.

The sky was a giant black onyx and all across it stars were exploding. He exhaled a wispy cloud that seemed to drift forever before it dissipated. Footsteps in the loft. They were coming. He scrambled down the slippery slope to the edge. One tile came loose and bounced over the drainpipe. He sat, stock still, listening to the throbbing silence and waiting for the deafening sound as the slate shattered on the tarmac of the drive. It sounded like a bomb exploding but there was no time to savour the moment. One of the gorillas had pulled himself up onto the roof, gasping and trying to shout but only a pathetic squeak came out of its mouth.

He laughed. No chance they'd get him! He would be free! He stood up straight, stretched out his arms towards the fireworks in the sky and took flight. But he wasn't going up to the stars. With a sense of bitter disappointment and a sudden realisation that he had failed yet again, he plummeted towards the earth that opened up to receive him into her unforgiving darkness. He felt nothing as he hit the ground.

Chapter 1

Four years later

Detective Inspector Russell McCord set down his tray on a table in the police canteen and draped his jacket carefully over the back of his chair before sitting down. Friday lunches were not too bad – Scotch broth, fish and chips, and custard sponge for dessert. He put all his dishes and cutlery neatly on the table in front of him and leant the empty tray against the legs of his chair. Detective Sergeant Gavin Fraser was less fussy about eating from a tray and started on the soup straightaway.

At first glance, they were an ill-matched pair. The boss was in his thirties although his sharp features and short, wiry frame made it difficult to guess his age. He looked no different now from when he was twenty and would probably look the same in his sixties. Neatly dressed in an inexpensive suit and tie, brimming with nervous energy, and forever chewing nicotine gum in his quest to beat his smoking habit, he was as single-minded as a sniffer dog when in pursuit of a suspect. His sergeant had twenty years on him, and it showed. Too many beers and takeaways had left their deposits not only on his waist but also on his shirts, and DI McCord had to tell him regularly to smarten up, reprimands which he took in good humour.

On their way in, McCord had briefly nodded at his colleagues, regarding this silent greeting as ample social interaction, while DS Fraser had heartily slapped every shoulder in his reach and enquired about the missus and the bairns.

"Has the post-mortem report on the Dalkeith stabbing come over yet?" DI McCord asked.

With affected indignation DS Fraser pointed to his soup.

"It's my lunch break, d'you mind?"

McCord smiled against his will. He liked Gavin Fraser, mainly because they came from the same place. Both had grown up in council houses in Niddrie but while Fraser had worked his way up from bobby on the beat to sergeant, a rank he was unlikely to leave behind, McCord had become a detective through the graduate programme and was on track to become a DCI. Despite the difference in rank, they had dispensed with all formalities and adherence to political correctness between them, which helped McCord to relax.

DS Fraser dipped a forkful of his battered fish into the tartare sauce and told McCord about the new shopping centre that was planned in Niddrie, which was ludicrous in his view because nobody there had money to buy anything anyway. People were either stuck in the hamster wheel of low-paid jobs that barely paid the rent or they sat at home merely existing rather than living on social security.

"It's because these folks don't have the get-up-and-go," Fraser said as some of the tartare sauce landed on his tie. "If ye wanna get anywhere in this life, ye've got to take a chance."

McCord nodded although it did not feel like he had taken a chance. His journey to DI had been more of an endless slog of studying, training and doing without.

"It's also about being *given* a chance," he said. "If my dad hadn't been on my back about education and my

5

teachers hadn't believed in me and got me into the scholarship programme, I wouldn't be here either."

"Teachers," Fraser snorted. "Don't get me started on them."

"Come on," McCord reminded him, "without good old Miss Balfour you wouldn't have two O-Grades to rub together."

Fraser grimaced at the memory of the belt.

"By Jove, the bitch could whack."

"You probably deserved every bit of it." McCord grinned. "By the time I got her, they had done away with the belt, but she still put the fear of death into us. Taught me how to write a good report, though."

Fraser tilted his head in acquiescence. "Still, if I could've, I would've taken the belt to *her*, I tell you."

He was interrupted by the buzz of his phone. He checked the screen and looked regretfully at his untouched custard sponge.

"Got to take this. Garage," he added, seeing McCord's questioning look. Ignoring his tray, he hurried out of the noisy canteen.

McCord was just debating with himself whether to eat Fraser's dessert as well or go back to his desk when DI Stuart Marshall approached his table.

"Do you have a minute for a chat?"

McCord pointed to the vacant chair. DI Marshall was a thoughtful, permanently stressed father of three, who worked in Vice. McCord had liaised with him on the case of the murdered prostitutes in Leith a few years ago, and the former hardliner had since taken a more moderate approach. A 'chat' with him did not mean idle gossip.

DI Marshall looked around to see if anybody was hovering around, but the tables were well spread out and there was no chance of anybody overhearing their conversation.

"Tell me, what can Homicide do for Vice?" McCord asked. "You're not telling me somebody has done the world a favour and bumped off Archie Turnbull?"

"I wish. That bastard with his lawyers has slipped through my fingers so many times I've lost count. He's about to spoil my career prospects."

"So, this is about Turnbull?"

DI Marshall threw up his hands in frustration. "Somebody is beating up and raping his girls."

McCord's lips curled in disgust. "I thought that was Turnbull's privilege."

Turnbull's 'girls' were usually underage and came from Albania, having been promised jobs in the 'hospitality' industry. On arrival, they found themselves without passports or money and at the mercy of one of the most feared men in Edinburgh.

"I was wondering if you had heard anything."

McCord's dark eyes narrowed.

"Why would I have heard anything?" he asked, although he knew exactly why.

DI Marshall shifted uncomfortably in his chair and lowered his voice to a whisper.

"Well, people say that you have a lot of time for the ladies of the night."

"Do they now," McCord replied coolly. "On the other hand, maybe I don't have time for unscrupulous men who exploit vulnerable women."

"It's just that you've been seen around The Orchard a few times."

"If you're that well informed," McCord retorted, putting his spoon down, "you also know that Dolly has nothing to do with Turnbull. She runs a decent establishment."

DI Marshall's mouth twitched. It was the first time in his career that anybody had called a brothel a decent establishment. McCord felt his blood pressure rise.

"Dolly's girls are grown women. The place has a licence, as you well know. The clients have a sauna and a massage, and if they want some of their private parts massaged, the girls do it if they choose to. No drugs, good hygiene. As far as I'm aware, there's been no trouble at The Orchard for ages. Dolly and I have the occasional chat, and believe it or not, she talks more sense than most of our esteemed colleagues."

"Fair enough," DI Marshall said soothingly. "I'm not accusing you of anything and I'm not judging. Just for your promotion's sake, be discreet. All I'm asking is that you keep your ear to the ground. The latest attacks have been particularly nasty."

"Did any of the victims come forward?" McCord asked, mollified. "It seems your only hope is for one of them to be brave enough to testify."

DI Marshall shook his head. "There have been rumours, but nobody is talking. Of course, the girls are terrified of Turnbull and wouldn't breathe a word without his say-so. But then again, I wouldn't have thought that he is thrilled about somebody going round messing with what he regards as his property. Ergo, this guy is either very foolish or he has something on Turnbull."

McCord scraped the last of DS Fraser's custard sponge out of the bowl. "So why is it so hard to nail that guy? We all know what he's up to."

DI Marshall bristled. "Knowing is one thing, proving it another. The last two raids we did led to nothing. No drugs to be found, half the girls had disappeared and the ones who were there weren't talking, even in custody with promises of getting them out of there."

DI McCord pulled his tray from under the table and neatly stacked his and DS Fraser's dishes. "Maybe one small fish leads to a bigger fish. I think it would be worth your while asking a few more questions about the rapist. Maybe send a female officer in undercover.

The girls might talk to someone they think is one of them. If somebody has something on Turnbull and is taking liberties with his girls, you need to find him."

The two men left the canteen and nodded goodbye. McCord went back to his desk, hoping for a quiet duty weekend with some birdwatching at Musselburgh Lagoons where a broad-billed sandpiper had recently been spotted.

Chapter 2

The evening rush hour had eased, and the Grassmarket seemed to take a deep breath before the revellers would come out to enjoy the quaint bars and restaurants lining the north end of the square. It was bathed in the diffuse twilight that seems to last for ages, unable to decide whether it is day or night. Amy Thornton, deep in thought, walked briskly along the pavement, oblivious to the sidelong glances and turning heads that followed her.

Whenever she had first toddled out of her mother's clothes shop on South Bridge as a little girl, she had had a crowd of cooing women around her within seconds. Now that she was a young woman, she drew wandering eyes to her effortless elegance and indifferent grace, as if she had stepped out of a 1960s film by the Italian director Antonioni: dark, petite, seemingly fragile and yet entirely self-contained. She ignored the inevitable attention of strangers just like the relentless easterly wind that made the Old Town shiver under its icy blasts, even now in early March when the first little daffodils in the planters on the square made a tentative promise of spring.

Cosy in her long, buttoned mohair coat and soft leather boots, her mind was occupied with the assignment that John Campbell, owner and editor of the small but respected magazine *Forth Write*, had given her, an article on the emerging fashion trend to wear trainers with every conceivable outfit, even seventies-style mini dresses. She applauded the notion that women should be comfortable rather than tormented by five-inch heels and be able to make a quick escape when needed. But having been brought up to be immaculately and stylishly dressed at all times, the concept seemed alien and plainly wrong. Amy sighed. If only John could bring himself to include a human interest and crime section in the magazine, how much more exciting her life would be!

Daydreaming about tracking down a notorious killer, she crossed the road at a green light. With her earphones rendering her deaf to the outside world, she did not notice the Toyota that raced up from a side street, until it turned the corner with squealing tyres heading straight for her. She froze, expecting the inevitable impact, but suddenly the car swerved and crashed into the low wall on the other side of the road. Amy snapped back into action and ran towards the Toyota, just in time to avoid a second car tearing round the corner. It slowed for just a second, before doing a 180-degree turn and speeding off towards Lothian Road, leaving behind the smell of burning rubber.

The front of the Toyota was smashed, the bonnet painfully warped with steam rising from the engine. She peered through the driver's window and saw a man, face down, motionlessly sprawled across the dashboard, his head covered in bloodstained glass splinters. Feeling nauseous, she averted her gaze, not daring to look again.

Instead, she fumbled for her phone to call 999 but her hands trembled too much to hit the tiny numbers. By now, the grim scene was surrounded by a crowd of onlookers, one of whom had already alerted the emergency services. A middle-aged gentleman, who identified himself as a doctor, opened the car door to see to the driver.

Amy put the phone in the pocket of her coat and turned away but stumbled on the uneven pavement. A dozen solicitous citizens asked her if she was okay, retrieved her handbag from the road, helped her over to the wall to have a seat, offering water bottles and even a flask of whisky. She just kept shaking her head until the sirens and flashing blue lights of police and an ambulance jolted her back into a state of some lucidity. She looked pleadingly at the man in the kilt who had offered her the dram, and he was only too happy to oblige. The sharp liquid burnt a trail of fire down her throat, but she felt immediately revived.

With amazing speed and efficiency, the road was cordoned off; the injured man was removed from the wreck and strapped to a stretcher to be slid into the ambulance. All she could see of him was his well-tailored suit and expensive-looking shoes. A paramedic made to come over to ask her how she was, but she waved away his offer of help, and he climbed back onto his driver's seat.

"Where are you taking him?" she called after him.

"Royal Infirmary," he shouted, slammed the door, put on the siren again and raced off.

Amy followed the ambulance with her gaze until it disappeared from sight and the sirens had given way to an eerie silence.

"Excuse me?"

A police officer, not much older than herself, sat down on the wall beside her.

"Are you up to answering a few questions, miss?"

Amy nodded and gave a clear account of the accident.

"So, you think the second car was chasing this one?"

Amy nodded again, thoughtfully.

"Yes, definitely," she said. "They slowed down for a moment as if to see what had happened to the man in the first car, then turned and accelerated away. Surely, they would have stopped unless they had something to hide?"

The young policeman continued to scribble into his notebook.

"You are going to look into this, aren't you?" she asked.

He gave a non-committal shrug.

"Do you remember anything about the other car?"

Amy screwed up her eyes in an effort to visualise the scene.

"It was Persian blue," she announced proudly.

The policeman looked up from his notepad, his face one big question mark.

"Excuse me?"

"Persian blue," Amy repeated, with the patience of someone who has to explain such obvious facts all the time, "a little lighter than Egyptian blue and with less of a purple hue than ultramarine."

"Right," answered the policeman doubtfully and added, without much hope, "make, model?"

Amy shrugged regretfully.

"Quite big, I think. Sorry, I don't know anything about cars. And it all happened so quickly. But" – she suddenly remembered – "the registration ended in AT, my initials."

He dutifully wrote this down and closed his notebook with a thud that betrayed his frustration.

"Never mind. Thank you, Miss…" He consulted his notes. "Thornton. If we have any more questions, we'll be in touch."

* * *

A little later, Amy climbed the stairs to the flat above Valerie's, her mother's fashion boutique, and suddenly it seemed as if her feet would not carry her one step further. All the way home, the events had played over and over in her head with the spectre of a lifeless, bloody figure flashing through her mind. It took her a while to insert the key into the lock and open the door. The delicious smell of her mother's chicken tikka masala pervaded the dark hall, and suddenly Amy became aware that she was starving.

At the sound of the door, her mother shot out of the kitchen, a damp strand of her pinned-up auburn hair dangling in front of her exasperated face.

"Where have you been? I've been out of my mind with worry. And the chicken is completely…" Seeing her daughter's drawn face, Valerie stopped dead in her tracks.

"What happened? Are you okay?"

Amy nodded and burst into tears. Alarmed, Valerie pulled her daughter into a tight embrace and kissed the top of her head. Amy cuddled into her mother's soft curves as she had done as a child. When the tears had finally dried up, she gently pulled away, wiped her face with a tissue and resolutely blew her nose. Then she stood on her tiptoes and gave her mother a kiss on the cheek.

"Sorry I'm late, Mum. I've got to make a call. Pour me a large malbec, would you, and while we eat your wonderful tikka masala, I'll tell you all about it."

While Valerie returned to the kitchen to open the wine, Amy found the number for the Infirmary on the Internet. It took three attempts to get through to the admissions desk. The car accident, yes. He was in theatre just now. No visitors, just immediate family. Was she immediate family? Amy hesitated.

"I was involved in the accident. I'll pop in tomorrow to see how he is. Thank you very much."

Cutting off the tired duty manager's protestations, she hung up and went through to the large dining kitchen. It was painted in the colour of a latte, which had been all the rage years ago, and the walls were covered in retro adverts for food and drink. Laid out on the large pine table was a veritable feast. While munching on poppadoms and dipping naan bread into the tangy sauce, she told her mother every detail of her adventure. Valerie listened with exclamations alternating between horror and relief.

"I really hope he pulls through," Amy interrupted her mother's musings. "It would be awful if he died because of me."

"Don't be silly." Valerie poured them another glass of wine. "Even if he did, he was speeding and putting *you* and others in danger, so on his head be it."

"But he was being chased! His life was probably in danger. Come to think of it" – she put down the glass again after taking another sip – "maybe his life is in danger even now. If they wanted something from him and realize he is still alive..."

"Hang on, hang on. You're getting carried away with your imagination. Maybe they were just boy racers."

Amy was indignant. "He is not a boy; he is a grown man. And boy racers don't wear suits and expensive shoes."

Valerie shrugged. "You know something? No more about car chases tonight. I'll find us a DVD, and then you'll get a good night's sleep."

Ignoring the dirty dishes on the table, she grabbed her glass and disappeared into the living room.

Amy nodded to herself. She did not want to think about blood anymore. She carried the dirty dishes over to the sink, rinsed them and put them into the dishwasher.

"*Fried Green Tomatoes*?" her mother's voice sounded from the living room.

One of their all-time favourites.

"Fine!"

Chapter 3

Tristan typed the hateful name into his search engine with incredible speed – he had been doing it for the last four years after all – stabbing at the letters and hitting the return key, grinding his teeth. Nothing. At least nothing new. Then, yet again, Facebook, Twitter, Snapchat, endless pages of faces but not the one he was looking for. Hours of relentless searching yielded nothing. Again.

He gulped down the last half inch of Famous Grouse straight out of the bottle. He knew by now that the alcohol would not wash away the shattered body on the driveway, but at least it blurred the image. Suddenly, in a fit of white fury, he swiped the empty bottle, Coke cans and pizza cartons off the kitchen table, sending them flying through the room.

"Where are you hiding, you bastard?" he screamed, hitting the wooden surface of the table with his clenched fist. "Where are you?!"

Chapter 4

On Saturday morning, Amy awoke with a jolt. Images from the accident flashed through her mind. Was the man in the crashed car still alive? Who was he and why had he been chased? He had almost run her over and yet, she felt responsible for the crash; after all, he had lost control of the vehicle while trying not to hit her.

Even before her first coffee, she called the hospital again but the woman at the admissions desk would not give any information over the phone. There was nothing for it; she would have to go there in person. But before that she was going to swing by the police station and make sure that the incident was investigated properly. That young PC at the scene had clearly not taken her seriously, while a superior officer might.

Her mother was already downstairs in the shop, so she popped a frozen croissant into the oven and reheated some coffee in the microwave. Flicking through *The Scotsman*, she chewed on the flaky pastry but neither gave her any satisfaction. She downed the lukewarm coffee and set off to find out what had happened to the man in the car.

* * *

The sky was a bright sapphire blue interspersed with cheerful white clouds, and St Leonard's police station was only a fifteen-minute walk away, so she made her way down Nicolson Street, turning left towards Holyrood Park.

The roads outside the squat brick building were busy that Saturday morning, but inside it was calm, and the desk sergeant greeted her with a smile. After a brief call, he pressed a button and waved her through the security door.

"DC Struthers will see you now, miss."

Detective Constable Alan Struthers looked Amy appreciatively up and down, clearly thinking that Saturday duty might have its compensations after all.

"How can I help you?" he asked in his best customer service voice and invited her to sit down.

Amy's first impression of DC Struthers was not favourable. She found herself wondering if the butterscotch tan was a result of an ill-chosen lotion or excessive use of a sunbed, and his eyes lingered on her chest a little too long.

He made a show of taking careful notes of her report, but Amy noticed the frown forming on his forehead when she mentioned the chase and saw the creases deepen during her account of the colour of the car and the fragment of the number plate. Anger bubbled up into her throat. Another PC Plod who did not take her seriously.

"I do hope you are going to investigate this case?" she asked, eyeing DC Struthers with scepticism.

He smiled winningly.

"Of course, miss. That's what we do, protecting the public. Leave it all to me."

Amy did not believe a word of it but there was nothing she could do.

"Goodbye," she said coolly, "please let me know what you find out."

"I will," he said and, with a slight bow he clearly considered gentlemanly, DC Struthers opened the door for her.

Having escorted a frustrated Amy to the exit, he breathed a sigh of relief when the door clunked shut behind her. Turning round, he was startled to find DI McCord standing in the corridor, still looking at the door Amy Thornton had just disappeared through.

"Who was that?" he asked curiously, popping a nicotine gum into his mouth.

"Nobody. A woman with a very long nose and a hyperactive imagination."

"What did she want?"

"It was just about a car accident yesterday, Traffic's already dealt with it. By the way, Gavin Fraser says he put the PM report on the Dalkeith stabbing on your desk."

* * *

The sky had clouded over when Amy entered the hospital and followed the signs to the Intensive Care Unit with mounting excitement, keeping her eyes open for a friendly, trusting face. The doors were locked, and only occasionally nurses and doctors in protective gear hurried in and out, clearly not up for a chat. Amy sat down on one of the chairs provided for waiting relatives and tried not to breathe in too deeply the smell of impending death, thinly disguised by disinfectant. In her head, she went over the speech she had rehearsed on the bus.

Eventually, an elderly nurse with short, silver-grey hair and kind eyes took pity on her.

"Can I help you?"

Amy glanced at the nurse's name tag and mustered her most charming smile.

"Yes, please, Fiona. My name is Amy Thornton, and I've come to see the man who was admitted last night after a bad car crash at the Grassmarket. I was involved in the accident and really need to know how he is."

"I'm sorry, but only close relatives are allowed to visit," the nurse said kindly.

"But he is still alive? He is going to be okay?" Amy insisted anxiously. "You see, he crashed because he was trying to avoid hitting me and I couldn't…"

Fiona spread out her palms in a soothing gesture.

"He survived surgery but is currently in a coma. I'm sorry," she added, seeing Amy's stricken face. "Most recover from that, you know. It's early days." She hesitated. "If you were involved in the accident, you'll have spoken to the police?"

"Only very briefly," Amy said, her heart beating faster. "Why?"

"They want to notify his relatives but are having difficulty identifying him, and nobody has come forward to report him missing so far."

Amy's nose twitched with the heady scent of a story.

"There was no ID in the car?"

The nurse was clearly mystified herself.

"Nothing, no credit card, only lots of cash in the wallet and an unregistered pay-as-you-go phone. The police checked out the car, of course, but the registered owner is somewhere in the Amazon on a trip of a lifetime and incommunicado, according to his mother, and she doesn't know who he lent his car to. They've asked us to keep an eye out for visitors who might know who he is."

"I don't, unfortunately. But I might have met him before. May I see him? Please?"

Fiona shook her head regretfully.

"I really am sorry, but I can't let you in."

Some machine started bleeping inside, and she rushed off.

* * *

Amy was not one to be thwarted by mere rules and regulations. The next day, she had taken up her seat at the ICU entrance again, looking out for a less fastidious NHS employee. To her disappointment, it was Fiona again who answered the doorbell.

19

Amy smiled apologetically.

"I'm sorry to trouble you again, Fiona, but I haven't slept all night worrying. How is he today?"

"There are positive signs," she said, "but he is still unconscious."

"Have his relatives turned up yet?" Amy asked, trying to sound compassionate rather than curious.

Fiona shook her head.

"Nobody. It is most odd." She had lowered her voice to a whisper as a tall, distinguished-looking gentleman in a white coat approached.

"Professor Singh," she called after him, and he turned.

"Yes, nurse?"

His dark, liquid eyes looked with slight amusement at the two women who seemed rather excited and for all the world looked like two schoolgirls accosting a teacher.

"Professor, you know the young man who came in on Friday evening who has still not been identified and has not had any visitors yet? This young lady here," she said, pointing at Amy, "was involved in the accident and is anxious to know how he is getting on."

Seeing the doubtful look on his face, Fiona quickly carried on. "I'm sure the patient would benefit from some company, and I really have no time to sit and chat. He's been lying there for two days now, and nobody has turned up for the poor lad. Could we not let Miss Thornton try to trigger his responses?"

Professor Singh considered this for a moment and turned to Amy, observing her closely.

"It is true that we think it is beneficial for a coma patient to be talked to, but this is usually done by close relatives whose voices they might recognize. May I ask how exactly you are involved?"

Amy recounted her story, emphasizing her sense of responsibility for the accident and her desire to help him regain consciousness and be reunited with his family. After she had finished, she held her breath waiting for Professor Singh to give his verdict.

"I suppose," he said eventually, "there are good medical reasons for making an exception here. But" – he raised his hand as the women's faces lit up with excitement – "only a few minutes at a time, please."

"Of course, Professor," Fiona hastily agreed.

She motioned to Amy to follow her into a room with several intensive care beds. All but one were occupied by very old people. Some of them were breathing heavily with their eyes closed as if gathering all remaining strength for their final journey; others were conscious but lost interest as soon as they had recognised her as a stranger. The bed in the far corner was surrounded by a curtain, and when Fiona pulled it aside, Amy saw the man she had been thinking of all her waking hours since Friday night. He was hooked up to a respirator and his head was heavily bandaged, but she could still make out a pale, attractive face.

"They inserted a tube into his skull to drain the liquid and relieve the pressure on the brain," Fiona explained. "But the CT and MRI scans showed no major trauma. They are quite hopeful that he will fully recover in time."

She pulled up a chair for Amy.

"There you are. I'll be just outside."

Amy pulled the curtains back round the bed and sat down.

"Hi, I'm Amy," she whispered, suddenly feeling silly talking to an unconscious man she had never met. "You had an accident when you tried to avoid hitting me. The police haven't found your relatives yet, but we'll keep looking. I hope they're also looking for the car that chased you. Don't worry, you're safe here and you're not alone. I wish you could tell me what happened, so please wake up soon."

She watched his face closely, hoping for a reaction but not even one of his long eyelashes moved. She lightly touched his hand with her fingers. "Bye for now."

She got up and left the room, nodding and smiling to the patients whose eyes were open. An old man, who had seemed beyond earthly cares when she came in, smiled back, clearly glad of any little entertainment that was to be had. Fiona was hovering at the door. Amy warmly thanked the nurse.

"I'll come back tomorrow if that's okay," said Amy. "But could you do me a favour? I'm sure that he was chased when his car crashed. Please be careful who else you let in. If you have any doubts, check with the police."

Chapter 5

On Monday morning, Amy returned reluctantly to the main office at *Forth Write* magazine. Spacious and airy, it had once been a reception room in the home of the original owner who had made his fortune in iron and steel, and her mahogany desk with numerous drawers and secret compartments stemmed from the same period. On a good day, the large Georgian windows allowed the light to stream in, but today raindrops ran down the panes as if somebody was crying in the heavens above.

The dreariness outside clearly did not affect the mood of her colleague Martin Eden, political editor and renowned cartoonist, who had noticed her muted greeting.

"Not a great weekend then?" Martin asked jokingly.

Amy shook her head.

Sensing a story, he sailed up to her desk, brightly coloured sleeves of enormous dimensions fluttering in his wake, and pulled up a chair. Grateful for a sympathetic ear, Amy told her colleague everything that had happened. Martin was in turn horrified and outraged at the events she recounted.

"Please don't worry, my darling. I'm sure he will recover. Best to distract yourself with your next article."

* * *

Amy spent a few hours listlessly collecting pictures and comments from fashion labels for the trainers-with-everything article. Every few minutes she looked at the large clock on the far wall and wished it were five o'clock. At eleven, Martin was solicitously placing a latte in front of Amy when he noticed the pictures on her desk.

"What on God's earth is *that*?" he asked, aghast.

"That," Amy said, raising her voice in disgust, "is a woman wearing Hearts socks and trainers under her wedding dress! Do you understand now what John is putting me through?!"

Martin pretended to faint when a gentle, melodious voice sounded above Amy's head, every syllable enunciated in received pronunciation.

"Remember, there is *never* anything wrong with wearing socks of the Heart of Midlothian club. My own grandfather was in the team."

Amy swivelled round, her face turning scarlet. John Campbell was as easy-going a boss as anybody could wish for, but she wondered if she had gone too far.

"Anyway, you were supposed to have fun with this," John continued, pretending not to notice her embarrassment. "Just do not be uncharitable. Not that you ever would," he added pleasantly.

Relieved, Amy nodded and looked at him with growing affection.

As always, he was dressed in chinos and an open-necked linen shirt that had clearly been ironed by a professional. This one matched the cornflower blue of his eyes. His perfectly cut, salt-and-pepper hair made him look distinguished rather than old, and the fine lines around his eyes and mouth were the result of smiles and laughter, rather than anxiety and frustration. Ignoring the trappings and supposed duties of his elevated birth, he had used the money inherited by his father to create his own little kingdom in this elegant town house in George Street, whose ground floor was occupied by the magazine's offices, while he lived in the spacious flat above.

"Well, I'll let you both get on with your work then," John said and withdrew into his office.

* * *

When the clock finally showed 5pm, Amy sent the finished trainer article to John for editing. Her temples throbbed. She logged off the computer, called goodbye to Martin and hurried to catch the bus to the Infirmary.

When she arrived at the ICU, eyes bright with anticipation, Fiona was clearly glad to see Amy again.

"No change, I'm afraid. And still nobody has reported him missing. How can that be? Such a lovely young man!"

Amy was disappointed. This was the third day after the accident, and no new developments, no leads. At least nobody had tried to get in to finish him off, she thought, but maybe they were just biding their time.

She made for the bed, more confident this time, pulled the sky-blue and primrose yellow NHS curtain around them and sat down next to her 'Mystery Man', whose file sat still empty in the documents of her laptop, waiting to be filled with an exciting story. Sheltered from the world by the colourful curtain, she took his warm, soft hand in hers and examined it. No pale marks to indicate a ring being worn. With every passing day, she became more intoxicated by the enigma surrounding him. Who was he? She dreamed up scenarios that could have brought him here and knew her sense of guilt would not release her until she had all the answers. Yet, until he woke up, there seemed little she could do.

Slowly she scanned his features, the slim, oval face, the smooth skin and the sensuous mouth. He had a strong chin and a long neck. The hospital gown had slid down, exposing on the side of his alabaster neck a maroon birthmark in the shape of a thumb.

"St Peter's Mark," she murmured, gently touching it with her thumb. It was a perfect fit. And just as St Peter had touched the fish and marked it forever, she had touched the life of this lonely, persecuted man, and she would solve the enigma that he was.

With her thumb resting on St Peter's, she suddenly had an inspiration: this was the story she had been waiting for, an intriguing mystery that was unfolding in real time. After finding out who was after him and having them arrested, she would reunite him with his family. This story would captivate her readers and show John Campbell that she was wasted writing about fashion.

Slowly, she withdrew her thumb from the birthmark and, careful not to disturb any tubes, squeezed his hand to say goodbye.

Chapter 6

It required just a wave with his police ID to get Russell McCord past the bouncer guarding the entrance to The Orchard in Clarence Street, a crumbling Victorian pile making a last stand in a road that had otherwise succumbed to squat concrete buildings whose blinking neon signs, rather than conveying a sense of cheer, reflected the misery of the sellers as well as the punters.

It was past 11pm, and the place was getting busy. In the bar area, a dimly lit Victorian lounge complete with threadbare velvety sofas and tasselled lamps, McCord saw a couple of men disappearing into a doorway labelled 'Sauna and Steam Room'.

Several of the girls, heavily made up and dressed in their professional gear, were having a drink to psych themselves up for another night's work. They smiled and gave the DI an inviting tilt of the head, but he marched straight into what was optimistically called 'the office'. It was a box room with a scarred walnut desk at the far end where the owner totted up the day's takings.

Dolly, a matronly, carefully made up fifty-something dressed in a navy skirt and a matching knitted cardigan, looked more like the landlady of a respectable B&B than a madam. When he entered the office, she was standing next to the desk, watering the huge gum tree, an incongruously fresh and clean-looking bit of décor that was far too big for the cramped space. When she saw McCord, she bared her yellow teeth in a big smile.

"That's how I like it," she rasped with a voice roughened from decades of chain-smoking, "I call, and the cops come running."

"One cop," McCord corrected her, "and in my own time."

"I appreciate that," Dolly said, suddenly serious.

The only seat was a small leather armchair covered in paperwork, so DI McCord decided to stand, and after checking the paint would not stain his suit, leaned against the wall.

"Drink?" Dolly offered, pointing to a bottle of brandy on the desk.

McCord shook his head regretfully.

"Driving."

The room was clouded in cigarette smoke. That was the one thing he hated about coming here. One second in this delicious fog, and the cravings came back with a vengeance. McCord pulled out a half-empty blister strip from his jacket pocket and popped a nicotine gum into his mouth.

"So, what's up?" he asked.

Dolly put down the watering can with a thud.

"Some scumbag has beaten up and raped one of my girls."

McCord was not impressed.

"And what am I supposed to do about it? I'm in Homicide, remember? Have you reported it?"

Dolly snorted.

"Don't be ridiculous. A girl like Candy reporting rape? She'd be laughed out of the station."

"I'm not laughing," McCord said. "Does she have a description? Distinctive features? A registration number? Did she keep any DNA?"

"No, she didn't," Dolly spat, suddenly furious. "I was looking for her because a client was waiting and found her on the bed, crying her heart out and with a shiner that won't go away for a week. The poor girl has completely gone to pieces."

"Maybe Jimmy should be more selective about whom he lets in?"

Dolly was about to swear at McCord but then remembered that he was probably the only person who was prepared to help.

"It wasn't one of our regular clients. You know very well that I don't run one of these slavery shops like next door. My girls are all of age and can leave any time they wish. But they don't. Because they get eighty per cent of their earnings and free lodgings, which is a damn sight better than any alternative they have. I look after my girls, McCord, and I've let Candy down big time!" She lit another cigarette. "The irony is that she wasn't even working at the time. She had just popped out to get some fags when that swine pulled up in his car. And the stupid girl got in."

McCord chewed thoughtfully on his gum.

"Can I speak to her?"

"Sure. She's upstairs, to the right. Her name is on the door. I told her you'd come."

He nodded and made to leave.

"Hey, McCord," Dolly called after him, "thanks."

"I haven't done anything yet," he grunted and shut the door.

* * *

When McCord knocked and called out his name, there was some hectic shuffling in Candy's room but then a shaky voice invited him to come in. Wrapped in an oversized terry bathrobe, Candy was sitting on the bed, holding a damp facecloth over her left eye. Without make-up and the hallmarks of the trade, she looked young and vulnerable, out of place in a gaudy boudoir decked out in flimsy red velvet. Her face was pale and spotty, her eyes narrowed in suspicion. McCord pulled up a chair and sat down.

"Tell me. Every detail you can remember."

Candy avoided looking at his sharp features and shrewd dark eyes. She had never seen him before and had no reason to like cops, but Dolly had told her that she could trust him. She focused on the drawn curtains of the small window looking out onto the back lane, and McCord's eyes followed her gaze.

It was there that punters had narrowly escaped when the newly established Police Scotland had made a spirited but misguided attempt to clean up the city six years ago, only to be told by a QC afterwards that the premises were licensed and that the police should back off unless they had reliable intelligence about drugs and unsanitary practices. DI Marshall had been fuming all week, and McCord's permanent grin had done nothing to assuage his feelings.

All this had happened before Candy's time, however, and to her the alley meant nothing but an additional fire escape.

"I was out for some fags and walking along the street last night when a car pulled up."

"What kind?"

Candy shrugged.

"Don't know. Posh, fast. He pulls up and asks quite nicely how his friend Mr Turnbull is. I say I don't know, and he says to get in, he would make it worth my while."

McCord frowned.

"What do you remember about him?"

"Old, white, clean-shaven, brown hair, a bit grey. Medium-height, podgy but strong. In a second, he had me in a grip and I couldn't do anything, I really couldn't." She started crying.

"What do you mean by 'old'?" McCord asked, having had experience with young people who classified everybody over forty as 'old'.

She shrugged.

"Forty? Fifty?" She briefly looked at his face. "Older than you, anyways."

"Thanks," he said drily but Candy did not crack a smile.

"Voice?"

"Normal like. Edinburgh, not posh but well spoken."

"Anything else? Any distinctive marks?"

"I don't know!" she cried out, tears streaming down her face. "I get in, he drives a few yards round the corner – it was dark, there was nobody else – and then he punches me and tells me he can do what he wants to me. I start screaming but he pulls a knife out from under the seat, holds it against my throat and rapes me. Then he chucks me out of the car and drives off."

McCord shifted uncomfortably in his seat until the sobbing subsided.

"Not much to go on, Candy," he said and got up. "I'll talk to Vice. A DI Marshall might want to speak to you. Don't worry, he's not a charmer but deep down he is a good guy."

At the door he hesitated.

"I'm sorry."

He waved goodbye to Dolly as he passed the office on his way out. The clapped-out Ford coughed and spluttered as if it was ready to give up the ghost, but after some encouraging coaxing by its owner which turned to exasperated shouting, it decided to take him home to Portobello after all.

Chapter 7

The following day Amy's phone finally rang. It was Fiona.

"I thought you would like to know – the young man has been moved out of intensive care."

"That is brilliant news." Amy beamed. "Has he said anything yet?"

"I'm afraid not, he is still in a vegetative state and unconscious. But do visit and talk to him if you like. Oh, and the police have just called. Somebody has reported a man matching his description missing and is coming tomorrow morning to identify him."

Amy just about managed to keep her voice steady.

"When is he supposed to be there?"

"Eleven o'clock, at the High Dependency Unit," Fiona said.

"Thank you so much. See you then."

Amy rushed across the room and knocked on the door of John's office.

"Come in," he called grumpily.

This was not a good start. She needed him in a good mood for what she was going to ask. Slowly, she opened the door and walked in.

Her boss was on the phone.

"Yes, Mama. Of course, Mama."

Amy smiled. She could make out the urgent pleadings of 'Mama', the stress being on the second syllable, even three yards away. John looked at her apologetically.

"She is lovely, you are right. I know, but I really cannot do lunch today... Listen, I have one of my colleagues here and we must finalize next week's issue today. I shall speak to you soon, okay? Bye now, bye!"

He put the receiver down and sighed.

"Sorry. My mother is on the offensive again. She has designated one of my distant cousins as a suitable wife. Her father commands a brewery empire."

"That is a pretty strong argument," Amy acknowledged. "And she? Bearing a striking resemblance to Mrs Doubtfire?"

He smiled wearily.

"Not at all. She is thirty-two, very attractive in a stick insect sort of way and speaks fluent French and Spanish."

"So, what are you waiting for then?"

He gave her a strange look.

"How is your mother?" he asked.

"Fine, thanks," Amy replied, surprised at the sudden change of subject. John had met Valerie a few times before when she had dropped Amy off or picked her up for lunch at the magazine by car if the weather was too inclement to walk. He had always made a point of coming out of his office to say hello and had even invited her to the office Christmas party. Hang on. How could she not have noticed before? He fancied Valerie! Surprised, she realised she liked the idea.

"Penny for your thoughts?"

She caught John's quizzing look and blushed.

"I was just thinking... Why don't you ask my mum out for a meal sometime?"

John sat up in his chair.

"Do you think she'd say yes?"

"Not sure," Amy admitted, "but it's definitely worth a try. I'll send you a text with her number."

His mind wandered off, no doubt composing this crucial message, and Amy grasped the opportunity.

"The reason I came, actually…"

"Yes?" he asked, absent-mindedly.

"Can I please have tomorrow morning off?"

His eyes focused on her again.

"May I ask why?"

Amy hesitated. It was too early to reveal her real motive. There was no story just yet. At least not one that warranted a redeployment of resources.

"I was almost run over last Friday," she said casually, noticing with satisfaction the horror on his face and pressing home her advantage. "The driver swerved to avoid hitting me and crashed. He's in hospital in a coma, and so far, the police have been unable to ID him. Tomorrow morning, somebody who might know him is coming to the hospital. I would like to see how he is and maybe speak to his relatives. After all, he is in a coma because of me."

John looked guilty.

"Of course, you can take the morning off. You should have said…"

She jumped out of her seat.

"Thank you, John," she said beaming, "you are the best!"

* * *

Outside Ward 117, Amy watched from a few metres' distance how a bored-looking PC interviewed the man who had come to identify the Mystery Man. He was a well-dressed forty-something who exuded energy and competence, the type who had a picture of his wife and two teenage children in his wallet. In other words, a reliable witness. Despite straining her ears, she could not pick up anything from the brief conversation, but it seemed to have been successful.

When the PC left, she made her move.

"Amy Thornton. Pleased to meet you."

She stretched out her hand.

The man looked at her in surprise but clearly did not mind being approached by an elegant and charming young lady. His pale, freckled face creased into a smile.

"Norman Mitchell, but everybody calls me Norrie."

Amy shook Norrie's hand and noticed favourably his dry, firm grip.

"Sorry to bother you but I was wondering if you could tell me who the man is who had the accident at the Grassmarket. I was there, you know."

Norrie nodded, and a strand of his ginger hair flopped sadly over his right eye. He swept it back with an automatic movement suggesting that this was a common occurrence.

"Geez, Angus, he's in quite a state–"

"So that is his name?" Amy butted in. "Angus…?"

"Aye, Angus Adamson. He's the owner of the pub I manage, The Pibroch. When the garage called yesterday to say he hadn't picked up his BMW after the service, and then he didn't turn up for our weekly meeting and didn't answer his phone, I thought something was amiss, so I contacted the police."

Amy tried to keep the indignation out of her tone.

"It has been five days, and you did not notice that he was gone before?"

"He often goes away for the weekend," Norrie said defensively. "Probably to see his fancy woman, I don't know. I asked him once, just friendly like, and he got quite shirty. And he is not exactly hands-on. He leaves the running of the pub to me. But he signs all the cheques. I wonder what's going to happen now."

"Are you two quite friendly, then? Do you know any of his family? It's just that I'd like to speak to them to say sorry about the accident."

There was a split second of hesitation before he answered.

"Not really. I hardly ever see him, and he's never mentioned any family."

Amy's heart sank.

"Anything at all you can tell me about him? Where is he from?"

Norrie shrugged.

"Down south, I reckon."

Amy frowned.

"England? Angus Adamson sounds Scottish, doesn't it?"

The manager shrugged.

"It does but he doesn't. Very plummy accent. Probably went to one of them posh schools, I shouldn't wonder, what with owning a pub and barely out of school."

One of those Scots with a general dislike of the English and suffering from social envy, Amy thought. Hardly surprising if a whippersnapper from the south rakes in all the money while he is doing all the work.

"He's a decent enough boss, though," Norrie added quickly as if worried about badmouthing his employer while he was in a coma.

Amy racked her brain for another question but could not think of anything that would help her further. Norrie shuffled his feet.

"Thank you so much for your time," Amy said, "I don't want to keep you."

He smiled gratefully.

"Yes, I need to get ready for lunchtime. The place is always heaving. I'm sorry I can't be of any more help. I really don't know much about him at all."

He waved goodbye and hurried off.

Amy sat down on one of the chairs, took a leather-bound notepad out of her handbag and wrote down everything she had found out. Not a lot. But at least she had a name. Angus Adamson.

* * *

The nurses' station inside the High Dependency Unit was deserted when she went in but soon a smiling young woman with spiky pink hair approached her.

"Can I help you?"

"Yes, please," Amy said. "I'm looking for Angus Adamson. Fiona said it would be okay for me to visit. Amy Thornton."

"Ah, yes. I'm Cathy. Nice to meet you. Fiona told me you'd come today. Follow me."

Cathy led her to room 3, with a name tag on the door which read 'Angus M Adamson'. It was a small room painted in the ubiquitous magnolia with a window overlooking a car park. It didn't really matter, thought Amy, after all, the patients here would not appreciate the view anyway. Angus Adamson lay on a bed surrounded by all kinds of machinery, but the tube had been removed from his nose and he was breathing unassisted. His eyes were closed.

"He is doing well, you know," Cathy announced proudly as if talking about her son winning a school prize. "His stats are improving, and he is out of immediate danger. Don't get a fright if he opens his eyes. He does that sometimes when he is awake, but he doesn't respond yet."

She pulled up a chair and motioned for Amy to sit down.

"It is nice of you to come. So many people are scared of hospitals and illness. And, you know, Angus has had no visitors until today, of course, because nobody knew who he was. It was weird talking to him without knowing his name. I always talk to them, you know, because nobody knows how aware people in a vegetative state are, and it is a terrible thought that they might just be lying there, hearing things but unable to move. Would you like a cup of tea?"

She had to pause briefly for breath.

"No, but thank you so much." Amy smiled. "Don't let me stop you from doing your job. I'm sure you are terribly busy."

Cathy nodded and made for the door.

"At least nobody is complaining." She winked. "I'll see you later."

Amy breathed a sigh of relief and turned to look at Angus Adamson.

"I bet you sometimes wish she'd shut up, don't you?"

She scanned his face for a reaction but there was nothing.

Most of his head was bandaged but enough of the face was left uncovered for her to scan his already familiar features. For all of Cathy's concerns he looked serene, and his breathing was deep and regular.

"At long last we know your name. Now we will find your family."

She lightly squeezed his hand, hoping for a reaction. It was warm as if he were just sleeping but his eyes did not even flicker.

"Come on, Angus," she whispered. She pulled out her phone and furtively took a picture of him.

Somebody dressed in white passed the door, and Amy hastily shoved her hand into her pocket.

"I'll see you tomorrow," she said quietly and left.

Chapter 8

McCord had just interviewed the prime suspect of the stabbing in Dalkeith, and after being presented with the results of the forensic examination, the young man had hung his head and confessed. Once he had been led away to sign a written statement, McCord returned to his desk. DS Fraser, who had been having a wee unofficial break, hastily slid his feet off his desk and ostensibly resumed work.

McCord dialled DI Marshall's number.

"Any news on Turnbull and the rapist?"

"Not the rapist, but we've managed to plant an undercover officer in Turnbull's organisation. Not right at the top but hopefully, he can pick up some intel on future operations. I'm a bit worried, he's quite inexperienced for such an assignment but he looks the part. Fingers crossed."

"Good luck."

McCord hung up and met DS Fraser's expectant gaze.

"Please tell me there is something more interesting going on than that stabbing," Fraser pleaded.

"Vice has placed an undercover agent trying to get to Turnbull. Mind you, if we nail him, the crime rate will drop so much that we might be doing ourselves out of a job."

Fraser chuckled.

"Unlikely. When one bastard goes, another one takes his place."

* * *

Back in her small but cosy room among her beloved Kandinsky and Macke prints, Amy spent all evening on social media but there was no trace of an Angus M Adamson anywhere, at least not one in Fife in the right age bracket, and the few she found in the rest of Scotland were not as attractive as he was. She thought that strange, for normally such a young and handsome man would leave a trail like a marauding army.

"This is not a good sign," said Valerie, who had come in to bring her a hot chocolate. "Nowadays everybody under the age of sixty leaves at least a tiny footprint on the web. My advice is to leave well alone."

Amy looked up from the screen with a frown.

"Mum, will you leave me to run my own life and choose whom I want to spend my time on?"

"I do," Valerie said defensively. "But does it have to be a vegetable that is involved with criminals? It seems to me that your interest in him is not purely professional."

Amy rolled her eyes. She really needed to get her mother off her back.

"Do you remember John, my boss, who was so attentive to you at the Christmas party?" she ventured.

Valerie nodded.

"I liked John, he seemed" – she was unused to finding positive adjectives to attach to a man – "posh but okay."

Amy laughed. "Quite so. I think he fancies you, but he is too shy to say anything. If he asked you out for a meal, would you go?"

Valerie automatically shook her head.

"Are you running a dating agency now? I thought you were supposed to find out what happened to the guy in a coma."

"One does not exclude the other. Come on, Mum, when were you last on a date? And John is quite a catch."

Valerie shrugged diffidently, but Amy could see that her mother was flattered.

"And by the way, it is work now. John has allowed me to write a weekly diary column called the Mystery Man, and the first one is coming out on Saturday, so I'd better come up with something for next week!"

Valerie sat down on the small armchair by the window. She had made the colourful curtains herself – a twenty-first birthday present for Amy.

"Anything new from the police appeal?"

"Nothing." Amy shrugged. "They're not investigating further for now because there is no crime apart from dangerous driving, and he was the only one hurt. There must be a way."

"Let's think methodically," Valerie said. "The only lead we have is this pub manager, what was his name?"

"Norrie," Amy reminded her. "He doesn't know anything. At least he says so. But I believed him."

"What did he say about Angus again?"

"That he didn't know of any family and rarely saw him. Angus often went away for the weekend, so he only realised he was missing when the garage called..."

Valerie jumped up. "That's it. Norrie doesn't know anything, but Angus's car does."

Amy began to fear for her mother's mental health. "The car?" she asked, anxiously.

"Yes! Angus's car. I bet he used the satnav. Young people nowadays don't use road maps. On the satnav there will be addresses he went to. But how...?" Valerie paused, pondering this.

Amy looked at her mother in astonishment. "You should have been a private detective, Mum."

Just then Valerie's phone rang. She looked at the screen, puzzled, and went next door to take the call.

Amy pulled out her phone and looked up the number for Angus's pub.

A harassed female voice answered.

"The Pibroch, can I help you?"

"Could I speak to Norrie, please?"

"One moment."

For a couple of minutes all she heard were murmuring voices, someone laughing loudly, a dismal attempt at singing that was shouted down in good humour and the clinking of glasses.

"Hello?"

Amy recognised the pub manager's voice.

"Hi, Norrie, Amy Thornton here. We spoke a week ago at the hospital about Angus."

He sounded surprised.

"Yes, I remember. Have you got news?"

"No, unfortunately he is still unconscious. But I had an idea how to find his relatives. Angus's own car was at a garage during the accident, wasn't it?"

"Yes, it was."

"Is it still there?"

"No, the garage didn't have space for it and after they couldn't get hold of Angus, they phoned the pub and asked if it could be picked up. Luckily, the boss keeps a set of spare keys in the office, so I did. Why?" He sounded suspicious.

"I thought I could check his satnav and see where he went..."

Amy held her breath.

"I don't know." He sounded worried. "I don't think we should... without his permission..."

Amy tried another tack.

"Who is signing off the bills? What if he dies? Who is then going to make decisions about the business? That would leave you in a terrible limbo, would it not?"

She could hear him agonize at the other end of the line and knew she had him where she wanted.

"Okay," he conceded. "I suppose you are right. Can you come tomorrow morning at nine?"

"I'll be there. Bye!"

Looking triumphantly at her mother, who had just come back into the kitchen again, she hung up.

But then a worrying thought crossed her mind.

"I'll have to ask John for the morning off – again." Amy sighed.

Valerie smiled cryptically.

"I don't think that is going to be a problem. He's just called to invite me for dinner on Saturday. Quite a coincidence, isn't it?"

She raised her eyebrows, but Amy just shrugged innocently as if she had no idea how this had come about. Valerie shook her head in mock disapproval.

"He seemed quite chuffed when I accepted."

Chapter 9

Amy arrived at The Pibroch on Cowgate precisely at the agreed time, a feat which in Edinburgh can only be achieved by walking. The pub was a neat-looking place cashing in on the tourists' demand for men in kilts and bagpipes. The sanitised and to the native obviously fake olde worlde feel was spoilt by a broken windowpane, whose cracks were crudely taped over, and a sprayed message telling somebody in less than polite terms to leave. Norrie had seen Amy coming and opened the door.

"Trouble?" she asked, pointing to the damaged window.

"Third time in two months. I've been wondering if somebody is targeting the pub because Angus is from down south. I mean, you don't have to like the English, but that sort of thing is not on. Or maybe they're just vandalising other people's property for fun. I think, we need to install CCTV. But with the boss away, I can't set that up, and I can't pay the glazier either."

"Did Angus report the incidents to the police?"

Norrie shook his head. "I told him he should, but he said no, there was no point."

Maybe there was no point because he knew who it was, Amy thought. Probably the same criminals who chased him into a coma.

"Would you like a drink?" Norrie offered politely.

"No, thanks, let's solve this case first," she declaimed brightly, but Norrie just looked at her without cracking a smile. Fair enough. He was desperately worried about the business and probably about to be complicit in a criminal offence.

The BMW stood in the tiny, still deserted parking lot of The Pibroch as if waiting for someone to pay it some attention. Norrie unlocked the car and hesitantly eased himself into the driver's seat. After a full valet, the inside of the car was immaculate and smelt of pine. Amy had hoped to get some more clues about Angus from things lying around in his car but there was nothing. She slid into the passenger side and pulled out her notebook, while Norrie started up the satnav.

He read out the postcodes, Amy scribbling furiously. Some of them he recognised as those of suppliers, and Amy crossed them out straightaway. When they came to the end of the list, Amy stroked her notebook as if it contained government secrets.

"What about that drink now?" Amy asked. "Let's go through the list and find out what these places are. When you hear the names, you might recognise them."

Norrie looked at his watch and sighed. "I suppose we'd better get on with it."

* * *

Amy had almost finished her glass of tonic light when they finally struck gold.

"Kingdom Country Club," she read as she scrolled down the website. "A posh place on the coast, just outside St Andrews. Spa, 24-hour room service etc. etc. That sounds like a place where you'd" – she looked at Norrie's M&S suit and corrected herself – "where he would spend a weekend."

She rose from her chair.

"Thanks for the drink. I'll see what I can find out there."

Norrie shook her hand, a glimmer of hope in his eyes. "Please let me know."

Amy checked her phone. There was still plenty of time to drive up to St Andrews and be back for lunch.

* * *

The Kingdom Country Club had a drive half a mile long and lined with accurately planted and brutally trimmed shrubs whose squat shapes would withstand even the howling winter gales in these bare, windswept parts. The drive curved round and ended up right in front of the main entrance, a modern monstrosity of steel and glass. As she drew up, a liveried minion bowed and beamed as if he had keenly anticipated her arrival for months. Now she wished she had gone to the car wash as she had planned, but at least her mum's ancient MG did not look entirely out of place. Amy dreaded the idea of relinquishing the keys of Valerie's most prized possession to a complete stranger who, to make matters worse, looked as if he was barely seventeen. But there was nothing for it; she had to look the part. In a fluid movement, she eased herself out of the low seat of the old-timer, assured the boy that she had no luggage he could take care of for her and handed him the key in a manner suggesting that she never parked the car herself. She could see his excitement at the chance of driving such a little gem and could not help but smile as he reverently approached the car and very gingerly drove off.

The reception area was the size of a cathedral although the only divine being worshipped here was the God of Luxury. A temple devoted unashamedly to pampering clients, it made her feel like an impostor being here on business, and a dubious one at that.

"Welcome to the Kingdom!"

The woman behind the reception desk wore a tight-fitting uniform complete with the company logo, a golden crown. "Do you have a reservation?"

Amy declined regretfully and pulled out her phone with the picture of Angus on the screen.

"I wonder if you could help me. This man is a regular guest here and…"

The receptionist did not even glance at the screen. Her smile had frozen.

"I'm afraid we can't give any information about our clients. Their privacy is extremely important to us."

And to most of them, I bet, Amy thought and wondered how many of them had something to hide.

"Of course." Amy nodded vigorously as if she was in complete agreement. "But the thing is that this man had a serious car accident, and I am trying to find his family."

The receptionist frowned.

"So why are the police not looking for them? You are not the police, are you?" she asked suspiciously.

"No, I'm… because no actual crime has been committed," Amy faltered.

The receptionist shook her head and Amy saw that she had lost her. She could have kicked herself. A clumsy amateur, that's what she was. But she wouldn't give up just yet.

"Well," she said quietly, "when I find his relatives and when he regains consciousness, I will be sure to mention how helpful you have been," – she leaned closer to read her name badge – "Stephanie. Goodbye."

She clicked Angus's picture away and made to leave.

Stephanie looked alarmed.

"I am sorry, it's not that I don't want to help. Would you like to speak to the manager?"

Amy swivelled round. "I would indeed," she said sweetly. "Thank you so much, Stephanie."

At being summoned, the manager sailed out of his office to smooth the choppy waters. He was clearly not happy to witness a dispute at the front desk where a steady trickle of guests was arriving.

"This lady is making enquiries about one of our clients," Stephanie told her boss and wrinkled her nose.

"Yes, thank you, Stephanie, I'll take it from here." He made a slight bow towards Amy. "James Kilpatrick. Would you like to step into my office, Miss...?"

"Thornton."

Amy surveyed his single-breasted suit and could not help admiring the delicate stitching on the step lapel. His obsequiousness seemed to make him an easy target, but she decided to be smarter this time. She knew that with the clothes she wore and her bearing, she looked like a member of the jet set, and yet she was asking questions as if she were a grubby PI.

He motioned to a leather armchair and offered her a drink. Amy refused on the grounds of having to drive later, hoping to exploit his obvious confusion. He listened to her story with increasing sympathy, and she was just about to congratulate herself on her interview technique when she showed Mr Kilpatrick Angus's photo. He blanched, blinked and said, a little too quickly, that this young man was to his knowledge no client of this establishment and that he was inconsolable that he was in no position to help her. Liar, Amy thought, you know him fine well.

She made a disappointed face and rose from her seat.

"Well, then I'll have to go back and just hope that he recovers soon and that his relatives contact the police eventually."

She stretched out her hand.

"I am sorry to have troubled you, Mr Kilpatrick. Goodbye."

His relief was palpable, and he even bowed to kiss her hand as she left.

"Goodbye, Miss Thornton. It was my pleasure."

The door shut with a discreet but decisive thud behind her.

* * *

Disappointed but undeterred, Amy stepped back out into the hall and surveyed the lie of the land. Stephanie was busy checking in an elderly couple, so she sneaked past the desk down the corridor leading to the restaurant and decided to have a coffee after all.

It was half twelve and the place was slowly filling up with people having a little apéritif before the strain of a three-course lunch. Amy chose a seat round the corner where she would not be spotted by a passing Stephanie or Mr Kilpatrick and kept her fingers crossed for a suitable waiter who had been on duty during weekends. And she was lucky. A tired-looking youth with an Eastern European accent that Amy could not identify took her order and was clearly taken in by her charm. She enquired about his family in Serbia and was confirmed in her initial assumption that he was here to make as much money as possible and sent most of it home to support his family. She told her story for the third time today but this time she casually left a twenty-pound note peeking out from under her wallet as she showed Miroslav Angus's photo. His eyes flitted between the two, and after a brief hesitation he came out with it.

"Yes, he come here often, every other weekend, with a woman."

Amy tried to breathe normally.

"A girlfriend?"

He shrugged.

"She's much older than him but quite attractive. I think he is a, how do you say it, gigolo? They hugged a lot and she take his hand during dinner."

Amy was puzzled. Angus seemed well-heeled as it was, without resorting to pleasuring lonely middle-aged women.

"Did they share a room?" she wondered aloud.

Again, Miroslav shrugged.

"A colleague of me did room service for her once, and she was in her own room."

He looked around nervously. Other customers had arrived, and he was clearly anxious to get away. Amy stroked her purse.

"Miroslav, can you remember her name? Or anything about her?"

"She always pay for both of them by credit card, and once she give me a big tip after she spilled half bottle of wine on floor. Mrs McAdie is her name. Big tip, I remember."

Amy lifted her purse and pushed the twenty-pound note towards the waiter.

"Thank you so much, Miroslav. Take care."

* * *

Amy left the restaurant trying not to whoop. She pretended to look at some of the glass cases containing hotel souvenirs until Stephanie turned round to fetch a client's mail and slipped out of the front door.

After she had reclaimed the MG from the liveried doorman, she drove off home towards Edinburgh mulling over what she had learned. Mrs McAdie. An affair with an older, married woman. Now she just had to find out if there was a Mr McAdie and if he knew.

Chapter 10

Amy stopped at a petrol station to pick up a salmon sandwich and a bottle of water and drove straight to George Street. Miraculously, she found a parking space in Queen Street and walked the few hundred yards to the magazine. The outer office was deserted; Martin must have gone out for lunch. On the off chance, she knocked on the door of John's office. She was lucky, he was spending the lunch hour working. He looked up, first alarmed, then amused at the excitement on her face.

"You have something, I take it?"

"I have." Amy beamed. "He has been meeting an older woman called Mrs McAdie in the Kingdom Country Club in Fife and kept it very quiet."

She looked triumphantly at John. "Do you agree now that there is a story? Can I follow that up?"

With a resigned look, he nodded.

"Fine. See what you can find out about this Mrs McAdie but be discreet. I do not want any lawyers at my door waving a libel suit. Use our newspaper archive. It looks like they are upper class, and the rags are very good at keeping tabs on them. Good luck and keep me posted. And," he added as she was already halfway through the door, "make sure you have some lunch."

She stopped. "By the way, well done getting my mum to accept your invitation. You should feel flattered."

Pleased to see John's beaming smile, she rushed to her desk.

The *Evening Star* could always be relied upon to hold the over-privileged to account. It did not take Amy long to find a reference to the McAdies from four years previously.

FIVE-STAR RESTAURANT OWNER IN THE DOCK ON TAX EVASION CHARGES

The mention of a restaurant reminded Amy that the salmon sandwich and water in her bag were getting warm. She took them out, gulped down some water and tore off the top layer of plastic from the sandwich and sniffed at the fish. It smelled delicious, and she took a big bite before reading on.

> *Today was the first day in the trial of Kenneth McAdie, 55, at the Old Bailey. Mr McAdie, who, among other venues, owns the five-star 'L'Accordéoniste' in Billingsgate as well as a two-million pad in Beechwood Gardens in Knightsbridge, is a well-known figure among the London high society. The exclusive restaurant, where a main course sets you back a week's wages, is a favourite with well-heeled politicians and celebrities. The Minister of Defence and even Oscar winner James O'Connor are said to be among the regulars. Mr McAdie appeared in court only to confirm his name and address and to hear the charges of tax evasion, to which he pleaded "not guilty". Contrary to persistent rumours before the trial, he was not charged with drug running.*

*His lawyer, John Morton-Oakley QC,
made a statement to the press
declaring that he is confident that Mr
McAdie will "swiftly be cleared of
those preposterous charges". A source
close to the family, who wishes to
remain anonymous, told the Evening
Star that there are numerous
witnesses who are willing to testify,
among them Mr McAdie's son, and are
"helping the police with their
enquiries". The CPS and Scotland Yard
declined to comment. Could this be
another case where somebody has
made his fortune on the back of the
suffering and ruined lives of so many?
Watch this space and follow our
campaign 'Death to Drugs' on
Facebook and Twitter.*

There was a picture showing Kenneth McAdie
shielding his face from the camera as he left the
courtroom. Oh Angus, what kind of people did you get
mixed up with? Amy whispered to herself. Rich,
powerful people, who always seem to get what they
want. And somebody like this Kenneth McAdie would
not have taken it lying down if he found out that a much
younger and more attractive man was having an affair
with his wife. But if he had hired some muscle to chase
Angus in a car, what would his next move be?

She took out her notebook and wrote down all the
details.

"Now let's see where this is going…"

As she took another bite and scrolled down the
pages, another article from the same week caught her
eye.

DOUBLE DEATH TRAGEDY AT LORD'S HOME

Genteel Knightsbridge was the scene of howling sirens and flashing blue lights last night when police and ambulances were called to the stately home of Lord and Lady Foveran in Beechwood Gardens after their younger son Fabian, 15, had fallen off the roof of the building. The family had hosted a party to celebrate the end of A-Level exams for Fabian's elder brother, which was attended by around a hundred young people. "It had been such a fun evening," one of the girls who was at the party told our reporter, choking on her tears, "and then it turned into a complete nightmare. I can't believe Fabian is dead. He was such a sweet guy."

But the family's suffering had only just begun. Lord Foveran, who is said to have had a pacemaker fitted recently, was at the scene of the accident within minutes and on seeing the mangled corpse of his beloved son, suffered a massive heart attack and died in the arms of his distraught wife. She, together with her elder son and some of the young people who witnessed the unfolding horror first-hand, was taken to hospital later to be treated for shock. The area of the roof where Fabian plunged to his death has been cordoned off for forensic examination and a post-mortem will be carried out, but there are widespread rumours that drugs were involved.

"I have never seen anything like it around here," Mrs Pomfreys, an elderly neighbour, who was woken up by the commotion, told us. "Who would have thought such a thing could happen here, of all places?"

Amy sighed. Rich people were not immune to tragedy either. Maybe she should do a feature on drugs in Edinburgh after this? After all, the picturesque city had a very nasty underbelly. She took another sip of her water. However, the tragedy that had befallen the Foveran family had not ended with two accidental deaths. A couple of days later the following article appeared, again in the *Evening Star*:

THIRD BODY FOUND AT KNIGHTSBRIDGE HORROR MANSION

Following our report on the violent and tragic deaths of Lord Foveran and his son Fabian, there has been another appalling development. The housekeeper, Mrs Linton, who had been tasked with looking after the house while Lady Foveran is recovering from a psychotic episode following the shocking events two days ago, made a grim discovery: yet another body at the ill-fated three-million-pound residence. "I get a phone call from the mum of one of the youngsters who was at the party. She was frantic; she heard about it the following morning and her son hadn't been in touch and didn't answer his phone. He was meant to stay over, you see. I tell her there is nobody here, but she begs me to look. So, I go through the whole place, every room and nobody is there," she told us. "Then I look out of the window and see the summerhouse and I think, maybe he is there sleeping off the booze with no idea what's happened. And there he was, lying on the floor, grey and cold as a stone. That's it. I'll never set foot in that cursed house again. Never." And who could blame the poor lady after all she has been through? The body has been removed for formal identification and a post-mortem.

Follow our campaign 'Death to Drugs' on Facebook and Twitter.

Intrigued, Amy scrolled down further.

LATEST DEVELOPMENT IN CASE OF KNIGHTSBRIDGE HORROR MANSION

The third body that was found in the summerhouse of Lord and Lady Foveran's residence on Tuesday has been identified as that of Daniel Littlejohn, 15, a friend of Lord Foveran's son Fabian, who fell to his death during a wild party hosted at the property. The coroner's verdict was "suicide by drug overdose". According to the police report, which we have been able to access, there was a glass containing residue of the drug methamphetamine, better known as 'speed', as well as a suicide note. Several witnesses have come forward with claims that Littlejohn had supplied some of his school mates, among them Lord Foveran's son Fabian, with drugs. The police have concluded that Littlejohn supplied his friend with a batch of meth, which caused hallucinations that led the fifteen-year-old to climb onto the roof. Witnesses say they heard him shout "I can fly! Watch!" immediately before he jumped to his death.

Littlejohn, having witnessed the horrific events caused by his recklessness and greed, must have been racked with guilt and unable to face the consequences, so he ran off to the summerhouse and took his own life. It seems that amidst the chaos in the villa itself, nobody thought to check the grounds and outbuildings.

Surely, uncomfortable questions will be asked of the duty officers who failed to deal with the situation in a professional manner. But the big question is: what will it take to purge our streets and homes from deadly drugs? How many more young people, privileged or poor, will have to end their unfulfilled lives shattered on a paved driveway or with a needle hanging out of their arm until society roots out this cancer of our society?

Follow our campaign 'Death to Drugs' on Facebook and Twitter.

Amy finished her sandwich. Suddenly, she craved a latte, but she had to find out what happened to the McAdie case, and thanks to the trusted *Evening Star*, it did not take her long.

McADIE TRIAL COLLAPSES

In a sensational twist during the McAdie court case, on which we have reported from the beginning, the prosecution has dropped all charges against Mr McAdie due to "lack of evidence". After his QC made a formal complaint about the way in which some of Mr McAdie's bank statements were obtained, the evidence was ruled inadmissible by the court. As his conviction seemed more and more uncertain, some witnesses retracted their statements, which fatally weakened the prosecutor's case. The CPS issued a statement that "the turn of events was most regrettable". One observer of the trial, who understandably does not want to be identified, put it more plainly: "The whole thing stinks to high heaven. What use is it chasing junkies when the big players are let off and don't even pay tax on their ill-gotten gains?"

Follow our readers' comments on our campaign 'Death to Drugs' on Facebook and Twitter.

Amy leaned back in her chair and closed her eyes, visualising the pale, handsome face of the young man, so vulnerable in his stillness. She shivered at the thought that Angus had made such a dangerous enemy. Surely now, thought Amy triumphantly, the police would have to listen.

Chapter 11

Emily pushed aside the pile of books she was supposed to read through for her history course, saved her notes on 'The European Enlightenment, c.1680-1799' and made herself a mug of tea. It was a dull, drizzly day, so she didn't resent being stuck inside. The house was quiet with her dad doing whatever he did in the city, her mum out boosting sales on Oxford Street and her brother Felix out with a friend. She was recovering from a mild bout of flu, but despite her protestations that she felt better, her mum had insisted she needed rest and should stay at home another day.

Sometimes she wondered if she shouldn't move out and enjoy the freedom other students had, but her parents argued that it would be silly to pay an exorbitant rent when she was studying at LSE and had a much more comfortable home right here. Emily had agreed, not least because she was much closer to Tristan if she stayed here.

She sat down at the kitchen table and listlessly browsed through the latest issue of *Forth Write* that her mum subscribed to because it made her feel in touch with her homeland. She read an article about the sorry state of Scotland's ferries after decades of underinvestment and shook her head at the picture of a bride wearing Hearts socks and trainers under her wedding dress. Then an article titled 'Mystery Man' caught her attention. Sipping her tea, she read the vivid account of the accident, but when St Peter's mark was mentioned, she put the mug back on the table.

She picked up her phone and googled St Peter's mark. An oval, maroon-coloured birthmark, also called the 'devil's thumbprint'.

"No," she whispered. "It can't be."

Frantically, she flicked the pages backwards and forwards, almost ripping them in the process, but there was no picture. She read the description again. And again. A young, handsome face, St Peter's mark where the neck met the shoulder. For a few minutes, she lurched from triumph to grief and back again, but then all she was left with was confusion. What was she going to do?

Chapter 12

DI McCord was sitting in front of his computer filling in forms. He enjoyed being on duty on a Saturday morning. There were rarely new reports coming in, so he had time to do the paperwork and go over his current cases without being constantly interrupted. He liked tidying up. Filing put information in the right place, not only on his desk and the computer but also inside his head. The sequence of events became clear and connections more obvious. Nothing got his goat more than these TV detectives who were unable to organise a clean shirt for themselves and only after five murders stumbled across a crumpled receipt in their pockets that finally made them realise who the killer was. In the real world, successful policing was all about detail: tedious, tenacious collecting and analysing of information. One bit of lost or contaminated evidence, and the prey escaped. And if you broke the rules, you had to be damn sure not to be caught because nobody cut you any slack.

He was just about to send his expenses claim for February to the accounts department when DS Fraser knocked perfunctorily and stuck his head into his office.

"Sorry..."

"What is it now?" McCord sighed.

"That woman who's been here before about the traffic accident is in the reception area. She only wants to speak to a senior officer. She says she has information that could prevent a murder."

"Murder?" McCord was sceptical. "Is she on drugs or just a general attention-seeker?" he enquired.

Fraser shrugged. "Looks clean but up to high doh."

McCord sighed again. "Show her in."

He looked the woman up and down whose slender back he had admired a week ago, and his heart sank. A dress that probably cost more than his monthly salary and walking on those heels as if she was born in them. Probably bored with her over-privileged life and looking for a stroll into the dark side. Under his breath he cursed Fraser for lumbering him with a deluded housewife from Morningside when she broke the silence.

"When you've finished gawping and wrinkling your nose as if I'm something the cat dragged in, you might want to hear what I've got to say? Your sergeant here" – she turned her head towards Fraser who was leaning in the door frame, blocking it almost completely – "didn't quite seem to grasp the situation."

Startled, he half-rose from his seat in a semblance of courtesy and pointed to the chair in front of his desk. He was used to people being weary of him, especially women, but this one clearly didn't take any shit.

"Fire away, Miss...?"

Against his will, he found himself fascinated by the long nose protruding from an otherwise beautiful face.

"Thornton," Amy announced.

She already regretted her outburst, not because she felt she was wrong but because he could just throw her out if he was so inclined. It was time for a peace offering.

"Thank you for seeing me. I understand you are the person in charge here."

She had taken in the detective's appearance with one glance when she came in. His powder-blue shirt was a poor choice, it made him look pale.

"I am. Detective Inspector McCord. Please have a seat," he said, remembering the superintendent's mantra: 'Hearts and Minds, Hearts and Minds.'

Amy lowered herself onto the chair and looked McCord straight in the eye.

"Last Friday I witnessed a car accident at the Grassmarket. A young man called Angus Adamson was chased by another car and crashed into a wall. He is in a coma in the Royal Infirmary."

McCord's interest waned.

"Did Traffic not make a report?"

"They did, but I don't think they took the fact that he was chased seriously although I *saw* it. And now, there have been further developments."

McCord tried to look anywhere but her nose. His eyes settled on the far wall.

"Developments?" he asked.

"He had no ID with him, and it took your colleagues four days to find out his name. Apart from the manager of the pub he owns, nobody has reported him missing, and there is no trace of him on the Internet."

McCord frowned. "What did you say your job was?"

"I didn't," Amy retorted. "I work for the *Forth Write* magazine but I don't see what that has got to do with anything."

A journalist. God help us, he thought.

"I spoke to the nurse who is looking after Angus," Amy pressed on before he could stop her, "and she told me that a woman came to visit him who refused to give her name but claimed to be a close friend. I'm sure it was a Mrs McAdie whom he's been having an affair with. They were meeting regularly in the Kingdom Country Club at weekends."

"You have been busy," McCord remarked sarcastically. "Anything else?"

"Mrs McAdie's husband is Kenneth McAdie, by all accounts a nasty piece of work. He was acquitted of charges of tax evasion and drug running because of a technicality four years ago. I think he is after Angus Adamson to punish him for the affair with his wife."

Kenneth McAdie. He was damned. This girl was poking at a hornet's nest and had no idea. But he wasn't going to let on.

"Okay, Miss Thornton, I'll look into it. The connection seems a little far-fetched, but I see your point. Leave it with me."

He rose from his seat as a clear sign that the conversation was over. But Amy was not going to be fobbed off so easily.

"And what are you going to do exactly?" she demanded to know.

McCord had to do some quick thinking because he had not planned to do anything at all.

"Well, since no crime has been committed, apart from dangerous driving on the part of Mr Adamson, I can't divert scarce resources to chasing jealous husbands on the off chance."

Amy's cheeks reddened.

"So, what you're saying is that you're going to sit here and wait until somebody kills Angus, and then you're going to investigate?"

McCord, registering the flushed face and heavy breathing of his visitor, suppressed a sigh. Angus, is it? he thought. A would-be detective in love on a magical mystery tour. You couldn't make it up. He attempted the soothing, reassuring voice and body language they had tried to teach him at Tulliallan, and failed.

"I'll have a look at the CCTV in the area to see if there is any sign of the car you said chased him, okay? That is all I can do for now, I'm afraid."

Reluctantly, Amy rose from her chair. There was nothing more to be gained from this oaf. DS Fraser, who had been listening to the whole conversation, turned sideways baring his teeth in what he seemed to think was a charming smile. Amy was wondering what the city was coming to if those two were in charge of protecting innocent citizens.

"Goodbye, DI McCord, I'll be in touch."

Fraser waited until she was out of sight, then whistled through his teeth.

"Not often we get someone like her in here, eh? Thornton, d'you think she's the heiress of the chocolate empire?"

"Haven't you got something to do, Fraser?" McCord growled. "Chasing killers, for example?"

DS Fraser wiped the grin off his face. Clearly the boss was not in the mood for banter this morning.

"I just need to write up the file on the stabbing," DS Fraser said defensively. "Forensics has not found anything that we didn't expect, and with the confession it is an open-and-shut case. Oh, and before I forget, DI

Marshall from Vice phoned. Not planning a transfer, are you?"

McCord waved the suggestion away. He leaned back and folded his arms behind his neck.

"Got a call from Dolly last week."

DS Fraser moved into the office and shut the door.

"Was she missing you?" he joked but McCord did not crack a smile.

"Somebody raped one of her girls last week."

"I thought that was a professional hazard." Seeing his boss's face, he stopped there. "Did she report it?" he added, more soberly.

"Considering the line of work she is in and the fact that she had a long shower afterwards and doesn't remember much about the attacker, they didn't feel there was a point."

Fraser sighed.

McCord looked up.

"What?"

"Just glad we don't have to deal with it. Lots of paperwork leading nowhere," Fraser said.

"I've told DI Marshall, it's really his area. Anyway, when you're done with the stabbing, get the file about the accident down the Grassmarket from Traffic and see if there is any CCTV of the area with a car chasing the vehicle just before the crash."

"You're not taking this Miss Thornton seriously, are you?" Fraser asked.

"Anything involving Kenneth McAdie is worth looking into," McCord decided. "And I have a feeling, she'll be back."

Fraser retreated with a sour face.

McCord sat up in his chair and woke up his computer that had gone to sleep. When the nosey Miss Thornton turned up again, he would at least have something to say.

* * *

A few hours later, there was a distinct feeling of the calm before the storm at the station. Soon the binge drinking would start in bars and pubs and later continue in clubs, with drugs added to the toxic cocktail. A&E would be inundated with bleeding limbs and broken bones, and those who could still walk ended up here, vomiting all over their cells and trying to remember why they had bashed somebody's head in. While the going was good, he put the last touches to the stabbing case file, which Fraser had returned. Satisfied that the evidence was irrefutable, he filed the report. His neck was stiff, his shoulders ached, and he longed for a hot bath, but it would have to wait. To his delight, Fraser appeared bearing two cups of cappuccino and lemon drizzle muffins from the coffee shop across the road.

"You must be telepathic," McCord said and fingered for his wallet to take out a fiver. He knew that the sergeant was on a modest salary and thought he must be struggling to pay the mortgage on his Stockbridge flat.

Fraser shook his head. "My treat."

"Thanks. My turn next time."

He took a tiny sip, careful not to scald his tongue. Sighing contentedly, he rolled his shoulders to loosen up the tense muscles in his upper body.

"Anything on the CCTV of the accident yet?" he asked.

Fraser shook his head. "Been busy with the stabbing file. Have you sent it away yet?"

"Five minutes ago."

McCord took a large bite out of the muffin. "Great choice." He examined the gooey, bright yellow filling. "Not too sickly, nice and tart–"

"Talking of which," Fraser interrupted his revelry, "any news from Dolly?"

"No, nothing yet. Maybe I should phone her and see if Candy remembers any more of the attack." He pulled out his phone.

"Surely she'd be in touch," Fraser said. "After all, you're as good as her personal protection officer."

"No need to be cheeky," McCord said, only half-serious, but put his phone away again. "DI Marshall is a good copper. If there is anything on that rapist, he'll find it. I just don't know why they can't put that scumbag Turnbull away. That alone would reduce the crime rate by thirty percent, I reckon, and keep the Super happy. By the way, I heard he's off to the Cayman Islands for a holiday soon, so we should get some peace."

"All right for some," grumbled Fraser. "Guys like us can only dream of places like that."

McCord shrugged.

"Too hot for me anyway," he said, "and full of bastards who don't even pay tax on their ill-gotten gains. I'd go for a week's birdwatching in the Algarve any day. Spoonbills, black-winged stilts, purple herons–"

His reverie was rudely interrupted by shouting and the sound of a chair being kicked over outside. With an air of resignation, McCord put down his unfinished cup.

"Welcome to Saturday night duty."

Chapter 13

Emily secretly eyed up Tristan, trying to judge whether this was one of his better days, and she was not sure. It was just after ten in the morning, and she had clearly got him out of bed. He was still in his boxer shorts, unshaven, and judging by the smell, he hadn't showered either for a while. All night she had debated with herself whether to tell him or not. How could she not give him what he had been looking for during four long years, four years of his life he had lost searching the whole country and beyond? A search that had reduced him to – this? On the other hand, if she told him, he was capable of doing something terrible and destroying his life completely. What had swung it, if she was being honest, was her own desire for retribution, and she knew that without him, she would not get it.

He knew something was up the minute she walked in.

"What is it?" he asked as she took his hand and guided him to the old-fashioned sofa.

When he sat, she kneeled in front of him, took hold of both of his hands and looked him in the eyes.

"You're making me nervous now." He pretended to laugh. "You're not going to propose?"

She did not even smile.

"You know I am your friend," she began after a long pause.

"Yes?" He searched her anxious, yet excited face for a clue.

"You trust me?"

"What is this about?" His eyes widened. "You haven't. You have!?!"

He tried to jump up, but she forced him back into the seat.

"Promise you will listen to me, promise you will not run off and do something stupid. If you don't, I'll take this to my grave."

"Okay, okay, I promise."

His hands were shaking.

Suddenly this felt like a mistake but there was no going back now.

"I think I've found him."

He sat motionless.

"Where?" he asked hoarsely.

"Edinburgh. But I could be wrong," she added hastily.

He still did not move.

"How?"

"A journalist has written an article about him – if it is him. He is in a coma in the Royal Infirmary. So, you see," – she held tightly on to his hands – "there is no need to rush into things. We can make enquiries to find out if it really is him, and when I'm on holiday next week we can maybe go up together. Agreed?"

He nodded, absent-mindedly. She stood up, pulled him towards her and hugged him hard.

"We've got him," she said. "We finally got him."

He hugged her back, but her beautiful, warm body distracted him from what needed to be done. Gently, he pushed her away.

"Time for a drink to celebrate," he said and poured them two glasses out of the half-empty whisky decanter that he had filled up only yesterday.

Doubtfully, Emily looked at the amber liquid. This was not her usual tipple and certainly not the time of day for a drink, but today was not a normal day. They clinked their glasses and while she delicately sipped the Famous Grouse, he downed his treble in one. She was immensely relieved how well he had taken the news. They talked for a while, about the past and, for the first time in ages, about the future, and then she left. She doubted she would do any more studying today for she was suddenly exhausted and just wanted to sleep. He gave her a kiss on the cheek and shut the door behind her.

He pulled out his phone. The next train to Edinburgh left at 12 noon. He phoned for a taxi and checked the time. No chance of a shower, just a quick shave and a splash of deodorant. The last thing he wanted was to draw attention to himself by looking like a hobo. He threw a few things in a bag and looked around his room wondering if he would see it again. When the taxi driver rang the doorbell, he was ready.

* * *

The Highland Chieftain left King's Cross exactly on time. Tristan had not been able to get a seat in the economy class, so he found himself in first class, at a little table all to himself. He had barely pulled out his laptop when a uniformed steward asked him if he would like something to eat. Seeing the surprise on the traveller's face, he handed him a menu and informed him that all food and drink was included in the price of the ticket. Although the word 'drink' had initially caught his attention, looking at the menu made him hungry. He ordered a steak sandwich and a small bottle of wine, to be followed by a fruit slice and coffee. When the steward had hurried off to process the order, he leant back in his seat and closed his eyes.

Soon they left outer London and were zooming through the north of England, past Doncaster and many places he had never heard of until the train stopped at York. Two and a half hours until Edinburgh. He'd better get ready. He logged into the train's wi-fi and googled the Royal Infirmary of Edinburgh. On his phone, he took pictures of the layout and of a map showing the way from Waverley to Little France Crescent on his phone.

He had not decided what he would do once he had Magnus there in front of him. The idea of putting a pillow over his face until he stopped breathing gave him immense pleasure but then, no. He wanted him to know. He wanted to see the fear in his eyes when he realised that there was no hiding anymore, that the time to pay had arrived at last. A couple of minutes' struggling for breath would not do. He realised that this was something that had to be planned carefully. Nothing would be worse than after all this time, after fantasising about this moment for four years, to barge in and make a mess of it. He must not fail, so he had to think this through.

They had reached Newcastle by the time he had read all the information on the website carefully. Soon they would be in Scotland. His hands started to get sweaty, and he could not stop his left leg from bouncing up and down.

The steward came back and offered more food and drink, but his stomach was clenched like a fist, and he knew he would not be able to eat a thing. Instead, he got up and made his way to the toilet. It felt good to stretch his legs, and while he was up, he had an idea. Who was the only person who might help him to get close to Magnus if he did not manage to sneak into the ICU? He slid back behind his table and searched the Internet for the *Forth Write*.

* * *

Tristan's upper lip itched. He had found a little joke shop on Cockburn Street, not far from Waverley Station, just before closing time, and bought a wig and a moustache. People gave him funny looks, though, and when he passed a well-lit shop window, he noticed in his reflection that some of his own hair was sticking out at the back. He angrily pulled off the wig and chucked it in a bin. He decided to keep the moustache but took a baseball cap from his bag and pulled it deep down over his eyes. He had read that there were CCTV cameras everywhere. He wondered about taking a taxi, but he did not want anybody to remember him, and, anyway, he needed to get rid of all the pent-up energy that had built up in him during the train journey.

It would take an hour to walk from the centre to the Infirmary and he did not want to arrive there while the place was too busy, so he had time to kill. Smiling at the pun, he pulled out his phone to look at a map of the town when he saw that Emily had sent him yet another message. Impatiently, he was about to lock his screen when he decided that he needed to tell her something, otherwise she would get suspicious and maybe even phone the hospital. He needed to sound normal. What did normal people do on a Sunday afternoon? He had forgotten. He wrote some nonsense about having fallen asleep and going for a jog and watching the box set of *Games of Thrones*. And that she should be reading her History books. Send.

He missed her but was glad that she was not here. No point in her screwing up her life as well. She deserved better. He would sort this out for her, and then she would be free. Free to lead a happy life with a nice, normal guy.

He turned right and went up the Royal Mile. He did not notice the majestic City Chambers under which lie some of the medieval streets of Edinburgh which were simply built over to make way for this building and which are said to be haunted by the ghosts of the former residents. He did not stop to admire St Giles' Cathedral with its iconic crown tower, under which John Knox had held his fiery sermons condemning idolatry. He was as oblivious to the colourful and often violent history of the city that shaped the grey sandstone buildings and smooth cobblestones, as he was to the street artists vying for his attention and a few of his coins, the living statues, jugglers and a woman who claimed to have the most piercings in the world. Blind and deaf to his surroundings, reliving the past and dreaming up a short-lived future, he was drawn towards his destination, far away from the places tourists come to visit.

It turned out to be much further than he had expected but his feet did not feel the unforgiving hardness of the tarmac or the northern chill; all his muscles were tensed up in anticipation of that moment. The moment he had waited for so long. His moment.

When he reached the Infirmary, his skin was clammy with sweat and his brain foggy. He marched straight into the reception area, looking for a sign for the ICU. When he reached the entrance, he was disappointed to find it was locked. On the telly, people always just walked in and out. Suddenly tired, he sat down on the chairs in the waiting area and observed what other people did.

Clearly the people who visited were relatives or close friends, and the nurses seemed to know them. There was no way he could get in without being questioned and drawing attention to himself. The disappointment weighed him down like a gravestone. He had come all this way, travelled all day, and now – nothing. Not even a glance to confirm it was him. But there was nothing for it. It was just a delay he had to accept. He had to find somewhere to stay the night and think.

It took him just a few minutes to book a room in a hotel in the city centre, and not for the first time today he was glad of his credit card. He got up and decided to get a taxi this time and find a place to eat.

On his way out, he passed the High Dependency Unit and noticed a young woman talking to a nurse. He did a double take, and his pulse started racing. It was her! It was the journalist who had written the article, the one whose picture he had seen online when he was on the train. She purposefully strode out of the building. He felt sure it was a sign. Just when he had been thwarted at every turn, the very journalist who was writing a series of articles on Magnus turned up, right here. She would lead him to other people who knew Magnus, maybe even to his home.

He caught up with her at the bus stop and positioned himself behind her at a safe distance. He pulled up his hood and pretended to look at his phone until the bus arrived. Feeling like a hunter closing in on his prey, he followed her into town.

Chapter 14

Nurse Cathy greeted Amy with a deluge of detail that boiled down to the one thing Amy wanted to hear: Angus had woken up. Finally, she would be able to speak to him, to get some answers. With a perfunctory 'thanks', she stormed past the nurse and hurried to the bedside of the man who would no longer be a mystery. When she pulled aside the curtain, Angus Adamson turned his head and tried to focus on his visitor. Amy sat down next to his bed and took his hand. He looked confused but did not pull his hand away.

"Hello, Angus," Amy whispered, her face flushed with excitement, "how are you feeling?"

"Not bad, thank you."

He scrutinised her face intensely.

"I'm sorry, do I know you?" he croaked. He had not spoken more than a few words since regaining consciousness.

Amy looked into his eyes, the colour of creamy milk chocolate, and tried not show her disappointment. So, he had not heard her news, her stories, her reading to him. For the past ten days, he had dominated every waking moment of her life, and yet, to him, she was a complete stranger.

Reluctantly, she withdrew her hand.

"I'm Amy, Amy Thornton. I was there when the accident happened."

She hesitated. Would it be rude to tell him? She decided, no. After all, it was all part of the grander scheme of things.

"I'm sure Cathy, the nurse, has told you. You almost ran me over."

He cleared his throat; it was probably still sore from the tubes.

"I'm sorry."

"Don't be," Amy reassured him. "It wasn't your fault. You were chased."

Amy saw with alarm that the bleep indicating his heartbeat became faster and the spikes on the machine he was hooked up to grew bigger.

"Don't worry, you are safe here. I told Cathy to look out for him."

Angus looked as if he was losing his tentative grip on reality again.

Amy sensed his confusion. She bent down to his face and lowered her voice to an almost inaudible whisper.

"I know about the" – she was looking for a suitable euphemism for the ugly word 'affair' – "meetings you had in the Kingdom Club. Cathy told me that your 'friend' was here asking after you; she must have heard from the manager of the Kingdom Country Club. I think her husband knows and is after you. He is not a nice person, by all accounts. As soon as you can get in touch with her, you must call it off. It is not worth getting killed for, and she is much too old for you anyway."

Angus looked as if he was in pain. He closed his eyes.

"You go to sleep, so you can get better," she whispered tenderly. "And I'll be back tomorrow."

* * *

When Amy was getting ready to leave, John called her into his office and carefully shut the door behind them.

"How is your Mystery Man feature going?" he asked by way of introduction.

Amy shrugged.

"Very slowly," she said. "The police are doing nothing, and Angus is still a bit dazed."

He cleared his throat.

"Please don't take this the wrong way," he said, "but I am a little concerned that you are perhaps a little too… emotionally involved in this case. You seem to spend an extraordinary amount of time at the hospital, are you not?"

Amy shook her head violently.

"This could be a really big story. And I can't help being involved. If he hadn't swerved to avoid hitting me, I would be dead or in a coma now, and not he."

John nodded.

"Fine," he said, "do what you have to do."

He hesitated, and Amy sensed that there was something else he wanted.

"I was wondering if your mum said anything about our dinner last Saturday. Do you think she enjoyed it?"

Amy smiled.

"You're still in one piece, aren't you?"

John's face fell, and Amy just wanted to hug him.

"How about having lunch with me, Mum and Martin tomorrow? Less pressure, more relaxed?"

John beamed.

"Excellent. Is there a particular place she likes?"

"There is a quirky little café just off St Andrew's Square called The Green Bean. That's halfway between the magazine and the shop. The tourists don't tend to come that far but I'd better reserve a table. Shall we meet here at half twelve and walk over together?"

John nodded enthusiastically.

"Great idea. Are you going to the Royal Infirmary now?"

Amy grabbed her handbag and made to leave.

"Yes, I hope Angus remembers more today; he seemed quite confused yesterday. My column needs to be ready on Thursday, and I have nothing new to report yet! See you tomorrow."

* * *

Shivering in the sudden cold after leaving the cosy office, Amy walked down George Street towards Shandwick Place to catch the number 33 bus. The sky was a fast-moving mass of grey that spat tiny half-frozen droplets of rain into her face. She wrapped her huge woollen scarf tighter around her head and neck and wished she were somewhere warm, somewhere with azure skies and lily-white sand, rather than this cold, grey place. In her head, she played different scenarios of her meeting with Angus, and she wondered if Mrs McAdie had been to see him again and whether the affair was over. Not that she was jealous, of course, that would be silly. Her concern had nothing to do with his fine cheekbones and the warmth of his hands. She was merely worried about Angus's safety. And although she would have loved to prove that obnoxious DI wrong and get hold of a sensational story, she did not want Angus to be the one paying the price.

As luck would have it, a number 33 had just pulled in, and less than half an hour later she reached the hospital entrance. The staff knew her by now, and she was greeted all the way along the corridors to Angus's room. Before she could reach it, however, Cathy waylaid her with news.

"You're not going to believe it," she told Amy, breathless with excitement. "Just before lunch, a man turned up wanting to see Angus. After you said to watch out, I was worried, so I said, 'May I ask who you are?' and he got really shirty and said that was none of my business. So, I said, 'Sorry, but the police warned us only to let in family,' and he looked furious. Then he said, 'Tell Mr Adamson that a Mr McAdie is here to see him.'"

Amy's eyes widened.

"And? Angus didn't ask him in, did he?"

"He did! So, I showed the man in but because of what you said, I stayed close by, just behind the door. Just in case he might attack him."

Amy nodded impatiently.

"Right you were. And what did they talk about?"

"I couldn't hear exactly," Cathy said, and seeing Amy's bitter disappointment, she added defensively, "they were speaking quietly but I could see from his body language that this Mr McAdie was angry, and Angus looked very worried after he had left."

"Just as I had thought," Amy said. "Thanks, Cathy, keep your eyes and ears open."

Cathy went ahead to announce Amy's arrival, and this time Angus was much more with it and seemed keen to speak to her.

"Hi Amy, nice to see you," he greeted her, and the scratchiness in his voice had gone. A lovely baritone. His skin had lost its ivory quality and his cheeks were rosy and his lips cherry-red. But Amy felt there was no time to dwell on that now, so she came straight to the point.

"I heard that Mr McAdie was here to see you this morning. Did he threaten you?" she demanded.

Angus looked bewildered.

"No, of course not."

Amy shook her head.

"You must tell the police. I think he is dangerous. Have you broken up with Mrs McAdie yet?"

Angus shook his head.

"No, but–"

"No buts," Amy interrupted, sternly. "Call it off, and that will get her husband off your back. If it is not too late, that is. If he comes again, tell him I've told the police, so he knows he can't get away with anything."

"You did what?"

Angus, now seriously angry, lifted his upper body off the pillows.

"You told the police?"

"Of course," Amy retorted hotly. "He's had you almost killed once already, and I'm not letting him try again and succeed!"

Angus fell back on the bed again and gripped Amy's hand.

"Amy, believe me, you've got it all wrong, terribly wrong. Please stay out of this. You have no idea what damage you are doing. What there is to sort out, I can sort it all out myself!"

Amy looked at him, still hooked up to a drip, too weak to get up or to hold a conversation for longer than five minutes. She shook her head in pity.

"Don't worry about me. You don't need to play the hero, you just need to get better. And do the right thing. Then everything will be fine."

She gently withdrew from his fierce grip and stroked the back of his hand.

Angus closed his eyes, suddenly looking exhausted. Amy saw that she would achieve no more today.

"Goodbye," she whispered. "Get some sleep and don't worry. You are not alone."

Chapter 15

By ten in the morning, Amy had put the finishing touches to an article she was writing and felt she had earned the right to spend some more of her work time on the case of the Mystery Man. The McAdies were still her only lead, so she started with old issues from celebrity magazines. After scrolling through endless pages of people looking glamorous at glamorous parties or in their glamorous homes, her eyes began to swim. She was just about to give up when a portly figure in a handmade charcoal suit caught her eye. Unlike the last picture she had seen of him, in this one he was grinning broadly and had his arms around a thin woman in a dress whose fuchsia colour did not suit her at all, and a teenage boy with a charming smile.

"No," Amy said aloud. "No way."

She read the caption and blew up the picture on the screen. She read the caption again.

> *Mr Kenneth McAdie and Mrs Colleen McAdie with their son Magnus at the fundraising dinner for TAD – Teenagers Against Drugs.*

There was no doubt. Angus was, in fact, Magnus McAdie. Amy slapped her forehead. How had she not noticed before? Angus M was an anagram of Magnus, and McAdie meant 'son of Adam'. She jumped up to tell John and Martin but then changed her mind and sat down again.

Her head was swirling with this revelation. She needed to think first. Again, she looked at the photo. Angus was Mrs McAdie's son? That meant her great theory about the affair was nonsense. So why was Angus, or Magnus, meeting his mother in secret in a hotel? Why was he hiding from his father? To have taken on a new identity seemed pretty drastic. It must have been something big... Of course, the trial! Magnus must have been a witness for the prosecution in the trial of his father, and when they failed to put him away, Magnus feared his father's revenge. Had she perhaps, through her column, led Kenneth McAdie straight to

Magnus? All her airways seemed to go into spasm, and she found it difficult to breathe. What had she done?! She had to go to the police, but not this arrogant DI McCord. She needed somebody who took her seriously. They needed to protect Magnus until his father was put away. She clicked on the picture, copied it into her 'Mystery Man' file and sent it to her phone. She grabbed her handbag, ran over to John's office and banged on his door.

"What's going on?" Martin shouted across the room.

Amy ignored his question and entered the office, interrupting John's phone call with the printer. John just looked at Amy's face and told the printer to call back later.

"What's the matter?" he asked alarmed. "Something happened to your mum?"

Amy shook her hand impatiently.

"No, of course not. I've just found out who Angus really is. Must go to the police, he could be in real danger."

"Okay, go," John said. But then something occurred to him. "Wait! What about lunch? We're meeting your mother here at twelve thirty, remember?"

"I'll be back by then. If not, just go without me."

She was already out of the door when he called her back again.

"Here," he said and pushed a twenty-pound note into her hand. "Take a taxi."

She nodded her thanks and was off.

* * *

Amy entered St Leonard's police station with the demeanour of somebody trying to prevent WWIII. The officer at reception obviously recognised her from her last two visits and put on his patient face.

"How can I help you today, miss?"

"I have important information regarding a current case," Amy recited the speech she had rehearsed on the way. "I need to speak to a senior officer, preferably not DI McCord."

"I'm afraid it is DI McCord who is on duty this morning," he informed her. "Would you like to come back another time, perhaps?"

Amy shook her head.

"No, it is urgent. Can I see him now?"

Looking harangued, he picked up the phone.

"Sir? There is someone to see you, a Miss" – he looked questioningly at Amy who mouthed her name – "Thornton. She says it's urgent."

The officer listened dispassionately to the voice at the other end.

"Yes, sir."

He put the phone down and pressed the buzzer for the inner door.

"Please go through."

* * *

DI McCord had just had time to pop in another nicotine gum before facing Miss Thornton again. She was shaping up to becoming one of those who visit a police station in regular intervals for no good reason other than to feel important.

"Miss Thornton, I am really busy," he started but Amy ignored his plea.

"Angus is really Magnus, so his father is after him because of the witness statement," she blurted out.

McCord chewed on his gum furiously. It was worse than he thought.

"Who is Magnus and what witness statement?" he asked, not particularly interested in the answers.

Amy realised she had not been clear enough for DI McCord's limited intellectual capacity and started at the beginning. She spoke very slowly.

"Angus Adamson, who was chased by a car and is just coming out of a coma, and who was secretly meeting Mrs McAdie, if you remember, in the Kingdom Country Club, is, or rather was, Magnus McAdie."

She waited for the effect this bombshell would have on McCord, but she was disappointed.

The DI leant back in his chair and laughed.

"Let me get this right. The lover boy chased by the jealous husband turns out to be his son? Are you saying that we have a modern version of King Oedipus on our hands?"

The surprise that this Neanderthal knew anything of either Greek tragedy or psychology showed in Amy's face, and McCord had always been oversensitive where social prejudice was concerned.

"Believe it or not, they teach these things in bog-standard comprehensives as well, not just in private schools," he said sarcastically.

Amy saw what was going on here.

"Not that it is relevant to the case," she fired back, "but I went to a bog-standard comprehensive myself. However, unlike yours, mine taught me basic manners."

McCord tried not to show his discomfort.

"So, what's the problem? If he is the McAdies' son, why should he not meet his mother?"

Amy tried to stay calm.

"Quite, but why the secrecy? He must have changed his identity four years ago, straight after his father's trial. One newspaper article suggests that he was a witness. It follows that he is hiding from his father, and now, unfortunately, his father has found him."

DI McCord chewed his gum with some glee.

"Ah, and remind me who led him to his son? It was you, wasn't it?"

"How was I to know that?" Amy said, defensively. "Anyway, what does it matter now? What matters now is that you protect Angus from his father."

"How do you know that Kenneth McAdie has found him? Has he threatened him?"

"He turned up at the hospital and one of the nurses says they had a heated conversation. Angus is clearly afraid of him but won't tell me what is going on."

"Let's assume your trial theory is correct."

The expression on his face showed clearly that he doubted this very much.

"Even then I can't see the motive. McAdie was acquitted, wasn't he? I'm sure he lives a very comfortable life somewhere in the sun."

"On Guernsey," Amy admitted.

"Well then. If young McAdie decides to disassociate himself from his father, he is well within his rights. As long as there is no evidence of a crime or an immediate threat to someone's life, there is nothing I can do, I'm afraid."

By now, Amy was furious. What was wrong with this guy?

"So, you're going to wait until Angus has another 'unfortunate accident' which actually kills him. Will you investigate then?"

DI McCord rose from his chair.

"You can be sure of that, but I doubt very much it will come to that. Thank you for bringing this to our attention. Meanwhile, if I were you, I would let people sort out their family affairs themselves. It is never a good idea to interfere."

So that is the help you get from the police nowadays, Amy thought as she was leaving. There was nothing for it; she would have to investigate this herself.

* * *

Amy had decided she needed a walk to clear her head and get rid of some of the aggression that had built up inside her during the conversation with DI McCord. Still muttering curses under her breath, she reached the office slightly out of breath at just after half past twelve. Outside the door lay a cream-coloured envelope. As she picked it up, John pulled open the door.

"At last," he sighed. "I was worried you would not make it."

Behind him, Martin was swirling his hand around his ear indicating that John was not in possession of his full faculties.

Just then Valerie arrived, radiant as always. Amy absent-mindedly gave her a peck on the cheek, John shook her hand awkwardly and Martin greeted her with an elaborate bow. Valerie smiled at the men, but then she noticed the expression on her daughter's face.

"Are you okay? You look upset."

"The police are just useless," Amy raged. "They won't do anything until somebody has been murdered in his bed."

"Who is getting murdered?" asked Martin. "Not your 'Mystery Man'?"

Amy thought she detected a trace of irony in her colleague's voice.

"This isn't funny! I've just found out that Angus' real name is Magnus McAdie. He is the son of a Kenneth McAdie who was on trial for tax evasion in London four years ago. Apparently, he's some sort of crime lord and–"

"See," Valerie interrupted triumphantly, "I told you to leave well alone!"

Amy ignored her mother's outburst. "I think Angus was hiding from his father here in Edinburgh, but now McAdie has caught up with him, and it was also McAdie who chased Angus in the car."

"But why on earth would a father want to harm his own son?" John wondered.

"The newspapers mentioned Angus in connection with the trial," Amy explained. "I told DI McCord to look into it to find out if Angus testified against his father, but he is not taking this seriously."

John looked sceptical.

"Shall we discuss this over lunch?" he suggested. "If we delay much longer, we might lose our table."

Amy was about to put down the envelope she still held in her hand when she saw that it was addressed to her. She opened the flap and pulled out a thick, cream-coloured card.

"'Mr Kenneth McAdie requests the pleasure of your company for dinner at The Royal on Saturday, 22 March at 8pm,'" she read aloud.

Bewildered, Amy looked up.

"What does that mean?"

"Angus's father is inviting you to dinner," John said as if this needed explaining.

"But why? What does he want from me?"

"You have such a suspicious mind, my darling," Martin said. "Maybe he just wants to meet his future daughter-in-law in civilised surroundings?"

"Don't get any ideas," Valerie butted in. "You're not going. You said yourself he is a potential killer. You're not getting involved with these people."

Amy's hackles went up.

"The police are not doing anything until there is some evidence, so what am I to do?"

"Stay out of it, I'm telling you," Valerie insisted. "You–"

"I'll do whatever *I* decide to do," Amy declared. "Stop treating me like a child!"

Martin and John exchanged a glance, and John decided to intervene.

"Let us think about it," he said, reasonably. "It would be quite an affront not to go. There is no point offending a man without needing to. Why not hear what he has to say? Then you can make up your own mind. But," he hastily added, seeing Valerie glaring at him, "you must not go alone. I shall be there as well, at a nearby table, keeping an eye on you, and if there is any nonsense from him, I shall take you home."

He looked expectantly from mother to daughter, quite pleased with himself for this diplomatic feat.

"No, no, no," interjected Martin. "If you dine on your own at The Royal, you stick out like a sore thumb and immediately make people wonder what you are up to. Especially if you keep staring at the beautiful young woman at the next table. Do that and McAdie will be chasing your car next – only joking," he added, as the three of them looked horrified. "No, what you need to do is take a glamorous companion and pretend to be out on a romantic dinner. Valerie, are you doing anything this Saturday?"

John saw the opportunity his old friend had created and grabbed it.

"Of course! This is the solution. We can keep Amy safe *and* enjoy The Royal's legendary lobster and champagne starter. Please allow me to take you out on Saturday?"

John looked at Valerie, clearly not prepared to accept a refusal.

Valerie was struggling to keep up with the conflicting feelings this conversation had triggered inside her. In the end, she focused on the words 'keep Amy safe' and 'lobster and champagne', ignoring the 'romantic dinner' bit.

"Okay, then," she said after a pause.

"Right." John beamed. "Let's go and have lunch."

Chapter 16

The flat above Valerie's had never seen such upheaval. Dresses had been pulled out of wardrobes, tried on and then discarded on the beds, shoes were strewn across the floor, and in the bathroom, there was a brief altercation as to who would get to wear the ruby earrings. Amy won this battle on the grounds that they perfectly matched her lucky brooch, and that her dinner engagement involved charming and catching a hardened criminal, while Valerie just needed to look pretty for John who would have thought her the most beautiful creature on earth even if she had been wearing a bin bag instead of the eggshell silk dress that showed off her curves perfectly.

"We should have fitted you with a bug," Valerie said while applying salmon-pink lipstick for the second time, "just in case."

"I doubt he'll confess to attempted murder of his son over dinner," Amy pointed out, stroking her narrow waist over the black lacy dress, "and anyway, I don't think there is room for anything underneath this."

Valerie regarded her daughter thoughtfully.

"You are my beautiful girl," she said. "Please be careful."

Amy leant across and kissed the air next to her mother's rouged cheek, so as not to destroy her make-up.

"I promise. And you'll be nice to John, you hear?"

Before Valerie could protest, the doorbell rang. Amy glanced at her phone.

"That'll be him. My taxi should be just a few minutes. Remember not to stare at me and enjoy your first ever lobster!"

Valerie put her lipstick away and made to leave. At the door, she hesitated but then turned to open it.

* * *

The Royal was housed in a Georgian terrace in Queen Street. It was easily overlooked by the casual passer-by because there was no menu displayed outside, and the discreet gold-plated sign on the outer stone wall could have pointed to a boutique hotel. The Royal did not need to advertise for business; it was the go-to place for those who drove cars that cost as much as a small flat and who did not want to rub shoulders with the hoi polloi. The fact that it offered no parking was not an issue for the guests who arrived in taxis or were chauffeur-driven. In the lobby, liveried staff relieved the illustrious guests of their designer coats along with a hefty tip.

Amy followed Valerie and John from little distance, trying to look as if she entered this place alone on a regular basis.

They ascended one of the semi-circular stairs leading into the dining area. The spacious, high-ceilinged room took up most of the first floor and looked out over Queen Street Gardens and Edinburgh New Town. Crystal chandeliers bathed the room in dim, soft light. The entrance to this hallowed place was guarded by Monsieur Brossard, the maître d'hôtel, who greeted John and his companion with reverence. Amy smiled as her mum tried not to look impressed and graciously accepted John's arm as they were led to their table.

Monsieur Brossard was about as French as the dry, flaky bits of pastry sold under the name of croissants in this country, but he was a master of the cheerful servility and food snobbery that is indispensable for the most exclusive restaurant in town. He adjusted chairs and waved about the embroidered linen napkins, all the while apologising for the inferior position of the table in the middle of the room. John reassured him that he was delighted to have managed to obtain a table at all considering his late booking. What he did not say, of course, was that the table gave them an excellent vantage point from which to observe the other tables. With a bow, Monsieur Brossard presented them with the heavy leather-bound menus and retreated to show

Amy to her table where the whole procedure was repeated.

Amy opened the menu but secretly scanned the room for Kenneth McAdie. She could not see him anywhere. When she met John's eyes, she pretended not to recognise him.

* * *

Just then Monsieur Brossard arrived at Valerie and John's table. After taking their order, he sailed off to the kitchen. Amy sneaked a look at her delicate silver watch, worrying if McAdie had changed his mind, when a short, fat man entered, his dark eyes shining and his belly bouncing in cheerful anticipation of a delicious meal and a drink. Monsieur Brossard greeted him enthusiastically and, engrossed in lively conversation that indicated a longer acquaintance, the men proceeded to Amy's table.

* * *

Tristan had just caught a glimpse of the Thornton woman entering the restaurant, but she was still on her own. She could not be meeting the couple who had left the flat just before her, because surely, she would have gone in their taxi, rather than taking her own. Luckily, she had spoken quite loudly to the driver when she told him where she was going, so he had waved down another taxi and followed her here. This was probably a complete waste of time, but he was curious whom she was having dinner with. Her flat, which she seemed to share with her mother, certainly did not look as if she had the money to dine in a place like this. He hung around for a while but when nobody else entered the restaurant, he decided to find a pub somewhere and come back later.

* * *

To Amy's surprise, Kenneth McAdie's handshake was warm and firm, quite unlike the reptile grip she had expected. He apologised for the absence of his wife, who was tending to her sick mother in Glasgow, and expressed his delight at her accepting his invitation. His Glaswegian accent and Govan upbringing had been almost erased by more than two decades spent in London high society. He used all the right words at the right time, but Amy could not help thinking that it sounded rehearsed, as if he had studied footage of the English upper class and become adept at mimicking them. His clothes were expensive but badly chosen, just like his wife's in the picture of the charity dinner. His pale green shirt, inexplicably all the rage this season, took the colour out of his ruddy face and gave his skin an unhealthy sheen.

When Monsieur Brossard brought the menus, McAdie explained the different dishes to Amy and suggested the wines to go with them. It was only after Monsieur Brossard had departed to the kitchen that it occurred to her that he had made all the decisions without her even noticing. She would have to be on her guard. Unfortunately, this meant that she did not speak at all for a while, and McAdie seemed to sense her discomfort.

"You do know why you are here this evening, don't you?"

Amy blushed because she realised her insecurity had shown.

"I'm not sure, actually," she replied.

"I thought that was perfectly obvious," he said with feigned surprise. "I wanted to thank you, of course, for looking after my son Magnus when my wife and I had no idea what had happened."

"It was a pleasure," Amy said and was just about to ask why Magnus had changed his name when the monkfish starter arrived. The lobster was famous but much overrated, McAdie had decided, and Amy shot a regretful glance at her mother who was trying to extract some meat from the claws with a peculiar-looking fork. John gave her a warning look, and she returned to her beautifully presented miniature kebab.

During the starter, McAdie learned everything about Amy's childhood in Edinburgh, her university years, the disastrous year in teaching Modern Languages in a comprehensive in Greenock, and finally her current position as fashion journalist at the *Forth Write*. He laughed at her article about the Hearts socks and promised to tell his wife to subscribe to it because she loved Scotland and all things Scottish, apart from the weather, of course.

* * *

They moved on to the pink guinea fowl breast. She threw a furtive glance towards her mum and John and noticed with some displeasure that they were engrossed in their own conversation. So much for John's protection. By now she was determined to learn something about McAdie and asked him about his life. He was a gifted storyteller, and his bumpy journey from rags to riches greatly entertained her, almost against her will. She was beginning to consider the possibility that she had been paranoid, and that all he wanted was to get to know the girl his son had recently been spending almost every evening with.

Monsieur Brossard was relieved that the main course had lived up to Mr McAdie and the young lady's expectations and served the cranachan, a classic Scottish dessert made from oats, double cream and raspberries.

As Amy dipped the long-handled spoon into the pear-shaped crystal dish, she realised that she had learnt nothing yet about Magnus, neither the reasons for his identity change nor the accident. After they had exchanged their life stories, she felt emboldened to ask the questions she really wanted the answers to.

"There is no secret," McAdie said, seemingly surprised that anybody could think such a thing. "Being a journalist, I'm sure you have found out that there was a lot of unpleasant publicity around my business affairs. It isn't easy working your way up from the gutter, and some people will never accept you into their circles. They'd throw muck at you knowing that some will stick just as long as they make enough noise. The accusations against me were completely unfounded, of course, and eventually I was fully vindicated. But the damage to my reputation was done, and I did not want Magnus to be dragged down by association. That's why I set him up with a small business in Edinburgh."

He managed to pile some oats, cream and a raspberry onto his spoon and screwed up his eyes in delight. He smacked his lips and looked at Amy with a disconcerting intensity. She had been busy trying to avoid the thick cream and fishing for the raspberries when she felt his eyes on her. She looked up and found herself unable to unlock her gaze from his.

"It was all going so well. Then *you* came along, Miss Thornton, and spoiled it all. You caused him to crash into a wall and as if that were not enough, you wrote an article about him and told all and sundry about his whereabouts."

Amy was about to protest but found that no sound escaped her mouth, so shocked was she in the face of this sudden, vicious attack. His eyes had gone cold, and his voice, though only a whisper, carried every terrible syllable.

"This is a dangerous world, Miss Thornton, and it will be much safer for you *and* for Magnus if you stay away from him. Do I make myself clear?"

He waited until she had nodded, and only then released her from his piercing eyes.

"Great," he said, suddenly jovial and jolly again. "Shall we have coffee?"

Amy shook her head.

"I'm feeling sick," she mumbled, not sure if that was down to the double cream or the fear he had struck into her. "I want to go home."

"Shame, the coffee is excellent, but as you wish," he said, quite the solicitous host again. "Allow me to call you a taxi."

Amy was about to protest but he was already on the phone, giving instructions for two taxis to pick up at The Royal.

Monsieur Brossard had noticed that something was amiss at table five and hurried across the room.

"Everything to your liking, Mr McAdie?" he enquired anxiously.

"Oh, yes, the dinner was splendid. Unfortunately, Miss Thornton is feeling unwell and wishes to leave. Could you get me the bill, please?"

Monsieur Brossard waved to an assistant waiter and offered to fetch water or call a doctor, but Amy just smiled weakly and reiterated her wish to go home.

McAdie paid the bill, complemented by a generous tip.

With expressions of deep regret and concern, Monsieur Brossard escorted them out of the dining room and left them in the care of the concierge who accompanied them down the stairs and helped them into their coats.

In a daze, she did not see her mother hurrying down the stairs into the lobby. Somewhere a clock chimed ten, and on the last chime, McAdie's phone rang. He answered, listened and said, "Good. The rest as arranged tomorrow."

He put his phone back into his pocket with a broad smile as the first taxi pulled up. He opened the back door for her.

"Thank you for a lovely evening, Miss Thornton."

The door slammed shut, and the taxi sped away.

* * *

Tristan's heartbeat quickened. Just as well he had left the pub early; he had almost missed them. And what a miss that would have been. McAdie senior, dining with Miss Amy Thornton. What was that all about? Was she a friend of the family now? On the other hand, she had not looked very happy when she came out, white as a sheet, and off, seemingly without as much as a goodbye. And now the couple from earlier, the mother and her boyfriend by the looks of it, appeared as well, clearly upset. Had they all been dining together? But why had they arrived and left separately? He could not figure it out. But whatever they had been up to, at least he was sure now that he was on the right track.

* * *

As soon as the taxi pulled away from The Royal, a terrible suspicion gripped Amy. What if McAdie had decided it was too tiresome to wait and see if she would heed his advice? The taxi had arrived awfully quickly, and the driver had not asked her for her address. They were cruising down Queen Street and turning right towards the bus station. She pulled herself up trying to catch a glimpse of the driver in the rear-view mirror. A pair of eyes the colour of mahogany met her glance.

"Everything okay, miss?"

"Where are you taking me?" Amy asked, immediately realising that this was a stupid question.

"South Bridge, isn't it?" The driver looked worried. He probably thought she was unhinged. "We're almost there."

With a huge sense of relief, Amy sank back into the leather seat, only to jump up again. Mum! She must have seen her leave and be worried sick! She fumbled for her phone and typed a quick message. Then she leant back again. The driver kept glancing into the rear-view mirror. When he pulled up outside Valerie's, she gave him a big smile and an even bigger tip.

Amy was still fumbling for her key when Valerie and John's taxi came to a screeching halt on the double yellow lines in front of the shop. Her mother jumped out and ran towards her.

"Is everything okay? What did he do to you?" she asked anxiously.

Amy shook her head.

"Nothing. But the way he spoke to me really frightened me."

"See, I told you to leave well alone. I hope you'll see sense now and stay away from that family."

The sound of a car door being shut made her turn round. John was standing next to the taxi looking guilt-stricken.

"What's the matter with him?" Amy asked.

"In the taxi he went on and on about how he let you down and how unforgivable it was that he had only eyes for me," Valerie scoffed, but there was a trace of pride amongst the scorn.

"But what could he have done?" said Amy reasonably. "It all happened so quickly."

John looked over to them, hung his head and began to fold his tall frame into the backseat of the taxi when Valerie called out to him.

"What *are* you doing?" she demanded. "Hurry up, or don't you want to hear from Amy what McAdie said?"

Like a shot, John was beside Valerie, and with her leaning against his arm to counteract the wobble on her high heels, they followed Amy up the stairs to the flat.

Chapter 17

McCord was just pouring boiling water over the coffee granules, when his mobile buzzed. DS Fraser. Quarter to eight? On a Sunday? Had he forgotten he had the Sunday off, for once? And even if he had been on duty, the shift would not start until eight. What was it that could not wait? Nothing good, anyway.

"What's up?" he asked without bothering with preliminaries.

"You'd better come straightaway." Fraser sounded shaken. "Two bodies found at Musselburgh Lagoons."

"I'm off duty, remember? Can't Jeffries do it?"

"He's called in sick. Tummy bug. Unless you want me to handle it?"

He sounded keen, which was not his usual attitude for work on a Sunday.

McCord shook his head, forgetting Fraser could not see him.

"I'll be over asap. Forensics there yet?"

"Any minute now, I'd think."

"I'll see you there."

McCord poured the coffee into the sink. No need for that now. The adrenaline rush of a new case had him wide awake in a second, and not for the first time he wondered if it was right to feel excited at the news of two lives being brutally cut short. But as always, he did not dwell on the deeper workings of his psyche. He rushed out to his ancient Ford, put on Motörhead and sped towards Musselburgh Lagoons.

* * *

The council still had not filled the potholes that were dotted cunningly across the dirt track so that it was well-nigh impossible to avoid damage to the exhaust or the suspension. Each time the ancient Ford complained about the injustice of being sent out to this dump, McCord swore.

He was also personally affronted that they had spoilt one of his favourite birdwatching spots. At least three pairs of short-eared owls were hunting here just now, and he had planned to come out later today to observe their long, streaked wings spread out magnificently during their silent, sweeping flight. Instead, he would have to look at two corpses.

When he finally pulled into the car park at the Lagoons, the circus had arrived. The SOCOs had cordoned off the site and were purposefully going about their business to preserve every bit of physical evidence that might lead to a conviction. One of them handed McCord a pair of blue plastic overshoes and waved him towards the burnt-out car. Fraser was already there to fill him in.

"Two bodies, badly burnt, each with a bullet wound to the head. Doc thinks two young men but needs them on the table first."

McCord was glad of the warning. As much as he loved the chase, he hated looking at corpses. In this instance, he smelt them before he saw them, although the worst of the stench of burnt flesh and hair must have been dispersed by the cold night air. It was exactly as Fraser had said. The bodies were so disfigured that they did not seem real, rather like the mummies he had once seen in the British Museum. In the forehead of the driver, he could make out the precise hole made by the bullet.

"Execution? Drugs?" he mused.

Fraser nodded. "It looks that way."

"Damn."

These cases were always difficult to solve. Hostile witnesses who had too much to hide or were too afraid to talk. McCord turned away. He did not want to look at the charred bodies any longer and focused on the car. Not much left of it but a burnt-out shell, just the right rear wheel cap had escaped the flames somehow and some blue paint was still visible. Something niggled in his brain, but he could not figure out what.

"Who found the bodies?" he asked instead.

"An old birder, looking for a broad-backed sandpiper–"

"Broad-billed sandpiper," McCord corrected him automatically.

Fraser just rolled his eyes. "Whatever. Anyway, he found the bodies."

McCord was waiting for one of Fraser's usual quips, but the sight had clearly shocked him as well. McCord surveyed the surrounding area. No houses nearby, awkward to access: the perfect place for a drug deal or a murder.

"Put out an appeal. Could be there were some teenagers around for bit of a smoke or sex, you never know." He did not sound optimistic. "Let's hope the PM gives us some identities, then we can take it from there."

Before he left, he looked back at the car. What was it that wanted to come to the forefront of his brain? Maybe if he stopped trying, it would reveal itself to him in its own good time.

* * *

Back at the station an incident board had been put up, and as information came in, it was added, hopefully to form a web of connections that might lead them to the killer or killers. At the moment, though, there were more holes than threads, and all they had were photographs of the car and the victims. McCord wished the colours of the photographs were less vivid against the white of the still empty board. There was nothing they could do until the doctor and the forensic people came back with tangible evidence. The enforced idleness drove him mad, so he phoned Vice to see if DI Marshall was on duty. As it happened, he was.

"Anything new on the rapist?" McCord enquired.

"Nothing," DI Marshall said. "I went to Dolly's and took a statement from Candy. She genuinely didn't seem to know anything but at least she's talking to us now and has realised that we are the good guys here. I haven't heard anything about any more attacks either. Maybe us sniffing around has made him nervous. I'll let you know if anything comes up."

"Thanks. Any luck with raids on Archie Turnbull?"

DI Marshall groaned.

"Another one that failed. I'm beginning to think that somebody must be tipping Archie Turnbull off."

"That thought had occurred to me as well," McCord admitted. "You sure about your team?"

"Of course," DI Marshall spluttered, indignant.

"No offence," McCord appeased him, "but investigating organised crime is tough. Sometimes the temptation can be too great."

"Not for my guys," DI Marshall insisted.

"If you think so. Good luck."

McCord put his phone away. He sat down at his computer and started on the incident file. He had just typed the first paragraph when Fraser edged into his office and closed the door.

"Don't shoot the messenger," he grinned, "but the posh totty is back to see you about the vegetable."

McCord's nicotine cravings suddenly came back, and he reached for a gum.

"I really don't have time for this. Tell her, I'm sorry but I have a double murder to attend to."

Fraser held up his hand.

"No can do. The Super met her downstairs, and when he heard that she was a journalist, he instructed me to assist her in any way possible. You'd better see her and be nice to her."

McCord chewed furiously.

"Damn. Did you check the CCTV around the Grassmarket?"

Fraser shrugged.

"No use – it doesn't cover that bit of road."

"Pity. Okay then, show her in."

Amy had deliberately chosen a black business suit with a white blouse, hoping to see a different DI, whom she could convince to take her concerns about Angus seriously. Instead, she seemed to be destined to having to deal with DI Bloody McCord.

"DI McCord," she said by way of greeting, "do you work every weekend?"

"No," he said curtly, putting a stop to the idle chit-chat. "What can I do for you, Miss Thornton?"

"There has been a development in the Adamson case," she said, trying to sound like a police officer on TV.

McCord swallowed the obvious reply that there was no Adamson case and even if there were, it would be dealt with by Traffic Division.

"Yes?" he asked in an indulgent tone as if talking to a child.

Amy had not been in the same room with DI McCord for more than twenty seconds, and already she wanted to slap him.

"I had dinner with Mr McAdie," Amy began but McCord interrupted her immediately.

"You had what? Did I not tell you to stay away from him?"

Remembering that Superintendent Gilchrist was probably hovering in the foyer, he checked himself.

"Would you mind telling me how you came to have dinner with Kenneth McAdie?" he rephrased the question.

"He invited me, ostensibly to thank me for looking after his son when nobody else did. He did his damnedest to be nice and to convince me that nothing untoward is going on."

McCord scratched his chin.

"Have you considered the possibility that there isn't?"

Amy stomped her right foot in frustration.

"Why would Magnus change his name then? And why is he afraid of his father?"

McCord leaned forward.

"How do you know he's afraid? Did he tell you?"

"He says no but I think he is lying."

"So, you're saying the father ordered the chase to get back at his son? Why did he not stay away then? Why did he come and draw attention to himself?"

"Maybe because he knew I was onto him. My article..."

McCord choked on his own saliva and Amy took the opportunity to explain while he was catching his breath.

"My article was very well received, and he must have felt it would look even more suspicious if he stayed away."

"Hang on," McCord gasped, "you wrote an article about the McAdies? Are you insane?"

Amy was offended.

"At the time I didn't even know their name. I was just trying to find out who this man lying in a coma was. His mother probably heard about me from the manager of the Kingdom Country Club. She could also have recognised Magnus from my description. She's the type who subscribes to our magazine although Kenneth McAdie seemed to think she wasn't."

McCord shook his head in despair. Amateur detectives were very near the top of the list of his pet hates. Amy read his face correctly.

"He said something to me. At the dinner," she said, desperately trying to convince him to stop arguing and to believe her.

The tone in her voice made McCord listen.

"What did he say?"

Amy hesitated.

"Nothing I could put my finger on. Just that it was a dangerous world out there and that it would be much safer for me and Magnus if I stayed away from him. He could have meant the car accident. But the way he said it gave me the creeps. It was a veiled threat, I'm sure of it."

McCord saw a glimmer of hope.

"Then trust your instinct and stay away. If nothing is going on, fine. If there is, believe me, you don't want to be involved."

Amy stomped her foot again.

"And wait until I read in the papers that Angus had another strange accident and is now dead? Never!"

McCord saw that his attempt had failed. She fancied herself as an investigative journalist and maybe was even in love with this Angus. Dear God. All he could hope for now was that she had just imagined the whole thing.

"I'll look into the trial and see if Magnus testified against him. And I'm telling you again, as a senior police officer, don't meddle with McAdie. But if you insist, at least be smart about it. Never let on that you are sniffing around, that you might be a threat, stop your articles at once and play the devoted girlfriend. By the way, is he returning your affections?"

Amy blushed and rose from her chair with an attempted air of dignity. She would not say another word. At least he had promised to look into the trial.

"Goodbye, DI McCord."

As she made for the exit, she noticed the incident board and, her curiosity aroused, drew closer. McCord was just about to call her back to tell her this was not for public consumption when a thought occurred to him. Maybe if she saw what some people were capable of, not on TV, not in a book, but here in real life, she might do the sensible thing and mind her own business.

But if he had expected Amy to recoil from the gruesome sight, he was wrong. She looked at the bodies without flinching and then moved on to the photos showing different angles of the car. She moved forwards and backwards between the two sets of photos for so long that McCord began to wonder if there was something the matter with her that needed professional attention. Eventually, she turned round and faced him with a look of utter bewilderment.

"That's the car," she announced without a shadow of a doubt. "The car that chased Angus."

McCord stared at her.

"Are you insane?" he asked for the second time today. "How...?"

Amy pointed to the right rear wing.

"Persian blue."

Chapter 18

Amy walked straight from the police station to Bernard Terrace to catch a bus to the Infirmary. She did not notice the crocuses bravely sticking out into the bitter wind nor the dark clouds tinged with purple drifting overhead, threatening an ice-cold downpour. She also did not notice the hunched figure following her at a distance. She kept her head down, just looking up briefly before crossing roads and finding her bearing at junctions before marching on.

In her head, she was trying to fit the pieces of the puzzle together, but no picture emerged that made sense. There was no evidence that the murdered men were the same ones that had chased Angus but there was no doubt in her mind. So, who had killed them? And why? She knew that she had to speak to Angus, regardless of his father's threats. She had to get him to trust her and tell her all he knew, and only then could she protect him.

As the bus turned into Little France Crescent, the clean, white exterior of the hospital reassured her. This was a place where wounds were healed, and good people looked after others who were in need. A place a million miles away from a potholed car park where people got shot in the forehead and then burned. Amy made her way to the unit, but Cathy was not on duty, which was a shame. Amy could always rely on her to report everything that had happened. By now, however, the other nurses also knew Amy, and she was led straight to Angus's bedside. He seemed to be sleeping but when she took his hand in hers, he turned his head and looked into her eyes.

"How are you?" Amy asked, smiling.

When she was here, everything seemed so easy and clear. Just him and her, against the big bad world out there.

"Better, thank you," he mumbled. "Still a bit dopey. Sleeping a lot..."

Amy patted his shoulder as if this might focus his mind.

"Angus, I need you to listen. They found the car that was chasing you with two men inside. They were murdered."

Angus's eyes suddenly opened wide, and Amy saw the realisation dawning on him that things were serious.

"You must tell me what is going on. The police don't seem to have a clue yet, but if they understand that your father is a threat, they will protect you."

Angus closed his eyes again, looking very pale.

Amy shook his shoulder.

"Angus, you must try to concentrate. Tell me what's going on!"

He slowly opened his eyes. The words came out very deliberately as if he had to think about every syllable.

"My dad has nothing to do with it."

Amy looked incredulous.

"He hasn't?"

Angus made an attempt to lift his free hand but winced when the intravenous tubes pulled at his skin.

"I swear."

"So, who is behind all this? Who are you running away from?"

Angus closed his eyes again, saying nothing. Amy shook his shoulder again.

"Angus, you must tell me!"

He seemed to be gathering strength for his next sentence.

"Phillips."

"Who's Phillips?" Amy urged him to go on.

"My dad's former associate. He did all kinds of dirty dealings and tried to pin it on my dad."

Amy could barely contain her excitement at the new lead.

"But why would he be after you? Is he still being investigated?"

Angus seemed exhausted. He closed his eyes again and did not respond to any more questions Amy asked. She stroked his hand gently.

"You must rest now. Don't worry, I'll make sure nothing bad happens to you."

* * *

On Monday morning the station was buzzing like a beehive. DI McCord had called a meeting of the whole team for eleven and was looking over the post-mortem and forensic reports one last time. He always felt a moment of stage fright before such meetings and made sure that he was so well prepared that nobody could catch him out. Just before eleven o'clock the corridors became quiet as everybody assembled in the open plan office.

"Good morning, everyone," he said without raising his voice, while still making his way to the incident board that had gained a few more additions since the previous morning.

They all fell silent immediately. Contrary to what his inferiority complex suggested to him, he commanded much respect among his colleagues. Nobody worked as hard as he did, and he treated everybody regardless of gender, race or social background with equal impatience. The clear-up rate had gone up so much since he had been in charge that even the assistant chief constable had felt obliged to visit the unit to pass on the congratulations of the police commissioner.

McCord cleared his throat.

"Right. Double murder at Musselburgh Lagoons. Saturday night between 9pm and midnight. Gunshot wounds to the forehead on one victim, to the temple of the other. Execution style. Ballistics are still working on the bullets. It looks as if the victims were shot inside the car because there are no traces of blood outside. It could have been one or more attackers. Registration plates were removed, and the car was torched with accelerant, which makes the identification of the bodies difficult. The Doc hazards a guess at two males in their twenties. Dental records are being checked and no DNA matches have come up yet.

"The bodies were found by an elderly birdwatcher early on Sunday morning. He spent the evening before in his favourite pub, and although he left there at eleven, I think we can safely score him off our list of suspects. Nobody has reported two men missing and no eyewitnesses have come forward since our appeal, apart from an elderly woman who claims to have heard two gunshots around 10pm when she closed her bedroom window before going to bed. She lives in Balcarres Road, which is at least three hundred yards away. One would expect the killer or killers to have used silencers, so we're treating this with a degree of scepticism.

"We need to do a house-to-house in the area just in case somebody has seen anything, maybe even before the murder. If this was a spot for drug dealing, we need to know. DC Collins and DC Beveridge, get on to that and liaise with the Drug Squad."

He paused. He could see his colleagues looking at him in anticipation.

"The only tentative lead comes from a young woman who is a fashion writer for the *Forth Write* magazine. Her name is Amy Thornton, and if I'm not mistaken, she will turn up here again soon. Her head is full of conspiracy theories that usually last a few days, but she has identified the car as the one involved in a car accident two weeks ago at the Grassmarket."

"How did she manage that?" Mike Turner, a bright, ambitious young constable asked. "If the registration plates are gone and the car torched?"

"Good question," McCord acknowledged. "My initial reaction was the same. The rear wheel arch was not entirely burnt, and she recognised the paint on it as a particular kind of blue. Persian blue, apparently. Forensics analysed the paint and found that the car had indeed been painted over with this colour, which is fairly unusual."

A murmur went through the room. By the sounds of it, nobody had heard of Persian blue before.

"She also" – McCord cleared his throat to bring their attention back to the case – "remembered part of the number plate. DC Sutton, I believe you are already on to this?"

DC Heather Sutton, a woman in her forties with short, untidy hair nodded.

"Now we are entering what could be the realm of fantasy or a way into an investigation that could be very far reaching indeed."

He paused, looking around the room.

"Miss Thornton says that this car with two men in it chased the car of one Magnus McAdie causing him to crash in the Grassmarket. He is recovering from his head injuries at the Royal Infirmary. Magnus McAdie happens to be the son of Kenneth McAdie who was acquitted of tax evasion four years ago. The Met was also investigating a drug angle, but it never made it to court. Some of you might be familiar with the name."

A few of the colleagues mumbled agreement.

"There were suggestions in the press that Magnus was a witness in the case. After the court case, Magnus changed his name to Angus Adamson and moved to Edinburgh where he runs the pub The Pibroch. Fraser will be looking into the pub's accounts. I've been in touch with colleagues down south to get access to the transcription of the trial and all the files connected to it. DC Jeffries, I want you to go through these files with a fine-tooth comb and look for anything that comes up in connection with Magnus McAdie."

Jeffries nodded.

"According to Miss Thornton, who phoned the station last night, Magnus McAdie claims to be on the run not from his father but from his father's former associate, a Mr Phillips, who, according to Magnus, was really the bad guy in the whole affair. DC Gillespie, you find me everything there is about this Phillips and liaise with Jeffries because his name might have popped up during the trial."

He looked around the room until he seized upon a young female PC. "Dharwan, I want you to get in touch with Magnus's old school and find out what he was like. Never mind the GDPR nonsense, this is a murder inquiry after all. I want to know everything, who were his friends, did he ever steal a chocolate bar from the tuck shop, everything."

McCord liked Surina Dharwan. She looked like an Indian princess and had most men in a tizzy after two minutes, but her sweet smile was deceptive. She was as sharp as a nail and tenacious as a terrier. If there was any dirt to be dug up about Magnus McAdie, she would find it.

"According to Miss Thornton, Magnus McAdie is the victim in all this and in serious danger. This may well be right, and we must not discount the possibility. On the other hand, I have the impression that Miss Thornton is a little biased where young McAdie is concerned. She seems to think that if a man almost runs over a woman, it qualifies him for romantic involvement."

A subdued giggle went through the room.

"However," McCord warned, "she has given us the only lead that we have, she certainly has an exceptional eye for detail, and she is close to Magnus. So, when she comes, treat her with courtesy, send her to me straightaway and if I'm not here, take careful notes of everything she says. Also, if you are dealing with anything to do with the McAdies, tread carefully. We are just making routine enquiries, dotting the i's and crossing the t's etc. If we go in too heavy, I'll have Kenneth McAdie's lawyers on my back the next day. So easy does it. If in doubt, check with me first."

He looked round the room. Some looked resigned that the long slog of the investigation had started, others were clearly itching to get onto their computers and phones to be the first to get a breakthrough.

"Off you go, then. Let's get those bastards."

* * *

Many hours later, McCord logged out of his computer, turned to the window and massaged his aching right shoulder. He could just make out the vague silhouette of Arthur's Seat against a moonlit sky, a craggy giant towering over the city. His jaws made a creaking noise as he yawned. It had been a long haul since Sunday morning with only a few fitful hours of sleep, interrupted by nightmares of car chases, gunshots and charred bodies.

He knew he could do no more today. His brain was mush, and he was beginning to feel emotional, which never helped solve a case. When did he last have a holiday? Christmas? A day down at Aberlady Bay, seeing which spring migrants had arrived, would clear his head and recharge his batteries but there was no way he could take a day off now, in the middle of a case.

He had a good team, and he was confident that they would come up with something tomorrow. Sleep was what he needed most but he knew that if he went back to his cold, silent flat, there would be no sleep. Numbers, words and pictures would be swirling round his head until the early morning. Maybe he should go to his dad's for a game of chess? He was so proud of his son who was doing such vital work, keeping the streets safe for decent folk. McCord liked being with his dad; unlike so many parents, he made no demands and was just happy to have his boy back for a little while. He liked to know about the cases that he was working on, and McCord was usually grateful for somebody utterly discreet to bounce ideas off.

But there was something about this case that got to him. Of course, he dealt with homicides all the time, drink-driving, drug-fuelled stabbings, heart-breaking suicides, but most of the time these were the actions of people who were not themselves, driven crazy by chemicals or the hopelessness of their lives. This one was different. A cold, clinical execution, and he had a notion of the killer or killers peeling off their blood-spattered clothes and gloves, disposing of them in a well-chosen place where the police would not find them, and then having a drink to celebrate the successful outcome of an evening's work.

He understood the fragility of the human psyche that wreaked havoc in so many lives and, on a normal day, he would have denounced the notion of the devil. But when he came across a killing that was so utterly devoid of feeling, he wondered what it was if not evil. And somehow he did not want to drag that poison into his dad's house and contaminate it with it. No, on an evening like this he needed to talk to someone who was at home in the darkness. Dolly might even have heard something about Archie Turnbull's latest moves. He said a brief goodbye to the night shift, went to the off-licence across the road for a bottle of Laphroaig and hailed a taxi to take him to The Orchard.

Chapter 19

Angus was much more alert today, and Amy was thrilled to find him bright-eyed and sitting up in his bed.

"You're looking so much better," she observed.

"Yes, I've stood up today for the first time since... since the accident. I thought I could walk to the bathroom but just managed two seconds on my feet. I couldn't believe that all the strength had gone out of my legs in such a short time. But the doctor said, I'd get stronger by the day now, just to take it easy."

He was clearly excited about the prospect of walking to the bathroom, and Amy rejoiced with him. Apart from a plaster on the forehead hiding a gash that had been stitched up, the bandages around his head now left his face uncovered, so that Amy could drink in every detail of his handsome features.

"And what have you been up to?" he asked casually.

"I phoned the DI, you know, that rude man, and told him about your father's associate and..."

Angus's face clouded over.

"Amy, I told you to leave it alone. What are you bothering the police for? I had an accident, that is all." He grabbed her hand. "I didn't know what I was talking about. The medication still makes me confused. Will you please promise me to stop asking about it? Please?"

Amy's heart made a somersault. She realized she would find it very difficult to refuse him anything.

"I promise not to ask anymore," she smiled, "as long as you give me no reason to worry."

As if he had read her thoughts, he stroked her hand with his thumb.

"There is nothing to worry about. What did he say?"

"Who?" Amy asked, already thinking of other things she would not refuse him.

"The DI."

"Oh, he said he would investigate it. But I'm not sure about him. I think he is just trying to fob me off."

Angus leaned back into his cushion and his grip relaxed.

"Please let it go. You should be looking after me," he said playfully. "Talking of which, could you do me a huge favour?" he asked, looking slightly embarrassed.

"Of course." Amy beamed. "What is it?"

"Now that I'm off the tubes and a bit more mobile, I'd like some of my things. Pyjamas, underwear, my washbag and my laptop. I would have asked my mum, but she is looking after my grandmother and my dad's gone back to Guernsey. Do you think you could get that for me?"

"Of course," Amy said again, relieved to hear that McAdie senior was hundreds of miles away. "How do I get into your flat?"

He leaned over to open the drawer of the bedside table but suddenly flinched with pain. Amy gently eased him back on his cushion and opened the drawer. She took out a set of keys.

"These are for the flat above the pub. The one with the yellow cap on it goes in first, at the top, then the green one, below. Once you're in, press 5612 on the keypad next to the door, but be quick about it. If you take longer than ten seconds, the alarm goes off. On the way out, you do the same, just in reverse, okay?"

"Geez." Amy chuckled. "What do you keep in your flat? The nation's gold reserves?"

She wrote down the numbers into the notes on her phone. Angus looked as if he wanted to say something but did not.

"Everything okay?" Amy asked, sensing his unease.

"Sure," he said brightly, "thank you so much."

Amy took her bag and brushed his cheek with her lips.

"See you tomorrow."

He smiled at her, and suddenly her chest seemed too small for her pounding heart.

"Yes, see you then."

* * *

The Pibroch looked spick and span as if it had been washed clean by the rain. The broken glass had been replaced and the graffiti removed. The pub was busy with tourists looking for a reasonably priced evening meal, and Norrie was scurrying around with platefuls of haggis towers and, for the less adventurous, steak and ale pie. When he caught sight of Amy, he signalled her to wait for him at the bar. As soon as he had served the table, he joined her.

"Can I get you a drink?" he offered politely.

"No, thanks," Amy said. "I just wanted to tell you that Magnus, eh, Angus is feeling better. If you need any urgent signatures or something, he is up for it now, I think."

Norrie nodded, looking pleased.

"I'm glad that he is coming round. Hell of a thing to happen to a young lad. Actually, his father has been round to pay the urgent bills, and he had the window repaired as well. He even gave me a bonus for looking after the place on my own, which was really nice of him. But thanks, there are some issues with suppliers I want to discuss with him."

Amy got up from her bar stool.

"He's asked me to get a few things from his flat, so I'll do that now. Bye, Norrie, take care."

"You, too."

Norrie rushed off to serve his customers and Amy pulled up the hood of her coat as she opened the door. Neither of them noticed the man who had been standing next to Amy at the bar. He waited for the door to close behind her, put down his half-empty glass and left the pub.

* * *

Amy quickly climbed the outside stairs leading to Angus's flat. A fierce wind had risen from the sea, and the rain had made the metal steps slippery, so she held on to the rusty railings until she reached the top landing. She took out the keys, mumbling the security code, worried she might get it wrong and have the police arrive to arrest her for attempted burglary. She wondered what DI McCord would make of that.

In the end, it all worked out, the door fell back into its lock and the burglar alarm stopped its frenzied beeping. Now she was in his flat; now she would see where he spent his time and get to know him better. To her surprise, it was warm; he must have had the heating on a repeat setting. Just as well, because there was still a night frost, and the pipes were always in danger of freezing. She switched on the lights, took off her coat and looked around.

A narrow hallway led into a tiny but very modern kitchen, all steel and black, and a spacious living room with a large bay window. The expensive cream-coloured curtains were drawn, shielding her from the gusts that made the old sash windows rattle. Squally showers threw water against the panes as if intent to smash them. The place could have done with an airing but the windows all had security locks and since there was a gale raging outside, she decided not to bother. It was a calm, comfortable room with a huge leather sofa and two armchairs in a semi-circle around a 55" plasma screen and an old-fashioned fireplace with a sheepskin rug in front on the opposite side of the room. A coal bucket stood next to it. Amy got momentarily lost, conjuring up romantic scenes in front of a roaring fire, until she remembered what she was here for.

She hesitated for a second before going into his bedroom. It seemed wrong to go in there for the first time without him. There were clothes spread on the bed and the chair beside it as if he had just got changed before rushing out. Amy picked up a shirt and held it to her face. She stayed like that for a while, intoxicated by his smell. Then she saw that some of her make-up had smudged the front of the shirt, so she threw it guiltily into the washing basket.

In a chest of drawers, she found a clean pair of pyjamas, pants and socks and stuffed them into her backpack. One corner of the room was taken up by a wooden desk. It was tidy and there was nothing on it that betrayed who he was. She carefully lifted his laptop and the cable and put them into the black bag leaning against the wall under the desk.

The drawers seemed to cry out for her to open them, and briefly she debated with herself whether it was right for her to invade his privacy like that. Eventually, she decided it was her duty to find out what she could; after all, she only wanted to help him. The first drawer contained a ledger with names, contact details and prices and other paperwork connected with the business. The other was full of stationery.

Disappointed, she went into the bathroom. She admired the classy fittings that must have cost a fortune. No thirty-year-old mixer taps here that managed to scald and chill you at the same time like at home. Home. Amy had never felt such a strong yearning for her own place before. Of course, it was out of the question with the exorbitant rents in the centre of Edinburgh, and it seemed ungrateful towards her mum who had always given her everything she could possibly afford – and yet, it was time to leave the nest. And now with John on the scene, she could see possibilities, many possibilities.

Raucous laughter from the pub below jolted her out of her reverie, and she started to look around for other things he might need. His washbag stood on the rim of the bathtub, and she packed shampoo, shower gel, toothbrush and toothpaste, and the electric razor. There was even a moisturiser on the shelf, and, approving strongly of men looking after their skin, Amy stuffed it into the bag. Just as well she had her backpack with her today.

In the hall, she stopped to think if she had remembered everything but even when she decided she had, she found it difficult to leave. Quietly, as if she could be heard, she went back into the living room. She examined the shelving unit in the lounge for clues to his tastes. On top of the unit, a framed photograph of him and his parents, but no photos of anybody else, which Amy noticed with considerable satisfaction. Angus was not a great reader, by the looks of it, but he had taken the Michael Morpurgo books from his childhood with him into hiding. Some science fiction, some fantasy and a pile of rugby and old school magazines.

Reluctantly, she made to leave the flat. In the hall, she put on her coat and the backpack and as she swung around, she brushed against the mirror that was hanging on the wall next to the door. Her heart stopped for a second as she expected it to crash to the ground and shatter into a thousand pieces. But it only swung to and fro and came to rest on its hook, just slightly tilted. Carefully, Amy took the sides to adjust it when something fell to the floor.

She hunched down to pick up the folded sheets of paper that had been taped to the back of the mirror. The Sellotape had deteriorated over time, and the knock Amy had given the mirror must have dislodged them.

Amy's heart thumped. This was it. This must be the answer to why Angus was hiding.

She sat down on the floor and, with trembling hands, unfolded the sheets of paper. Each said the same thing, written in capitals with angry strokes that had dug into the paper so deeply that it was torn in some places. Angus must have kept them behind the mirror, out of sight of any visitors but as a constant reminder to be vigilant every time he left his flat. Amy's mind was racing. Should she confront Angus with what she had found? Maybe he would think she was snooping around in his flat and would never want to see her again. Should she take the letters to the police? But what if he noticed they had gone? He would know it was her who had taken them.

After staring at the odious objects for a few minutes, she came to a decision. She took a picture of each of the sheets on her phone and folded them again exactly the way she had found them. Then she went to the desk and found some double-sided Sellotape in one of the drawers. Carefully, she stuck the tape in the same place and fixed the sheets to the back of the mirror. Now nobody would be able to tell they had been removed. She put the tape back in the same place and looked around. The joy she had felt exploring his world had turned to fear. Suddenly, she could not wait to get out. She grabbed the bags, quickly typed in the code and locked the door twice from the outside. All the way home, oblivious to the driving rain, she whispered the one awful sentence:

> *YOU WILL PAY FOR WHAT YOU HAVE*
> *DONE TO MY FAMILY*

On South Bridge, the lights from her mother's shop flooded the pavement and gilded the little stream of dirty rainwater that ran across the bumpy tarmac. What was going on? At this time of night her mother would have long locked up and gone upstairs. The hatred emanating from those letters had seeped into Amy's world, and in a sudden panic, she ran the last twenty yards with Angus's bag awkwardly swinging from her shoulder. The old-fashioned bell almost somersaulted as she burst open the door and gave Valerie, who had just come in from the back room, the fright of her life.

"What on earth happened, sweetheart? You look like a ghost, and you're soaked to the skin. No, don't touch anything!" she shouted suddenly as Amy, still gasping from the sprint, was about to collapse on an old, rickety chair.

It was only now, after her mother's torrent of words had reassured her she was fine, that Amy noticed the state of the shop. The floor and all surfaces had been covered with old sheets that were splattered with paint, as was Valerie herself, who was holding a dripping brush. Amy tried not to move although her shoulder was hurting.

"What *are* you doing, Mum?" she asked, suddenly very weary.

Valerie wiped the sweat from her forehead, covering it with even more emulsion.

"John is right. This place is in a mess. We got a lovely sofa and matching armchair today, and they're going to be delivered tomorrow. So, I thought, I'd give the shop a lick of paint before they arrive."

Amy saw the sense in that and looked at the three walls that had been done.

"Vintage taupe? Classy," she decided. "Let me put my bag down, and I'll give you a hand."

* * *

Tristan could barely contain his excitement. After following this woman for what seemed like five hundred miles, he had been about to give up. But here he was, at Magnus's flat, above his pub. It had given him a thrill to stand just two yards away from Amy

Thornton and the guy in the pub and to listen in on their conversation without them realising it. Angus Adamson! So that must be the name Magnus used nowadays. He cackled and was annoyed at the same time that he had not thought of the obvious transformation of the names. What a gift that this Thornton woman was in and out of his flat! He must have charmed her even in a semi-conscious state. That was Magnus all right, the great seducer. But now, with the help of this girl, he could have some fun with him before he struck the final blow. But it would have to wait until tomorrow because the shops were all shut now. Time to go to his hotel and have some food and a rest. Sleep would not come, he knew, until it was done.

Chapter 20

It was a hectic morning for all of them, so Amy had to wait until noon before she could finally share her news over a brew and a light lunch at The Green Bean. For the first few minutes, John could not keep his eyes off Valerie's beautifully shaped ear where a tiny spot of emulsion had escaped her vigorous scrubbing, but eventually Amy managed to get his full attention. She told them every detail about the visit to Angus's flat, leaving out only her thoughts on wanting her own place. Then she showed them the pictures of the letters on her phone.

"What shall I do now?" she asked, genuinely at a loss.

"Show them to the police and stay away from that boy," Valerie said, without a moment's hesitation.

"I knew you would say that." Amy was disappointed. "And anyway, I can't, I need to take him his stuff, don't I. But what am I going to say to him?"

"I would say nothing just yet," John argued reasonably. "Clearly, he does not want you to know, otherwise he would have confided in you, and we have no idea what it is all about. If you tell him, he will just suspect you of going through his things and having betrayed his trust. You must show it to the police, though. It might help them to solve the case, or they might well have found out something already that explains it."

The thought of facing this uncouth DI yet again did not appeal to Amy at all but, on the other hand, it would give her an excuse to go to the station and maybe pick up some news.

"I think you're right, John. Is it okay if I go straight after lunch?"

John sighed. "I do hope this ends up as a breaking news story because I seem to be spending a lot of manpower on it."

"Don't encourage her," Valerie complained. "Do you really want her mixed up in this?"

"It seems that she is mixed up in this already, whether we like it or not," he replied mildly.

Amy shot him a grateful glance and looked again at the pictures.

"What could it mean?" Amy said. "What is he supposed to have done to a family that is so awful? He can't have! He's..."

She stopped herself before she betrayed too much of her feelings but need not have bothered. Valerie and John got the picture anyway.

"Why didn't he go to the police with them then?" Valerie asked. "It's a clear threat, and it was repeated. Surely there's a law against that."

"Well, either he has something to hide that he does not want the police to look into, or," John continued, seeing Amy shaking her head violently, "or he is being persecuted by a nutcase."

Amy nodded approvingly.

"Maybe that's why he is hiding. That means, however, that the letters refer to something that happened when he was still Magnus McAdie. He was still at school then and living in leafy Knightsbridge, so what could anybody have against him?"

"Bullying?" wondered Valerie.

"But why the mention of a family? It doesn't make sense." Amy lowered her head. "We're just treading water with this story."

John suddenly put his cup down.

"That day you went through the newspaper archives," he said, "you told me about this family that was in the papers at the same time as the McAdies. Some drug tragedy you wanted to write about later, remember? Did they not live in Knightsbridge as well?"

Amy perked up. "You're right! The Foverans!"

"Who are the Foverans?" asked Valerie.

"The family of the late Lord Foveran," Amy explained. "During a wild party, their son jumped off the roof because he was high on drugs. Lord Foveran died of a heart attack when he saw the body of his son, and the friend who had supplied him with the drugs killed himself with an overdose straight afterwards."

"How awful," Valerie said. "Did you know them, John?"

John smiled.

"I don't know every titled person in the country, you know."

* * *

At St Leonard's, Amy was greeted solicitously by DC Struthers who winked at her suggestively as he showed her into the DI's office. She just managed to uncurl her lip before shaking DI McCord's hand. There was a shadow of a beard showing on his face, but she approved of the maroon shirt that set off his mocha eyes. There was a crease across his chest where the iron had slipped but then, he was a busy, and, judging by his temperament, a single man.

"Any news about the associate?" Amy enquired without any preliminaries and sat down without being offered a chair.

DI McCord gave her the already familiar look.

"Not yet," he enunciated clearly, as if speaking to a toddler, "you only told me about him two days ago. What can I do for you today?"

If she was not mistaken, the sarcasm had given way to a mild irony.

"The question you should ask instead is, what can *I* do for you," she retorted.

She tapped on her phone and held it out to him. Reluctantly, he took it and enlarged the first photo with his thumb and index finger. Amy noticed that his fingernails were clean and neatly cut. Who had said that a man's fingernails were more important than his business card? He looked up.

"What are these?"

"Anonymous letters I found in Magnus's flat yesterday. Four of them, all the same. They were hidden behind a mirror."

"Did you have a warrant to search his flat?" he asked with a frown.

Amy was about to protest when she saw the twinkle in his eye. Still, she did not want him to think she was a nosey parker.

"He had asked me to get some of his things," she said defensively, pointing to the laptop bag and her bulging backpack, "and as I was leaving, I knocked the mirror in the hall, and these letters fell down."

"Interesting," DI McCord admitted. "They could explain why he went into hiding."

Amy lifted her chin.

"Do you believe me now that he is in danger?"

McCord shrugged.

"If every threatening note led to a murder, the bodies would be piling up in the streets. But," he added quickly when he saw the expression on Amy's face, "of course we monitor such threats. What has he said about them?"

"I haven't asked him – yet."

"And I don't think you should. One does wonder why he didn't report them."

"That's exactly what my mother said."

"Is your mother investigating this case, too?" he asked, enjoying her reddening face.

Then his grin faded.

"Listen, Miss Thornton, I do take this seriously. You were right about the car. If the people inside were the same, they are now dead, as you know. Please, keep your eyes open but don't go round playing detective."

Amy got up to leave. She had just about had enough of this patronising moron. Playing detective indeed! As if she was seven years old. If he didn't take her seriously, she would not tell him about the possible Foveran connection. She would uncover that herself, and he would end up with egg on his face. With her head held high, she marched out of the office. With a sigh, DI McCord went back to his investigation.

* * *

Angus returned her peck on the cheek when she arrived. He was excited like a little boy about having his own things back and wondered when he could have his first shower. Although Amy normally was not inclined to act as a nurse, she did envy Cathy that particular job.

"Everything okay at the flat?" he asked.

Amy looked at him sharply but could not detect any urgency in his question.

"Yes, the heating's been on a timer, so the pipes are all fine. Nice place you've got there."

"It does me for now," Angus said, "as long as I'm single, anyway."

Amy wondered what that sentence implied and came to an encouraging conclusion.

"Hopefully that won't be too long. It is not good for people to live on their own," she added hastily so as not to seem desperate. "I talked to Norrie as well. The pub is looking great, the broken glass has been replaced, all the graffiti cleaned off, and the place was buzzing. Norrie said your dad had been and sorted things out."

She smiled innocently and waited for some revealing comment.

"Yeah, I know," was all Angus said as he leaned back into his pillows. "I'm sorry, I just get very tired still."

Amy took the hint. She grabbed her empty backpack and leaned over for a kiss goodbye.

"Get some rest. I'll see you tomorrow."

* * *

Back at the office, Amy opened the folder 'Mystery Man' where she had collated all the information and speculation she had gathered on the case. She quickly found the link to the newspaper articles from four years ago and read them again, this time a lot more carefully. The Foverans lived in Beechwood Gardens, number 10. She checked her file on the McAdies and found their address: 12 Beechwood Gardens. They were neighbours. It was the school-leavers' party for the elder son, and Angus, then Magnus, had also done his A-Levels that year. Surely, he would have been invited to that party? And only a couple of months later, he had become Angus Adamson, the owner of The Pibroch, and had got rid of his history.

Amy decided to start with the housekeeper, Mrs Linton. She must have known everything that was going on. She googled the BT phone book and typed in her name and Beechwood Gardens. Nothing. Not surprising that a housekeeper could not afford a place in Knightsbridge, and she would no longer be there as she had said she would not set foot in that house again. So maybe Mrs Pomfreys, the nosey neighbour, was a better bet.

Please let her be in the phone book, Amy thought, please... A number came up. Amy whooped. She got pen and paper ready and tapped on the number. It rang four times. Maybe she was out. Maybe she was dead?

A vigorous female voice answered.

"Yes?"

"Mrs Pomfreys?"

"Yes?" The voice sounded suspicious.

"Amy Thornton here from the *Forth Write*."

She paused a moment to let this information sink in.

"I'm writing an article on the human cost of recreational drugs and how they destroy not only the lives of the people taking them but also those of their families. I was wondering if you would be happy to share your views. I understand that you know the Foverans, and it seems to me that there are few families who have suffered as much as they did."

Mrs Pomfreys was flattered and relished the idea of seeing her name in print again.

"I'm happy to help, of course," she said, "but that happened almost four years ago, and it was all over the papers at that time."

"What I'm interested in," said Amy, "are the long-term effects. There is always a great splash when it happens but afterwards the families and their suffering are forgotten. And that is not right, is it?"

"It definitely isn't," Mrs Pomfreys agreed, feeling good about the fact that she was being supportive of the

Foverans rather than just an ordinary gossip. "This business really has destroyed the whole family."

Amy had switched the speakerphone on, and her pen was poised.

"So do they still live in the same house?"

"Well, Lady Foveran has never been there since, and who can blame her? Losing her son and her husband in the same night, the poor woman. Nice she was, too, no airs and graces. I often met her at the local shop, and when we organised the street party for the Queen's Jubilee, she helped out a lot and we chatted for quite a while."

"So where is she now?" Amy butted in before Mrs Pomfreys could relate the whole conversation word for word.

"First, she was at Bethlem Royal for a few months. Word is that she tried to kill herself. Now she is in a private care home near here. I went to see her once, but she didn't recognize me. She just stared at the wall and didn't say a word."

That could be proof of a very lucid mind, Amy thought but scolded herself for being unkind.

"How awful," she said instead. "Is there not an elder son as well?"

"Yes, Tristan," she said. "Poor boy, you could say he lost his whole family that night."

"He's not still living in that house all by himself, is he?"

"He is! Not healthy at all, if you ask me. I rang the doorbell a few times to see if I could help but nobody answered."

There's a surprise, Amy thought.

"He is often away, though," Mrs Pomfreys continued. "I'm not sure whether he stays with relations or has a job that involves travelling."

Amy could hear how the lack of information pained Mrs Pomfreys.

"One really worries about the poor boy, but at least he's got Emily."

Amy perked up.

"Who's Emily?"

Mrs Pomfreys voice brightened.

"Emily was the girlfriend of the drug dealer who gave the drugs to Tristan's brother before he jumped. At least he did the decent thing and killed himself after all the misery he caused. You wonder why Tristan is so friendly with her, but people say that she knew nothing about the drug dealing."

Amy scribbled furiously.

"What is her second name?"

"Fullerton. Nice girl. She is studying History at the LSE now, but she goes and sees Tristan regularly when he's at home."

"Are they a couple then?" Amy asked.

"Not sure. I don't think she stays over if that's what you mean."

Amy felt sure the neighbours would know if she was.

"Do you think Tristan or Emily would be prepared to give me an interview?"

"I doubt it," Mrs Pomfreys said, "they're very private people."

No wonder, Amy thought.

"Could you possibly give me Tristan's phone number and Emily's address, just in case?"

"Hang on, I must have the phone number of the landline in my diary. I phoned his mother a few times about the Jubilee. Here it is."

Amy jotted down the number.

"And Emily's address?"

"She lives just round the corner, in Oakbank Road, number 5. I don't know her phone number, I'm afraid. Young people nowadays only use their mobile phones, don't they?"

Amy thanked Mrs Pomfreys profusely and promised to send her a copy when the article appeared.

She leaned back and chewed on the back of her pen. She had to speak to Tristan and Emily.

Chapter 21

It was after midnight, and still there were people hanging about the pub. Tristan had thought they had strict closing times in Scotland what with their Calvinist heritage and all. It was a clear night but the bonus of not getting wet was cancelled out by the fact that the temperature had dropped to minus five. The cold sweat that lay like a thin film over his skin had chilled him right through, and he had to make a conscious effort to keep his teeth from chattering.

On the plus side, he had had time to think, and he had finally made up his mind about the grand finale. Now that he knew how he would get to Magnus, it was all unbelievably simple. He pulled out his phone. His fingers were so cold, he could barely move them but eventually he managed to place the order for the stuff he needed and arranged for delivery to his hotel. Everything was taking shape.

As he stowed his phone away, the last group of drinkers tumbled out into the street and dispersed on the pavement amid cheers and overly sentimental goodbyes. Time to strike some terror into him, a little apéritif, so to speak, before the last supper. First, the flat. The stairs were round the side and in the shade of the neighbouring building, so he was confident that nobody would notice him. It took only a few seconds for him to run up and back down the stairs. The pub was trickier. He hung about a bit, waiting for a taxi and some people on their way home to pass. Eventually, there was nothing for it, he just had to risk it. He pulled his balaclava down and jumped out of the shadows.

Chapter 22

"The guys are waiting for you," DS Fraser said cautiously. It was not like his boss to be late for anything, and he suspected correctly that DI McCord was therefore not in the best of moods.

"I know," McCord growled, slamming the phone down. "The Super wants an update on the double murder so that he can show off his uniform at a press conference where he tells them all what a marvellous job we are doing. Just a shame he is stopping us from doing exactly that."

He got up and gathered his notes for the staff meeting but found his exit blocked by bloody Miss Thornton.

"Not now," he said, about to explode, "I'm already late for a staff briefing."

But instead of moving out of the way, she held a plastic bag in front of his face.

"What's this?" he demanded, impatiently. But when he looked up from the bag into her eyes, the usual cockiness had disappeared and been replaced by naked fear.

"What the hell is this?" he asked again.

She pushed the bag into his hands. It was not very heavy, and whatever was in it had an untidy oblong shape. He knew from her face that he would discover something unpleasant but if he hesitated a second longer, he would look like a wimp. He undid the knot and looked inside. The bulging amber eyes of a tabby cat, frozen wide open in terror, stared at him. A thin rope had squeezed the neck to the diameter of a finger and the little furry limbs were so rigid, he was afraid they would break off if he moved the bag.

"It was hanging from the doorknob outside my flat this morning," Amy said in a barely audible whisper, "and this note was pinned onto the door frame."

She held out a note, carelessly torn from an ordinary pad of lined A4, written in capitals with felt-tip pen.

CURIOSITY KILLED THE CAT.

McCord swallowed and turned to Fraser who had hung back.

"Take a photo of this," he said brusquely, shoving the bag into his hands, "have the rope dusted for fingerprints and checked for DNA, and then get rid of it, for Christ's sake. Then process the note. It doesn't matter if you miss the meeting, you're up to date on the case anyway."

DS Fraser hurried off in disgust.

McCord took a deep breath and turned to Amy, who fully expected a self-satisfied 'I told you so'. But his expression had softened, and he stretched out his arm to pat her on the shoulder as he would have done to a child, pulling back only in the last second.

"I'm sorry," he said quietly, "that must have been a nasty surprise."

Amy nodded, almost more shocked now by his reaction than the threat.

"We're working flat out on this and making progress. Leave it to us. Go to work if you must but stay at home the rest of the time, and don't wander about on your own."

He handed her a card with his name and scribbled his mobile number underneath that of the station.

"Call me, day or night, if anything else happens that worries you. Understood?"

Amy nodded again.

"Is anybody at home?"

"My mother is working in the shop below," Amy said.

When she had left, her mother was still having a shower. On making the grim discovery, she must have just put the cat into a plastic bag, run to find a taxi and come straight here. She couldn't really remember and wasn't sure why. She was wondering whether to tell her mum. She would be off her head with worry.

"You need to tell your mother," McCord said, as if reading her thoughts. "Your family and friends need to watch out for you as well."

Seeing how shaken she was, he needed to think of something to reassure her.

"Clearly somebody wants you to back off. Stay away from the McAdie boy. If you do that and they don't see you as a threat anymore, the poor cat will have served its purpose and they will leave you alone."

"Do you really think that?" Amy asked meekly.

"I do," he said, fervently hoping he was right. "Now phone your boss, take a taxi home and have a long hot bath. And a drink."

He was already a few yards down the corridor when he turned back.

"You can do so much better than the son of a crime lord, believe me."

As Amy watched him hurrying to his meeting, she managed a little smile.

* * *

All eyes were on him. They knew that if he was late, there was a good reason. Did they have a breakthrough? McCord's face suggested otherwise, and everybody hoped they had not cocked up without even noticing.

"Right. The two victims have been identified as Fergus Tait and Josh Murales. No job or regular income, as far as we can see, but they have been paying rent and on occasion splashing it about. Some evidence of drug use in their flat but not enough to prove they were dealers. The bullets that killed them lead us to a guy last known under the name of Katz Kaminski. The colleagues from Organised Crime tell us that he is a first-class assassin for hire for a first-class price. So, we can assume that Tait and Murales were annoying somebody big time, somebody with a lot of influence and money. The name Archie Turnbull springs to mind but we can't be sure. The question is, what did two small-time pushers do that provoked such drastic action?"

He paused for effect, not expecting an answer, when DC Sutton lifted her hand.

"Yes, DC Sutton?" he asked, surprised not just by the interruption but also because DC Sutton hardly ever spoke, and some colleagues suspected that the only language she understood was computer language. And to some extent that was true, as she would much rather have sent an email.

She cleared her throat, but her voice was hoarse as these were the first words she had uttered that day.

"Chasing this Angus Adamson slash Magnus McAdie caused him to crash and almost die."

The obvious conclusion was that either someone was angry that they chased and almost killed him, or they were angry because they did not manage to kill him.

McCord barely concealed his impatience.

"I know. This was a suggestion originally put forward by Miss Thornton. Unfortunately, there is no evidence and we have only her word for that. She had been almost run over at the time and was probably mistaken."

One could see the pain in DC Sutton's face at having to speak again.

"They definitely did. There is CCTV in the area for the time of the crash. They were right on his bumper for 1.25 miles. Then the cameras stopped."

McCord did not quite manage to hide his surprise.

"Really. Very interesting. Well done, DC Sutton."

His mind was swirling. What did that mean? He needed time to think. But for now, he needed to concentrate on the briefing.

"This supports the theory that the accident, and therefore Magnus McAdie alias Angus Adamson, is closely linked to the murders. The question is how. DS Fraser has looked into the accounts of the pub Magnus owns, and there is…" – he hesitated – "there seems to be nothing dodgy going on. The manager is clean and there have been no suggestions of any criminal activity at the pub. However, when we interviewed him, he told us that the pub had been vandalised on a regular basis in the past few months. He did not report it because Magnus told him not to bother. The question is why."

He pointed to the board where a photo of Kenneth McAdie had been pinned up.

"For a while, we considered the possibility that Magnus may have been hiding from his father, who, as you know, was acquitted of tax evasion on a technicality round about the time Magnus came to Edinburgh. But we have checked the trial transcripts, and there is no evidence at all that Magnus was called as a witness for the prosecution. We know that Kenneth McAdie paid for the pub that Magnus now owns. He also appeared on the scene last week and paid for repairs of all the damage done during Magnus's absence, so it doesn't look as if he is after his son."

McCord was suddenly overwhelmed by a sense of futility and failure. Little crooks like Tait and Murales ended up with bullets in their heads, hundreds of police officers were running round in circles, and guys like Turnbull and McAdie lived a life of luxury and then retired somewhere in the sun. He felt dozens of eyes fixed on him and forced himself back on track.

"Strangely, when Miss Thornton asked Magnus who he thought was behind the chase, he claimed it was a Mr Phillips, an associate of his father's, who he says was behind all the wrongdoing his father was accused of. He told us the same story when we interviewed him. But again, the notes about the trial and the police reports leading up to it give no hint of that. So, I am inclined to think that Magnus McAdie is telling porky-pies, whether out of fear or because he has something to hide, I don't know. He was certainly very jumpy when we came to visit."

He looked at his notes, momentarily at a loss. What a mess this case was! They didn't even know how many cases there were yet.

"To complicate matters, there might be yet another strand to this investigation. While fetching things from Magnus's flat, Miss Thornton came across threatening letters that seem to have been addressed to Magnus."

He missed out the fact that the letters had been hidden.

"We don't want to let on that we know that yet, but we need to find out who might have written them. Dharwan, what have you found out about Magnus from his school days?"

Surina Dharwan shook her head regretfully.

"Nothing, I'm afraid. I'm getting the impression that he was a spoiled, arrogant boy. His former headmaster says he was not particularly popular but there is nothing untoward in his school file and he swore he wasn't holding anything back. I believed him."

"Shame," McCord commented.

He scanned the room. Most of the officers looked as if they had a headache, just like him.

"So much we know, or rather think we know, about the background. There have been more recent developments, though."

His throat was dry, and he wished he had taken a drink with him. He could not even remember when he had last talked so much.

"Last night, somebody sprayed the word 'killer' on the front door of The Pibroch; then a Molotov cocktail was thrown through the side window. The only reason the whole place didn't go up in flames was that the manager was there later than normal to tidy up. He heard the noise of breaking glass and managed to put out the flames before too much damage was done. Again, the CCTV coverage from across the road is interesting. It only covers the front and shows a hooded figure in a balaclava doing the graffiti just after midnight, but then there is a gap of fifteen minutes before the fire starts. What was that person doing in those fifteen minutes? And this morning, just before the meeting, Miss Thornton popped in to show me a strangled cat that had been hung onto her doorknob, accompanied by a note telling her to stop asking questions."

He paused again and when he spoke, his voice sounded worried.

"I don't like where this is going," he said. "I don't like this one bit."

* * *

When the officers had dispersed to continue their parts of the investigation, McCord called DC Sutton aside. With her broad, elongated face, square chin and big limbs, she reminded him of a Clydesdale horse. Her large eyes were deep-set and seemed even bigger behind the blue-tinged glasses she wore, no doubt a result of a lifetime staring at a screen. She had only been in his unit for a couple of weeks. The Super had called him into his office one morning and informed him that DC Sutton would from now on be assigned to him. The barely suppressed glee in his face immediately aroused McCord's suspicion, so he had asked where she came from. Glasgow, he was told, Child Protection Unit. Left under a cloud, Gilchrist had said, darkly, all very hush-hush. She was on her last warning but, by all accounts, was a very gifted officer 'in her own way'.

The next day she had arrived, demanded a secluded desk space all to herself and told him not to partner her with anybody. Normally, DI McCord would have made it immediately clear to her who the alpha male was in this unit but, oddly, the way she said it had been less insubordination than a mere statement of fact. Some instinct had told him it would not be wise to fight this particular battle.

After a few days he had asked Fraser how she got on. According to him, the colleagues called her 'Heather the Hacker' because as a dare, she had managed to pull a suspect's financial records in under ten minutes without having any clearance. McCord should have reported this but the information from the records led to an immediate arrest, followed by a confession, which made it unnecessary to include the hacking into the final report. So, he had kept shtum. That it was also a snub to the Super had nothing to do with it, of course.

It would be a risk involving her, he knew, but he needed somebody who could keep their mouth shut, knew their way around a computer, and was not completely averse to breaking the rules.

"Well done, DC Sutton, for taking the initiative about the CCTV. Now, I need someone reliable and discreet to do some confidential checks for me. Without anybody else knowing," he added, just in case. "Are you up for that?"

DC Sutton shrugged as if this was a stupid question that did not deserve an answer.

DI McCord nodded.

"Come to my office when everybody on this shift has gone, and I'll explain."

Chapter 23

Tristan was sitting at the small desk in his hotel room, tearing open the parcels he had ordered, and which had been delivered that morning. He inspected the contents with satisfaction, tore off a sheet of plain white paper and tipped out all the blue pens from the pack.

The helpful lady at reception had printed out the sheet he had emailed her without looking at it too closely, so now all he needed to do was practise the logo – the unmistakeable sky-blue bracket underneath the dark blue letters. Of course, he could have had the whole thing printed professionally but that might have aroused suspicion. And he did not want to draw attention to himself, not just yet.

After the fifth attempt, the logo looked about right. He cut out the drawing and the text and carefully slid it into the lanyard. All being well, nobody would get too close a look anyway. He leant back in his chair and went through every step of the mission that lay before him. In his head, he imagined his encounter with Magnus. At that very moment, his phone rang.

"You need to come home, now," Emily's voice at the other end sobbed. "It's your mum."

Chapter 24

After the prescribed hot bath in the company of a large gin and tonic, Amy felt light-headed and restless. What was she supposed to do – sit around all day waiting for someone to tie another strangled cat to her door? She did not like being alone in the flat. Her mother was out but her assistant was holding the fort in the shop. Amy was annoyed with herself for being so easily scared and felt guilty about lying to John when she had asked him for the day off this morning. Just a touch of flu, she had said. Now the initial shock had worn off and it was time to come clean. She called his mobile so he would know it was a private call.

He answered immediately.

"Amy? Are you okay?" he said, and she could hear the concern in his voice.

"I am," she said, "but I have a confession to make. I'm not ill."

When she had told him about the cat, there was a brief silence at the other end of the phone.

"Don't come in to work, Amy," John decided. "Have a rest, and when you are ready in a few days, you can work from home until they have found the culprit."

"I don't want to sit around here," Amy complained, "I'd rather do something to take my mind off this whole business."

"There is nobody in the office just now," John said, "Martin and I are both in town, so you had better stay home this morning. And if you do not feel up to coming in later, please take the day off."

* * *

By midday, Amy had done her nails, tidied her room, cleaned the kitchen and watered the plants on the windowsill. She was desperate to see Angus but every time she imagined seeing him, a tabby cat with bulging eyes stretched out his paws in a silent warning.

She looked out of the window onto the houses opposite which looked bright and clean in the sharp spring sunlight. The road was as busy as always and ordinary-looking people were hurrying along the pavement, some dragging suitcases towards Waverley along the uneven pavement. Surely, nobody would dare to attack her in broad daylight in the city centre? And anyway, she would not be reduced to a cowering wreck just because some thugs were trying to intimidate – she jumped as her mobile rang, and instinctively moved away from the window.

The number was not familiar. It rang and rang while she was wondering whether to answer it or not. Just when she had decided it would be worse not to know, it stopped ringing. Furious, she flung the phone onto the kitchen table where it landed with a painful thud and started ringing a second time. She ran over and almost dropped it again because her fingers just would not obey her. She managed to press the green icon and heard somebody breathing at the other end. She wanted to shout, to scream but only a pathetic little squeak came out.

The voice at the other end was reassuringly familiar.

"Miss Thornton? Amy? Are you okay?"

Amy exhaled slowly and felt her heartbeat going back to almost normal.

"DI McCord? Yes, I'm fine, thank you."

"Where are you? Not visiting your boyfriend, I hope?"

"He's not my boyfriend and I'm at home," she said.

"Good. Stay away from the Infirmary and The Pibroch. Did you hear that somebody sprayed graffiti on the pub door and then threw a Molotov cocktail through the window?"

Amy felt faint.

"Is Norrie okay? It didn't burn down, did it?"

"No, luckily, Norrie was there and put the fire out. So, you see, there are a lot of unpleasant things going on."

The tone of his voice belied the understatement. Suddenly she was glad DI McCord existed and that he was now on her contact list.

"There is something you should know," she said.

"Yes?"

The question was laced with scepticism.

"There might be a connection with the Foveran family."

"Go on?"

Amy told him the whole story.

"I can't think of any direct link, but it seems a strange coincidence that these deaths coincided with Magnus's disappearance," she concluded.

"I suppose there *could* be a connection," DI McCord said dismissively, not wanting to fan her enthusiasm for detection. "But I'll *definitely* look into it," he added hastily so that she would not feel the need to do it herself.

"Is it safe to go to work? I'm going mad here on my own doing nothing."

"I think so. But don't accept any lollies from strangers."

"Cross my heart, hope not to die."

They both called off with a smile.

* * *

When Amy returned to the magazine, Martin looked up with a face that was one big question mark asking where she had been this morning. She signalled to him to meet her at the coffee machine, and there she updated him on the latest developments. Horrified, Martin implored Amy not to go anywhere on her own and assured her that John would be happy to hire a bodyguard for her. Amy laughed the suggestion off, sat down at her computer and wondered what to do next. With the food supplement ready to go with a few adjustments that could be done just before publication, John had told her to work on a new fashion feature, but at the moment nothing interested her less than the latest length of skirts or the question of whether torn jeans were still 'in' or so very 'last year'.

In the Royal Infirmary there lay a handsome young man, apparently friendless and gradually getting stronger. He would be wondering where she was if she did not turn up today for the first time since the accident. She should let him know but what should she say? 'Sorry, the police think you could be a villain'? 'Seeing you might get me killed'? And if she did stay away from him and the investigation, who was going to answer all these questions swirling round in her head? They would be niggling away at her forever. There was nothing for it. She needed to speak to the elder son of the late Lord Foveran. The landline at 10 Beechwood Gardens rang for several minutes, but nobody answered.

Chapter 25

Tristan was sitting at the mahogany dining table that had once seen cheerful dinner parties for a dozen people. Now it was cluttered with the paperwork regarding the settlement of his mother's estate. He looked around. So, this was all going to be his, his alone. To do with as he pleased. A little fortune. Or, actually, not so little, he thought, considering the sums on the documents he had just signed. He was the sole survivor, as the solicitor had so succinctly put it. The last in the line. Who would inherit all this when he died? This did not feel like such an outlandish idea, rather a distinct possibility in the near future. Emily should have it, he decided.

She didn't need it, really, but she would know what to do with it. She would invest in microbusinesses in Africa and environmental schemes. She would rescue abandoned dogs in Greece and abused donkeys in Hungary. She would do all the things he laughed at her for, while secretly envying her belief in the good in human nature and in a better future. Without her, he would probably have killed himself, early on, so in that sense, he owed her his life anyway.

Without her barging into his life, forcing him to cook meals with her and eating them afterwards, occasionally pouring his whisky down the drain, dragging him out for a walk and playing hours of Uno and Monopoly with him, he would not have made it to this point. The point he was meant to be at, to put to rights what had been so terribly wronged.

Since they had discovered where Magnus was, he had furtively, bit by bit pushed her away. He had told her he was just trying to find out some background information on Magnus. After he had come back to find his mother dead from a stroke, Emily had offered to stay with him, to be there when the solicitor came, to support him in his hour of need, but thankfully, she had eventually accepted his wish to do this on his own. She did not understand what he needed. He did not need her light, her warmth. On the contrary, they made his task more difficult, even impossible. She would have been going through his parents' things, asking him questions about his past, when they still had a life and the illusion of a future. She would have forced him to remember things that made his eyes sting. He did not want to remember the happy times. He needed to remember that night, every detail, and that would give him the strength to see this through.

He didn't know what lay beyond, and he didn't care. The solicitor had pointed out that all his father's papers were still in his study and needed sorting out, but who cared? On the other hand, the thought of shredding the past, a few sheets at a time, appealed to him. There should be no trace left of his family because they had been obliterated, annihilated that night, and every object perpetuating the idea that they were still here was an insult to their ghosts.

He carried the shredder to the desk, opened the drawers and, without looking at the papers, began to feed them into it. They were sucked in with a shrill whining sound as if they were complaining of their destruction. He imagined the sound Magnus would make when it was his turn, and smiled mirthlessly. Just then the whining stopped and was replaced by a choking noise. The shredder was full.

Angry at having his reverie interrupted, Tristan tipped the thousands of strips of paper onto the floor and replaced the lid. When he picked up the next sheet of paper, one word caught his eye: 'summerhouse'. He lifted the paper up to his face and read the whole page. He could not believe it. He read it again. He wheeled the leather swivel chair up to the desk and opened his father's laptop. He had figured out the password long before in order to watch some 18-certificate films when his father was away on business. He had never looked at any of the files again after discovering the first few had been boring business letters. But now he opened every folder until he found what he was looking for in a file called 'Orwell'. Tristan smiled at the irony of it.

"Dad, you are a bloody genius," he whispered.

He scrolled down the file until he found the date and time. He was just about to click on it when something made him stop. He could not possibly do this without Emily. He went into speed dial and listened to the ring tone. His fingers drummed on the table until Emily's voice on loudspeaker filled the room.

"Tristan? You okay?"

"Oh yes, come over here now. You've got to see this."

Chapter 26

McCord was sitting at his desk, deep in thought. Eventually, he dialled DI Marshall's number. His colleague answered straightaway.

"Any news on our rapist?" McCord asked.

"Nope. Seems to have gone to ground. Maybe Turnbull sorted him out himself. No murder or assault that fits?"

"No, only a double murder that could be his style. Getting nowhere fast with that one. I was wondering – any chance you could email me the dates and times of the attacks?"

"Sure," DI Marshall said. "What's on your mind?"

"Just an idea I want to check out. Use my personal email, I don't want tongues wagging."

"No problem. By the way, we've got wind that Turnbull has a new batch of girls from Albania arriving soon. No details yet, though. Fingers crossed we get him this time."

"Good luck, Marshall."

He punched in the next number.

"DI McCord, Edinburgh, Homicide Division. Could you please put me in touch with the investigating officers in the Foveran case?"

The officer at the other end clearly had never heard of the Foveran case. He sounded as if he was still at school four years ago, McCord thought, but he was keen to help. McCord spoke slowly so that the youth could keep up taking notes.

"June 28th four years ago, the younger son of Lord Foveran, Fabian, accidental death after drug misuse, and Daniel Littlejohn, suicide by drug overdose. Both happened on the same day at the same place, but Littlejohn was not discovered until the following day. I need all reports connected to both cases and would like to speak to the investigating officers. Could you ask them to get in touch and send a copy of the reports?"

He gave the officer, who promised to do this immediately, his email and phone number and rang off.

He got up to look for Fraser but could not find him anywhere, and nobody seemed to know where he was.

After a few minutes, Fraser finally emerged from the stairwell putting his phone away.

"Where have you been?" demanded McCord.

"Just car trouble," Fraser explained. "What's the urgency?"

"We've got a double murder to solve, that's what."

* * *

Amy spent a depressing weekend trying not to think of Angus and failing miserably. When her phone buzzed during dinner on Sunday night, an unknown number showed on the display. She swiped the phone to read the incoming message.

> *Where've you been? You ok? Missing you. Any chance of a visit tomorrow eve? Angus xx.*

Her heart leapt. For a brief moment, she saw the amber eyes of the tabby cat, bulging in terror at the suggestion, and heard DI McCord's warning voice, but then she tilted the phone to hide the screen from her mother who was sitting opposite her and eyeing her suspiciously.

"Who was that?" Valerie asked.

"Just an old school friend," Amy answered, hoping that counted as a half-truth at least.

Quickly, she typed the answer.

> *I'm fine. See you tomorrow xx.*

She leant back in her seat and lifted her glass. Suddenly, she felt alive again. Tomorrow.

* * *

Amy barely slept that night. Visions of her and Angus kissing alternated with an inner debate whether to tell her mother or not. Obviously, she would not tell DI McCord.

Her alarm clock showed 4am when she decided she would take a taxi from Waverley to the Infirmary after work. That way she would be home more quickly and might be spared questions why she was home so late. Again, she felt with complete certainty that she would have to get her own flat as soon as possible. Daydreaming about solving the case and starting a life with Angus in their own home, she finally drifted off.

* * *

Amy had spent the late afternoon watching the hands of the clock. She had made good progress with the fashion article and felt entitled to a full evening. It now being five o'clock, Amy was ready to go but John was standing around, discussing the new educational policy of the SNP with Martin. She had booked a taxi round the corner for five past but feared she would be questioned by John with regards to her plans this evening. After waiting for a couple of minutes, there was no sign of the conversation ending, so she made a dash for it. With a breezy 'See you tomorrow', she hurried out of the office before either of the men could reply.

* * *

Unfortunately, her plan had a flaw. She had not thought about the evening rush hour, and the taxi was crawling through the city centre at walking speed. A few times she was close to telling the driver to stop and let her out, but the gentle drizzle had turned to rain, and she did not want to appear at Angus's bedside looking like a drowned rat. It was a quarter to six by the time she paid the driver and hurried through the familiar corridors to the High Dependency Unit.

Angus was already waiting for her. He heaved himself up and kissed her lightly on the mouth. It was the first time, and although Amy had been dreaming of this moment for days now, she was completely taken by surprise. Slightly dizzy, she sat down on the chair next to his bed and held his hand.

"Where have you been?" he asked. "I've missed you."

"Working," she said vaguely. "How did you get my number, and a phone, for that matter?"

"My dad gave me one, and then I just asked Cathy for your number. Elementary, my dear Watson."

"Is your father around?" Amy asked lightly, as if just making conversation.

"He's gone to see some relations in Glasgow today. You're not going to tell him I called, are you?" he asked sharply.

Amy squeezed his hand.

"Of course not. Angus, you must tell me..."

He suddenly sat up but, wincing with pain, fell back onto his pillow.

"I have good news, Amy, that's why I called. They're going to move me to a normal ward soon, and if all goes well, I might be discharged next week."

"That's wonderful news." Amy tried to sound happy but worries about his safety moved like dark clouds across her mind.

"So," he continued breathlessly, ignoring her concern, "I need more clothes from my flat. Would you mind?"

"Of course not," Amy repeated.

Angus regarded her thoughtfully.

"You are an angel. The key is in the drawer and the dirty washing in the bag over there."

Amy opened the drawer and found the key amongst bags of sweets and tissue packets. Next to it lay a brand-new iPhone XR. Daddy was certainly not stingy. She was just about to start an innocent conversation about him that might lead to Angus opening up to her, when she saw that his eyes were closed.

She squeezed his hand, and he briefly squinted at her.

"Thank you," he mumbled, "I'm feeling very tired again."

Amy checked the monitor but there were no alarming dips or spikes in the lines running across the screen.

"You get some rest. I'll come back tomorrow evening with the clothes. Call me if..." – she was about to say 'your dad is around' but decided against it – "if it isn't convenient."

"Will do."

She bent down, and he turned his mouth up for a lingering kiss that left her heart hammering and her brain buzzing. He smiled dreamily.

"See you tomorrow."

She slid the keys into her jacket pocket, fetched the bag from the corner of the room and reluctantly left.

On her way out, she hung around until Cathy appeared from another room.

"Where have you been?" the nurse asked. "We've missed you."

"Just busy at work. By the way," Amy said, "there is no need for Angus's father to know I've been here, okay?"

Cathy winked conspiratorially.

"Got it. Will you be back tomorrow?"

"Definitely."

* * *

As Amy walked out of the ward, it occurred to her that a bag full of men's clothes would attract her mother's attention and elicit unwelcome questions. She would have to drop off the bag just now and pick it up tomorrow. This secrecy would cost her a fortune in fares but there was nothing else for it.

She took a taxi to Angus's flat. She unlocked the door, dropped the bag on the floor and was about to lock the door again when she remembered the code. She pushed the door open again, just wide enough to slip inside. She punched in the numbers, shut the door, waited for the bleep and repeated the procedure, all the while muttering curses.

She checked her phone. Normally, she would be home now, and she was sure her mother would worry, as it was dark by now. A quick message would do. 'Home in ten min. Xx', send. And she did not even have to lie.

* * *

Amy hurried up the iron stairs to the flat but hesitated on the landing halfway up. She had done something she should not have, and the little girl in her feared immediate punishment. What if there was another dead cat hanging on the door? Or worse? It occurred to her that her mother had not replied to her text. Panicking now, she ran up the last steps. There was nothing hanging from the handle. She opened the door. The reassuring smell of dinner bubbling on the stove flooded her nostrils and she heard her mother rummaging in the kitchen.

"Hi, Mum," she shouted. "I'm home!"

"About time," Valerie's voice came back from the kitchen. "Tea will be ready in five minutes!"

* * *

Having got away with one misdemeanour, it is human nature to be emboldened to commit another. Now that she had seen Angus and even been to his flat without any immediate ill effects, Amy continued her efforts to solve the mystery surrounding him the following day.

As soon as John had retired into his office and Martin was hunched over his computer, she dialled the London number scrawled on a Post-it note that was tattered from being fingered so often.

The phone at the other end rang and rang. The longer it went on, the more uncertain Amy became. She heard DI McCord's warning voice but before the tabby cat could start pleading, the ringing stopped, and an irritated voice snapped, "Hello?"

Amy tried to keep calm.

"Could I speak to Tristan, son of the late Lord Foveran?"

There was a pause.

"Who are you?"

This was not an auspicious start, but Amy bravely plodded on.

"Amy Thornton from the *Forth Write*."

There was another, even longer, pause.

"A-ha?"

At least he had not slammed down the phone immediately.

Amy put on her most sympathetic voice.

"Tristan – may I call you that? – I'm working on a feature about the long-term effect of drug abuse on the families of the victims and I was wondering if you would be prepared to give me an interview. Nothing," she added hastily before he had a chance to say no, "will be published without your prior consent."

She expected a pause, but the reply came immediately.

"Sorry, no," the quiet voice said curtly. "My mother passed away last week and I'm busy with the funeral arrangements."

Amy was shocked.

"I am so sorry," she whispered, and her compassion for the young man who had now lost all his immediate family was sincere. "So sorry to have bothered you."

She ended the call.

After a few minutes contemplating the magnitude of the tragedy that had befallen the Foveran family, her journalistic instincts kicked in. She banged the top of the desk with her fist in frustration. She had not even left him her number in case he changed his mind.

Chapter 27

DI McCord had declined the offer from DS Fraser and DC Struthers to keep them company for lunch and cited work overload as the reason for just having a coffee and a sandwich at his desk. Two minutes later, there was a cautious knock on the door, and DC Sutton entered quickly.

"People might watch and ask," she explained.

McCord nodded.

"If you're uncomfortable, you can send me an email instead in future," he suggested.

She looked at him in bewilderment. McCord wondered what he had done wrong now.

"Emails are not secure."

Knowing now what she could do, he nodded apologetically and resolved never to entrust a secret to the email system ever again.

"Of course. What have you got?"

DC Sutton took a few seconds to build up to her report.

"Unexplained funds are going in and straight out of the account. Two thousand each time."

She handed him several sheets of paper.

McCord's face fell.

"Can you trace where it comes from and where it's going to?"

"Not yet. Soon."

DC Sutton looked confused. McCord suspected that she was never quite sure what people were thinking. That was why he tried not try to make her do things that she hated, like working with people or talk more than was absolutely necessary.

"There's more," she said.

McCord looked up, trying not to show his emotions, because he understood by now it would just trouble her.

"Yes?"

"Dates of major transfers coincide with failed raids by Vice."

He stared at her.

"How did you get into their...?" He stopped himself. He still had to get used to the idea that DC Sutton could get into any computer software she chose. He shuddered to think what she could do if she went over to the other side.

"Would you mind telling me what happened in Child Protection?" he asked. "You must have been their best asset."

DC Sutton had a pained expression on her face. Explaining the whole business was an almost insurmountable challenge to her. But she tried.

"A witness said people in high places were involved, so I hacked into the police commissioner's account. He wasn't. But he might have been," she added defiantly.

McCord coughed into his hand to stifle a laugh.

"Well, I hope you never suspect me of anything," he said, only half-joking.

"Me, too," she replied, entirely serious, and as there was nothing more to say, she left.

McCord looked at his sandwich but had lost his appetite. He was desperate for a cigarette and fumbled in his drawer for the nicotine gum. He popped one in his mouth and chewed furiously. One of his own. Although he knew in his heart of hearts that it was true, he decided to wait until Sutton had sniffed out the whole trail. And then he would have to eat humble pie and tell DI Marshall.

* * *

Amy had worked hard all day on her fashion article and just about finished it. John seemed pleased that she was so immersed in her work and had not mentioned the McAdie case at all.

"How have you been feeling about walking around town on your own?" he asked her earnestly. "Your mother and I have been worried."

Amy felt guilt tightening her stomach again.

"It's fine, I feel quite safe out and about during the day, and I'm not going out at night, anyway."

John was still not convinced.

"I have made enquiries at an agency; they can provide security at any time, as long as we give them 24 hours' notice."

Amy shook her head violently. That would put an end to her secret meetings with Angus, and she was not having that.

"Thanks, John, that's very kind of you, but absolutely not. It would make me even more nervous. If anything happens, anything at all, that worries me, I'll let you know, okay?"

He reluctantly acquiesced.

"I shan't force you, of course. But I have agreed with your mother that a CCTV camera is going to be installed that covers the entrance to your flat. If nothing else, it will at least deter burglars."

She did not say anything, and he interpreted her silence as criticism.

"I must seem like an old fusspot to you, but I make no apologies for being worried about you and your mother," he said hotly. "If anything happened to either of you…"

His voice trailed off.

Amy walked round the huge desk and planted a big fat kiss on John's cheek.

"Nothing is going to happen to us. You just concentrate on Mum. She is already talking about going to Paris, and when she says 'we', she means you, not me. I should be really upset, you know. And now I'm off. I've had enough of dresses for today."

* * *

Amy pushed open the door to Angus's flat with some difficulty. When she had hurriedly dumped the bag the previous day, one of the straps had become wedged under the door. She switched on the light and listened. There was no sound but the muffled noises from the pub downstairs.

She closed the door, releasing the strap. She picked up the bag and only then noticed the sheet of paper on the floor. She felt cold despite the stuffy warmth in the flat.

"Please, no," she whispered.

She picked up the note, unfolded it and read. Then she read it again as if she might have misunderstood the meaning the first time. Suddenly she had an idea. She lifted the mirror off the wall. The bubble of hope burst. The four old letters were still in exactly the same place on the back of the mirror where she had taped them.

Her innocent pleasure at being in Angus's flat and sorting out his clothes turned to dread. The dark entrances to the rooms either side of the corridor stared at her menacingly, and it was not until she had switched on all the lights in the flat that she felt safe again.

Hurriedly, she emptied the bag into the washing basket, picked up some new clothes and stuffed them inside. She switched off the lights one by one until only the hall was awash with a cold, fluorescent glare. The odious note was still lying on the floor where she had dropped it. She picked it up, folded it and slid it into her jacket pocket. This time she would show it to Angus, and this time he would have to give her an answer.

* * *

The ward was busy with people visiting their loved ones after work, and Amy waited impatiently until the man saying goodbye to Angus's neighbour had left. When he was out of earshot, she slipped between the gaps in the curtains, dropped the bag on the floor with a thump and sat down. No smiles or kisses this time.

"Hi, Amy," he said, hesitantly. "Thanks for getting my stuff."

"Never mind that," she said, pulling out the letter from her pocket and throwing it on his chest, "explain this."

Angus looked from her to the letter, and she could see how it slowly dawned on him what it might be. He picked up the note and took a very long time to read the eleven words. He pushed it away and slid his hands under the duvet to hide the fact that they were trembling. Amy looked at his pale face and the eyes widened in fear and felt sorry for having been so brutal.

"Who's doing this, Angus?" she said with quiet urgency. "What is this letter about? And the other four? Why are you being threatened?"

He just shook his head.

"My father's associate..."

"Stop lying," Amy hissed, aware that the other people in the room could hear them. "They know where you live, Angus, they've been at your door. You *have to* tell us."

Angus sat up, furious.

"I don't *have* to do anything. And who is *us*? You just run to the police with every little thing that is not your business!" He paused. "Did you go to the police with this?"

"Not yet," Amy said, "but I will if you don't tell me."

"It's got nothing to do with you, so back off!" he shouted.

"Somebody's been following me and left a strangled cat on my doorstep," Amy said through clenched teeth, "so it *is* my business now, and I will find out what's going on whether you help me or not!"

Both jumped when the curtain was pulled away and a male nurse Amy had not seen before approached them.

"Everything okay, Mr Adamson?" he asked. "I think you should rest now," he added, with a pointed look at Amy.

With a scowl, she yanked her handbag off the chair and stormed out. It was not until she sat in the back of the taxi taking her home that the tears came.

Chapter 28

"I should go to the police with that," Emily said. "Surely, that would convince them."

Tristan was pacing up and down the living room. Not only did he doubt that, he was also reluctant to hand the punishment over to others. The revenge is mine, he thought. It should be hers as well. How could she not see that? By going to the police, all she would do is draw attention to him. He shook his head.

She grabbed his arm to calm him down.

"Let's do the right thing. It'll work out. You need to have some faith."

He burst into a bitter laugh. Faith. He had irretrievably lost that four years ago. But he needed to be careful if he were to succeed. He needed to dissemble.

"I suppose, you're right," he conceded. "Go tomorrow and give me a call when you're done."

She smiled and hugged him.

"I promise. Soon this will all be over."

Yes, he thought, it will.

Chapter 29

DI McCord was out at Dalry speaking to the parents of a joyrider who had hit and killed a child. His mobile vibrated in his pocket. He threw a furtive glance at it, and seeing that the call was from Amy Thornton, he made his apologies, handed the interview over to DS Fraser and went outside.

"Are you okay?"

He was relieved to hear that the voice at the other end was calm, but he detected something unfamiliar that he identified only after a few sentences: sheepishness. It also took only these few sentences for him to explode.

"You did *what*!? Are you actually *trying* to get yourself killed?"

It was unprofessional, he knew, but this young woman really infuriated him. He needed to get a grip.

"Okay," he added, making an effort to cool down, "and what did Angus have to say about it?"

He listened as Amy recounted the conversation.

"Maybe it's good that he is rattled. Then people make mistakes... No, I'm sorry, Miss Thornton, I don't buy the Angus-the-Martyr version of events anymore. If he were innocent, he would talk to us, or at least to you. Could you bring in the letter to the station asap for forensic examination?"

"Eh, I left it at the hospital with him. One of the nurses interrupted us and, kind of, threw me out," Amy said, again sounding sheepish.

"Damn."

"There is another thing."

McCord rolled his eyes. There was always another thing with Miss Thornton.

"Yes?" He sighed.

"I thought the letters must be connected to the Foveran family. 'You will pay for what you have done to my family,' the letters said. They and the McAdies were neighbours, and very soon after Fabian and his school friend die, Magnus McAdie changes his name and disappears. It seems too much of a coincidence, doesn't it?"

"You could be right," McCord admitted reluctantly. "What makes you think the two events are not connected after all?"

"I was on the phone to the elder son, Tristan, this morning, on his landline in London. His mother passed away and he was making arrangements."

"And the reason you phoned him was merely to express your condolences, of course?" His voice dripped with sarcasm.

"Well, it's not as if you are getting anywhere fast, is it?" Amy retorted hotly. "At least I get some new information occasionally."

McCord was stung but not ready to admit his frustration, and certainly not to her.

"Remind me when you found the first letters behind the mirror at Angus's flat?"

"Last Monday," Amy said without hesitation.

"The attack on the pub and the cat incident were on Wednesday, a week ago – *if* that was him. Plenty of time to get back to London, depending on when the mother died and when he got back. We need to find out."

He took some notes.

"I just don't see a motive. We – and I don't mean *you*, Miss Thornton – need to speak to him. I'll get in touch with our colleagues in London again."

Amy was pleasantly surprised.

"So, you've already spoken to them?"

"I did ask for the files on the Foveran incident and for a chat with the investigating officer, but they haven't got back to me yet."

"Good," Amy said, "please let me know when they do."

McCord was incredulous.

"Miss Thornton, do you understand that *you* are not investigating this case, if indeed there is a case?"

Amy ignored his remark.

"At least we know where Tristan is at the moment, and it isn't anywhere near Angus. Or my flat."

McCord sighed.

"Even if he is in London just now, don't be complacent. Somehow this whole business does not make sense. I know you're not going to listen to me, but I've got to say it again: stay away from the McAdies. Whatever is going on, it has to do with them."

Amy did not answer, which told him enough. She thanked him perfunctorily and rang off.

He fished out a nicotine gum from his pocket just as Fraser came out of the flat. He looked accusingly at McCord for having deserted him at such a critical moment.

"It was complete mayhem in there," Fraser complained. "Mother in denial, father threatening to beat the son to a pulp if he shows his face again."

"Sometimes I hate this job," McCord said. "On those occasions, I'm glad that I don't have kids."

"God, no," Fraser agreed, "cost a fortune and nothing but trouble."

"Nice motor," McCord observed, circling Fraser's sporty Mazda cabriolet, "that must have set you back a bit."

"Not really," Fraser said lightly, proudly patting it on the roof, "I got it second-hand, and I've got a chum at the Mazda garage who gave me a good deal."

"Look at those tyres," McCord said, bending down. "What's the acceleration?"

"It's 60mph in five point five seconds," Fraser announced proudly. "Not that you get to try that very often in this shitty country. If you're interested in cars, why do you drive that wreck of yours?"

"Sentimental reasons."

"Had your first shag in it, eh?" Fraser grinned.

"Actually, my dad gave it to me when I got into Tulliallan. It was all he could afford then."

They slid into the black leather seats.

Fraser turned on the engine that started immediately and purred like a contented cat.

"I really should get a new car," McCord reflected.

"You really should."

Fraser pulled out of the parking space, turned into Gorgie Road and accelerated so fast that they were pressed into their seats.

"See what this baby can do?" He beamed, turning to McCord.

The traffic soon slowed their progress, though, and as they crawled behind a double-decker bus towards the town centre, the phone conversation with Amy

Thornton pushed itself into the forefront of McCord's mind.

"Drop me off at the Infirmary," he told Fraser.

"Why?" Fraser asked, surprised.

"I want to speak to McAdie junior."

"Was that what the phone call was about?"

"Yes, might be nothing, though. It has to do with the threatening letters he got."

"I might as well come with you and drive you to the station afterwards."

McCord looked out of the window as they turned into Dundee Street. An idea was forming in his head.

"No, I'm meeting people afterwards. You go ahead and write the report on the joyride. It needs to go to the procurator fiscal asap. I want the report on my desk by the end of the day."

"Sometimes I hate this job," Fraser echoed his boss's earlier comment.

Fraser sulked for the rest of the journey and only muttered 'see you at the station' when he stopped at Little France Crescent.

* * *

McCord entered the hospital, still unsure of his strategy. It had been a spontaneous decision to speak to McAdie junior, but as he prepared his little speech, he realised that he had nothing at all apart from the anonymous letter. If he challenged him about it, and the previous ones, he would undermine any trust the young man still had in Amy. It sounded as if there was something going on between the two, and he did not want to lose the one source that might give him an insight into Angus's mind.

He slowed down as he reached the HDU. Another thought had occurred to him. Supposing Angus *was* involved in major crime and just using Amy, he might put her in danger by revealing to Angus that she had told him everything. He stopped suddenly in the middle of the corridor, annoying the staff, who were hurrying back and forth and had to take evasive action.

One doctor, seeing that he just stood there motionless, stopped beside him.

"Can I help you?" she asked kindly.

McCord shook his head.

"No, thanks. I was just thinking."

He turned round and hurried out of the hospital, feeling like an idiot and, not for the first time, glad to be in plain clothes. Outside, he blinked in the bright midday sun. It occurred to him that he had barely left the station since the murders and decided to walk to St Leonard's. It took him the best part of an hour. He was surprised how much he enjoyed it, and when he reached the HQ, he went straight to the car park to pick up his old Ford. There was somebody else he wanted to speak to.

Chapter 30

Valerie approached the new customer with a smile but blanched when McCord pulled out his ID and introduced himself. He got this look from people all the time when he visited them unannounced.

"Please don't worry," he reassured her hastily, "there is no bad news."

He was surprised to find a tall redhead in the shop when he had expected a petite, dark woman, and wanted to make sure.

"You are Valerie Thornton, Amy's mother?"

"I am."

Valerie had regained her composure and shook his hand. She pointed to John, who was standing next to her.

"This is John Campbell, Amy's boss and... and a friend of ours," she added.

"Pleased to meet you," John said formally.

McCord had taken his measure of them when he came in. Heads close together, bent over a portfolio of designs. Remembering where Amy worked, he deduced that John Campbell was the owner of *Forth Write* magazine and clearly more than just a friend. Upper class. The prince and the dressmaker – an odd couple.

Valerie in turn, with undisguised curiosity, examined the detective she had heard so much about.

"Would you like a coffee?" John offered. "Please have a seat."

He pointed to the newly acquired sofa.

Realising that John played the host while she was gawping at the visitor like a rude teenager, Valerie blushed.

"Yes, please do," she added hastily.

John turned on the coffee machine.

"Espresso? Cappuccino? Americano?"

"What a service," McCord said, "I hope this does not count as police corruption. An Americano would be great, thanks."

When McCord began to slowly stir some sugar into his coffee, Valerie could not hold back any longer.

"Why are you here?" she blurted out.

McCord smiled. At last, he could see one similarity between mother and daughter. No beating about the bush. But then he became serious.

"I'm concerned about Amy's safety," he said. "Mildly concerned, there is no need to panic," he added quickly when he saw the look of horror on Valerie's face. "Has she told you about Angus?"

Valerie nodded.

"Of course."

"The dead cat?"

Valerie nodded again, this time with a shudder.

"Yes, she told us everything. We'd been trying to persuade her to leave well alone, but…"

"I know," McCord said, "I've met her, remember?"

Valerie smiled.

"It's the anonymous letter that I worry about," McCord continued. "Somebody, who is not exactly Angus's biggest fan, has found out who and where he is. He might be the one responsible for the cat, but we don't know."

Valerie and John stared at him, uncomprehending.

"What letter?"

McCord's heart sank. He always hated the moment when he had to break it to parents that their children did *not*, in fact, tell them everything.

"The letter she found in Angus's flat when she got him his clothes."

Valerie's face lit up.

"Oh, those letters. Yes, she showed us the pictures. Horrid. Why would you keep them behind your mirror?"

"There has been another one," McCord said gently. "She found it yesterday."

Valerie's smile froze.

"Yesterday?"

"Are you saying that Amy has been seeing this Angus again since the incident with the cat?" John asked, clearly hoping that he had misunderstood.

"I'm afraid so," McCord said. "I take it she didn't tell you about that."

John shook his head. He looked hurt and bewildered.

"I suppose, it's understandable," McCord heard himself say. "We've all been telling her not to, and in her mind, she is just doing what a decent person would do to protect someone they're in love with."

He could not believe he was sitting here, defending the utterly irresponsible actions of a wilful, wayward twenty-something.

"I'm sorry," he said, referring to the hand grenade he had just lobbed into their familial harmony. "I just wanted to reassure you that I have Amy's best interests at heart, but she seems to be her own worst enemy sometimes."

Valerie still sat there speechless, storm clouds gathering on her forehead, so he handed his card to John instead.

"Try not be too angry with her," he said to Valerie. "We can't stop her from seeing Angus unless we lock her up, which, unfortunately, is illegal, so the best plan is for her to tell us at least what she is up to and to keep a close eye on her."

John nodded his agreement.

"Call me any time if you are worried."

"Thank you," John said.

McCord looked at Valerie, but she was still sitting motionless. Fear, fury and disappointment were fighting for supremacy over her face.

John, almost imperceptibly moving his head, indicated to McCord that he would look after her.

The men shook hands.

McCord thanked them for the coffee and departed.

Weird, he thought as he stepped out onto South Bridge. Total toff, but nice guy.

* * *

Back at the station, McCord called Jeffries and Gillespie into his office.

"Any more on the McAdies?"

Jeffries shrugged. "We have been through all the files and have also spoken to the officer who oversaw the case."

"What did the officer say about McAdie senior?"

"That he had never been so scared in his life when he was called to testify against Kenneth McAdie. The London colleagues are sure that he was the mastermind behind a large chunk of the crime committed in the city. Drugs, prostitution, trafficking, slavery, you name it. They were desperate to nail him for *something,* so they tried to do an Al Capone and get him on tax evasion and money laundering first. Once he was safely tucked away in prison, they had hoped to have free rein to go after him for all the other crimes. It would have worked, too, but one of the investigating officers was a little over-enthusiastic and accessed his accounts before securing a warrant. Kenneth McAdie's lawyer found out and that was the beginning of the end. When the trial collapsed, nobody was prepared to come forward as a witness."

"Do we know what he is up to now?" McCord asked.

"It had been a close call, and the colleagues think that McAdie decided to retire and enjoy life on Guernsey," Jeffries said bitterly.

"Any sign that he had groomed his son Magnus to be his successor?" McCord wondered.

Jeffries shook his head. "On the contrary. The colleagues had the impression that his whole aim in life was to make sure his son never had to resort to crime, or hard work, for that matter, and have a carefree existence."

"So, who took over from him?"

"Previous rivals who are still fighting over the spoils. Sometimes our London friends wish McAdie were back because then they would be dealing only with one bad guy. On the plus side, they're killing each other off occasionally, but that's still a lot of hassle for Homicide," Jeffries said sarcastically.

McCord turned to Gillespie.

"Anything on the associate, Phillips?"

Gillespie shook his head.

"Zilch. He was the respectable front for some of McAdie's businesses. He knew that McAdie was dodgy but by the looks of it never did anything illegal himself. McAdie used the businesses to launder some of his money putting it down as 'investments'."

The detectives shared a glance.

"Sorry, boss, that it didn't get us any further," Gillespie said.

McCord looked up.

"Don't be sorry. A negative result is also a result. We now know that young McAdie has been leading us a merry dance talking of this associate. He's been lying through his teeth. We can now work on the assumption that McAdie is prepared to go to any lengths to protect his son and that the threat has nothing to do with the trial. We must concentrate on the Foveran connection. I still haven't heard back from the Met. I must chase them up. And see if you can help find this Kaminski. There is no evidence that he has left the country. If there is unfinished business here, he might be here right under our noses. Get a picture and check out all accommodation round the city."

He saw that his men were about to protest.

"Do you have any better ideas?"

They shook their heads.

"Right. Until you have one, get your walking shoes on."

* * *

When Jeffries and Gillespie had left the office, McCord made for DC Sutton's desk. Approaching slowly, so as not to startle her, he handed her a note with the name Kenneth McAdie on it.

"I want you to look into his accounts," he said quietly.

Heather the Hacker fixed her enlarged eyes on him.

"Has he not retired from business?"

"Might have been dragged back into it. Just want to know, don't need evidence, wouldn't be admissible in court anyway. Make sure you don't get caught, though. I don't want a cock-up like the Met had."

Without further acknowledging his presence, she put the note into the shredder and started clicking on her keyboard.

McCord, equally fond and frightened of DC Heather Sutton, returned to his desk and dialled the London number again.

* * *

When Amy came home straight after work, she intended to have a quick tea and then withdraw to her room to mourn the missed meeting with Angus. She had debated with herself all day whether she should go and see him or not. In the end, she decided not to, as painful as it was. She was still angry about his refusal to confide in her and thought a day or two of lonely reflection might make him see sense.

On entering the kitchen, however, she found Valerie and John sitting at the kitchen table, returning her greeting without a smile.

She knew only too well that expression on her mother's face. When she eventually retired to her room, although forgiven, she felt deeply ashamed.

Chapter 31

DI McCord was enjoying his drive home for once, listening to *Sounds of the 70s* on Radio 2. The evening was calm and dry, and the traffic out of the city had flowed nicely. All being well, he should be home by eight. When his mobile rang, he glanced at the display. Unknown number. Frowning, he pushed the green button, keeping his eyes on the road.

"McCord."

"Hi, DI Giles here from the Met. I got a message that you were interested in the Foveran case?"

"Yes, last week," McCord said.

The woman at the other end laughed.

"One of those days, is it?" she enquired with a chortle. "Sorry I didn't get back to you sooner, but it's been hectic here recently. Well, it always is. Why are you so interested in the Foverans?"

"We think that the older son, Tristan, has a grudge against a certain Magnus McAdie who calls himself Angus Adamson these days. We think he has written threatening letters to Magnus alias Angus and vandalised his pub, but we don't understand his motive. Did you come across any link between the two that might explain it?"

"I have," DI Giles said as if announcing her engagement.

McCord's nerves were jingling, and he regretted not having taken a gum out of his pocket before setting off. Why was this woman so bloody cheerful?

"And just as well I didn't phone you earlier because yesterday, I had a visit from Emily Fullerton."

"Who is she again?" McCord asked, annoyed that he had not looked more carefully at his notes.

"The girlfriend of Daniel Littlejohn, who gave the drugs to Fabian. Do you know who Fabian is?"

There was no sarcasm in her voice, but McCord became more and more irate.

"Yes, I do," he muttered. "Lord Foveran's younger son. The one who jumped off the roof."

"Exactly."

DI Giles seemed genuinely pleased that he was getting a grip on the story.

"Well, Daniel Littlejohn left a note saying how sorry he was about Fabian's death and downed a large vodka laced with speed, which caused a fatal heart attack."

"Yes, yes, I remember," McCord said, impatiently.

DI Giles was impervious to her counterpart's bad mood.

"Emily made wild accusations the first time round, claiming that Daniel would not have written such a note, but we didn't believe her. She was hysterical and admitted herself that she'd had no idea that Danny was selling drugs. We thought she was clutching at straws trying to make out her boyfriend had been a victim rather than a grubby little dealer."

"And yesterday?"

McCord contemplated stopping the car to get a gum, so bad was the craving.

"Yesterday she came and showed me something that you would be interested in."

And then she told McCord in her bright children's TV presenter voice the story of the almost complete annihilation of the Foveran family. McCord listened, and as she went on, he forgot all about his craving.

"Bloody hell," was all he said when DI Giles had finished.

"Isn't it awful?" she chirped. "And the worst thing is, there is nothing we can do."

McCord tightly gripped the steering wheel of the Ford.

"Did you tell Emily that?"

"Yes, I thought she deserved an honest answer."

McCord snorted.

"And if she told Tristan, he would see only one way out of this. Shit, do you know when his mother's funeral is?"

"It was today, Emily told me."

"Shit!" McCord shouted again and banged the steering wheel, which wobbled indignantly in response. "He could be here in Edinburgh right now! Do you have Emily's mobile number?"

"Yes, somewhere."

"Can you text it to me, quickly, please?"

"Okay, I will."

McCord hung up and pulled the car into a petrol station, willing his mobile to buzz.

After less than a minute, the text came up. He called the number, letting it ring until it went to voicemail. A nice-sounding voice, apologising for not picking up and inviting him to try again. He did, without success. He wondered about sending a text, but what if DI Giles had been wrong and Emily was not as nice as she thought? Maybe she was on a train with Tristan, plotting to kill Magnus as he was sitting here?

He called DI Giles back who answered immediately but did not sound quite as cheerful anymore.

"DI McCord, what else can I do for you?"

"Listen, I can't get through to Emily. Could you please send someone to the Foveran villa and check if Tristan is there? And if not, try Emily, she lives just round the corner. I need to know where those two are, or we might have another tragedy on our hands."

There was a pause.

"You know that I'll have trouble justifying that to my boss?" she said. "Sending officers out on somebody else's hunch?"

McCord ground his teeth.

"If he asks, tell your boss that as far as you know it is a matter of life and death. I'll speak to him if necessary. Just get over there and check. Now. Please."

DI Giles sighed, which McCord guessed was her version of a torrent of abuse.

"Okay. I'll call you back. And by the way," she said, and this time there was a hint of annoyance in her voice, "my boss is a woman."

She ended the call.

McCord leant forward and banged his head on the steering wheel, which wobbled even more.

"Shit!" he shouted for the third time.

He dialled the station.

"DI McCord here. I might need some back up in a minute. Who is on duty?"

"Sutton and Dharwan," the duty officer said. "The others are on a call-out to an incident at Easter Road. Do you want to speak to Dharwan?" He naturally assumed that nobody in their right mind would want to speak to DC Sutton.

"No, but tell her to be on stand-by to meet me at the Royal Infirmary's main entrance. Tell her to put her vest on. I'll call in a few minutes to confirm. And, yes, get DC Sutton on the phone."

There was a stunned silence, then a shuffling of feet and a shout in the distance. Presently, DC Sutton was on the phone, an activity she obviously did not relish.

"Yes?"

"Can you trace a mobile? As in *now*?"

"Of course."

McCord smiled. Heather the Hacker was turning into a prime asset.

"Find me the mobile number of Tristan, the son of Lord Foveran, resident at 10 Beechwood Gardens, London, and his location. Also, the current location of this mobile." He read out Emily's number. "As quickly as you can, please."

He had barely finished the sentence when the line was cut.

He was about to call the Infirmary but decided to wait until he had more to go on. At the moment it was, just like DI Giles had pointed out, nothing but a hunch and he did not want to cause a full-scale alert in a hospital until he had a clearer picture.

* * *

He dialled Emily's number again. While it was ringing, he looked longingly at the lit window of the shop in the petrol station and fought a brief but fierce battle with himself over whether he should go in and buy a packet of cigarettes as he had often done in the past. This time the little angel on his right shoulder won. He kept trying Emily's number, while he fished out a gum from his pocket.

He looked at the time display on his phone. How long did it take for a bobby to get round to one of the wealthiest addresses in the UK?

This was all taking too long. He'd better make a move driving back, even if it turned out to be a wild goose chase.

He turned the key. All the red lights on the dashboard flashed in alarm, the engine made a sound that evoked the strangled cat on Amy's door handle, and then everything went dark and quiet. Swearing profusely, McCord tried again and again to start the Ford, but the engine had clearly decided enough was enough.

He exhaled long and deliberately several times, then took his mobile out of its holder.

"McCord again. Get Dharwan on the phone, please."

A few seconds later he heard the bright voice of the PC. She sounded excited.

"Yes, sir?"

"Pick me up at the Morrisons petrol station in Portobello, off the A1. Have you got your vest on?"

"Yes, sir."

He could hear that she was dying to ask what was going on, but he could not bring himself to explain this whole shambles.

"Good, get going."

* * *

McCord checked the time. She would be at least twenty minutes. The golden shine from the shop windows seemed to beckon him again. Then he remembered that PC Dharwan ate for lunch seeds and berries he had never seen before. She was not the type that would tolerate passive smoking. To make matters worse, at the station they all knew that he had quit, and he was damned if he was going to look like a pathetic junkie. He needed to stop thinking about cigarettes and concentrate on the task in hand. They could be a while at the Infirmary, and he was hungry even now.

He got out of the car, slammed the door as if to punish the useless motor for letting him down at such a critical time, and entered the shop. He thought he could smell the tobacco behind the counter but forced his attention on the aisles. He stood a while in front of the chocolate bars, deliberating which to buy for a health-conscious colleague. He settled on a sugar free, high protein yoghurt bar with cranberries and took a dark chocolate bar with nuts for himself. He grabbed a couple of bottles of water and crisps and carried it all to the counter. Trying not to look at the wall of temptation behind the spotty youth who was serving, his eyes wandered over to the little oven next to the till.

"I'll have a Scotch pie as well, please."

He piled the snacks on the counter and quickly paid by credit card before he could change his mind. The water bottles stuck under his arms, he knew he cut a ridiculous figure trying to carry the hot, greasy pie as well as the chocolate bars and crisps. He was already congratulating himself when he realized he would not be able to open the car door without dropping something. Just then his phone rang. He dropped the pie, the chocolate bars and the crisps, and pressed the green icon.

It was DI Giles.

"Yes?"

"Two PCs have been round. No sign of life at the Foveran villa. They rang the bell and banged on all the doors, but no answer. Emily's not home either. She told her parents after the funeral that Tristan wanted to be on his own but then, later, she said that she was going to Tristan's to keep him company and that she would stay overnight. She left in quite a hurry, which they wondered about at the time. They've been trying to call her but she's not answering. Obviously, they're frantic with worry. Let me know as soon as you hear anything."

"I will. What time was the funeral?"

"Not sure. Usually they're late morning, aren't they?"

"When did Emily leave?"

"Around three, half three."

"Thanks. I'll be in touch."

* * *

He had just thrown the pie in the bin, picked up the chocolate bars and crisps from the tarmac and wiped them with a tissue when a Fiat Punto screeched round the corner into the car park and came to an abrupt halt next to the Ford. PC Dharwan lowered her window.

"Hello, sir."

"I know, I need a new car," McCord pre-empted any comment.

He stuffed the food between the front seats and belted up.

"Royal Infirmary."

It was good that he had to explain to his colleague the whole story because it helped him clear his frazzled mind. He was just at the point where Emily entered the story when his phone rang.

"Both phones located," DC Sutton informed him. "Royal Infirmary of Edinburgh."

"Shit!" McCord shouted into his phone. Then, hastily, he added, "Sorry, DC Sutton. Not you. You are brilliant." He hung up.

Dharwan looked at him, surprised.

"Step on it!"

She did not need to be told twice.

Chapter 32

As they were racing back towards the city, McCord googled the number for the Infirmary.

"Detective Inspector McCord, Homicide Division. We have information that there are intruders in the hospital. Possibly armed. They're looking for Angus Adamson in the HDU."

He listened for a couple of seconds.

"No, this isn't a bloody hoax! We're on our way. Approach with caution. I don't believe he is intending to harm anyone else, but one never knows. Get security over there, now!"

He called the station.

"McCord here. Backup required at Royal Infirmary. Possibly armed intruders, one male, one female, targeting Angus Adamson in the HDU. Cover all exits. We're on our way."

* * *

When they turned into Little France Crescent, the hospital entrance was blocked by three police cars.

A young PC ambled towards McCord.

"No sign of any intruders, sir. Mr Adamson was sleeping peacefully when we got here. No signs of interference but the nurses have changed the drip, just in case. Colleagues are doing the upper floor now; everywhere else has been checked. Looks like a false alarm, sir."

McCord heard the insolence in his tone.

"Well, it's good news we don't have a murder on our hands, isn't it?" he snapped.

Just then another PC approached McCord, altogether more cautiously, having heard McCord's last comment.

"The whole building has been searched, sir. No sign of any intruder inside."

McCord took a deep breath.

"Thank you. Leave one officer on guard with Angus Adamson, the rest of you can go back."

The PC nodded. "Yes, sir."

When both PCs had gone off, McCord turned to Dharwan.

"Something's not right. Sutton said they were here."

"Maybe they were but we scared them off?" Dharwan suggested.

McCord scratched his chin, where stubbles had begun to appear.

"Maybe."

McCord signalled her to follow him and entered the hospital. Nurses were hurrying around, trying to settle patients, some of whom were worried about the police raid, while others were clearly excited and kept asking the nurses what was going on.

At the HDU they found an officer guarding the room McAdie junior was in, and McCord told him to keep alert as the intruders might well be back now that the police cars had left. A nurse with hair the colour of candyfloss was with the patient, checking the machines again. McCord glanced at her name badge.

"Cathy, hi, I'm DI McCord."

He showed her his badge, but Cathy seemed more reassured by PC Dharwan's presence than by his ID.

"Amy said this was going to happen, you know."

Here we go, McCord thought but bit his tongue.

"I would just like a word with Angus," he said.

"If you must," agreed Cathy reluctantly, throwing a protective glance towards the young man. "Angus must rest. There was quite enough excitement tonight. He is still not well, you know. And the other patients…"

"I do know that," McCord said, irritably. "It won't take long."

He waited until she was out of earshot before he turned to Angus, who, to McCord's great satisfaction, looked pale and anxious.

"Did you catch him?" the young man demanded.

"Catch who, Angus?"

He swallowed.

"Well, the intruder, eh, intruders."

McCord shook his head in mock regret.

"No, we haven't. Did you see them tonight, by any chance?"

"No, I was asleep until the police barged in."

McCord bent down, almost touching Angus's temple with his nose, so that he could whisper in his ear.

"I'm surprised you sleep so well. Have you not been expecting a visit for a while?"

Angus's eyes darted from the short menacing detective to the beautiful officer beside him who did not look sympathetic either.

"No, why?"

"All right, no need to worry then, is there." McCord pulled himself up and smiled mirthlessly. "Good night, Magnus, I'm sure we'll meet again."

* * *

Outside the hospital all was dark and quiet again, apart from the light forming little white pools outside the entrance and the windows.

McCord pulled out his phone and sent a brief message.

"Sutton?" Dharwan asked.

He nodded appreciatively.

Almost instantly, there was a buzz. He read the message and put his phone away again.

"They're still here. Let's have a look round."

He turned left and started to walk round the building. Behind the pharmacy, it was very dark, and there were some trees and bushes lining the car park. He nudged Dharwan, put a finger to his lips and took small, deliberate steps along the path. About fifty yards in, he heard a noise. Dharwan had stopped at the same moment. They looked at each other, trying to work out what it was. It was a choking sound, like someone struggling for breath. They inched closer, trying not to breathe too loudly, and praying they would not break a twig under their shoes.

The sound was coming from behind one of the bushes, and McCord pointed to the other side, indicating a pincer movement. They surrounded the bush and almost stumbled on two figures huddled together in the grass who froze when the beam of Dharwan's torch hit them. The detectives saw a young man, dressed in a nurse's uniform, whose eyes were red and swollen. A young woman was hugging him protectively as she squinted up with a terrified expression into McCord's face, whose lean features seemed skeletal in the indirect light.

McCord pointed his torch at them.

"Tristan and Emily, I presume."

He hunched down on the grass next to them, but Surina Dharwan remained standing, just in case they decided to make a run for it. She need not have worried. Tristan seemed utterly exhausted, and Emily was not letting go of him anyway.

McCord broke the silence.

"I know why you're here, and believe it or not, I have some sympathy."

Emily looked up at him in surprise.

"You do?"

"I've spoken to DI Giles, and she filled me in. For what it's worth, I'm glad you didn't get in," he said to Tristan, "and not for Magnus's sake but for yours. Nice touch, by the way." He pointed to the home-made lanyard with the fake nurse's ID.

The young man's voice was hoarse from crying all the tears pent up over the past four years.

"I did get in," he croaked. "I stood over him with this at his throat."

He pointed into the shapeless night next to him. Dharwan pointed her torch in that direction, and the blade of a kitchen knife gleamed in the dark. Slowly, her eyes fixed on Tristan, she moved towards the knife. Tristan did not stir as she picked it up with a gloved hand.

"And then..." His voice broke as more tears streamed down his cheeks. "I just couldn't do it. Four years," he suddenly screamed, "four years I had been waiting for this, prepared for this, *lived* for this, and then I bottled it! A useless coward, that's what I am."

Sobbing loudly, he was rocking back and forth, while Emily held him and shot a pleading glance at McCord.

"You're not a coward," Emily said. "Just a decent human being who was pushed to his limits. Thank God, you've not done anything wrong."

"Aye, right," Dharwan could not help uttering.

McCord had to admit that his colleague had a point. Tristan had done nothing wrong, apart from making threats, vandalising a pub, plotting to kill, impersonating an NHS nurse and wasting police time with an operation costing a few thousand pounds. But in the greater scheme of things, McCord felt, Emily was right. It could have been much worse.

"I understand Tristan's anger but I'd have thought that you might have had more sense," McCord said to Emily.

"She had nothing to do with it," Tristan burst out. "She just followed me down here trying to stop me."

Emily nodded.

"After the funeral Tristan said he wanted to be alone. But I had a bad feeling and went round to see him. When he wasn't there, I checked his phone. We had set up the search function after he'd lost his old one. It showed that he was at King's Cross. I missed his train but there was one half an hour later. When I got here, he just came out of the building, and then the police arrived, and we hid here."

"Why didn't you answer your bloody phone?" McCord asked. "If you'd picked up, we could have got here in time and possibly prevented a tragedy."

"I never pick up calls from unknown numbers," Emily said indignantly.

McCord sighed.

"Go on, call your parents. They're frantic with worry."

She pulled out her phone.

"Oh my God, I've got fifteen missed calls from them!"

"Ironic, when normally you youngsters are never off the damn things," McCord observed.

Emily got up and moved a few steps away, but the others could still hear a shrill voice ranting at the other end.

"Yes, Mum, I'm *so* sorry... I was worried about Tristan and followed him to Edinburgh."

Another outburst at the other end.

"We're both fine... We're with two police officers at the moment."

That was clearly not the smartest thing to say, judging by the torrent of questions coming from London.

"No, we're not in any trouble," she reassured her mother, looking at McCord, who raised his eyebrows. "I'm going to get a hotel room. I'm coming straight back home tomorrow. Promise."

The voice at the other end had calmed down but still had a lot to say.

"Yes, Mum," Emily said eventually. "Will do. Yes. Love you too. Bye."

She exhaled loudly.

"Sometimes I wish they would chill," she complained. "It's not as if I'm still fifteen years old."

McCord exchanged a look with Dharwan that said 'kids!' and turned to Tristan. It suddenly occurred to him that Tristan had nobody left to call. He put a hand on the young man's shoulder.

"You okay?"

What he meant, was, of course, 'can we let you loose on society without you sticking a knife into somebody?'

Tristan understood.

"Yes."

He sat there, broken, unable to muster the energy to get up. Dharwan was worried, McCord could see that, and the same thought had occurred to him. Now that Tristan had given up on revenge, he had nothing to live for – apart from a brave, loyal young woman who clearly felt more than friendship for him. But McCord doubted that Tristan was able to see that just yet.

"What happens now?" Tristan asked, completely lost.

"We'll get you something to eat and a room, and then, after a good night's sleep, you'll feel yourself again."

Tristan shook his head.

"I mean, what happens to Magnus? Nothing at all?"

McCord scratched his itching stubble. He hated not being shaved.

"I think there is one way for you to get justice," he said. "But it will take a little while and both of you will have to do exactly as I say. If it works out, this meeting will never have happened, and I'll do my best to stop you from being charged with anything. Do we have a deal?"

Tristan scrutinised the detective's face, uncertain.

"This is your only chance," McCord reminded him.

"Deal," he said, and finally got to his feet.

On their way back to the car, McCord remembered something that had been bothering him for a while.

"Just out of interest, what did you do in the fifteen minutes between spraying the graffiti on the pub and throwing the petrol bomb?"

Tristan stared at him, uncomprehending.

"What petrol bomb? I did the graffiti but then I went back to the hotel. I just wanted to frighten him and somehow tell people the truth."

McCord watched him closely.

"So that petrol bomb wasn't you?"

Tristan shook his head.

"I swear."

"And the cat?"

The expression on Tristan's face was blank.

"What cat?"

"The strangled cat somebody left at Amy Thornton's door."

Tristan was horrified.

"God, who would do something like that? She seems a nice girl, too."

"So, you know her?" McCord asked, prepared to find out another of Miss Thornton's secrets.

"Not really," Tristan admitted. "I knew that she wrote the article about Magnus, so I was hoping she would lead me to him, and she did." He paused. "I followed her around for almost a week, and I tell you, my feet are still sore."

* * *

Tristan booked a twin room in the same hotel he had stayed in before, and McCord reflected how nice it must be to have this kind of money just at your fingertips. On the way, they all agreed they were starving. Dharwan stopped at a fish and chips shop, and they polished off their fish suppers, eating with their fingers and talking. Tristan was quiet but Emily was telling them about her History course and how she had no idea what to do afterwards. She threw a telling glance at Tristan, and McCord winked.

"I'm sure, you'll figure something out."

Once this business is finished, he added silently.

* * *

When Dharwan pulled in at the hotel, McCord turned to Tristan and Emily with a grave face.

"Now listen," he said. "It is *vital* that you keep out of the way until I'm ready. Emily, *don't* tell anybody where you are or going, apart from your parents or us. You'll be getting a train home tomorrow first thing. Text me when you're on it and once you're home. Get on with your studies and keep your head down. No blabbing on social media or anywhere else, understood?"

Emily nodded anxiously.

"Do you really think we are in danger?"

"Not tonight," McCord said, "but I'm not taking any chances. I've got two men in the morgue with bullets in their heads, probably because they annoyed Magnus, and I don't want another corpse or two on my hands. I take it you want him caught and punished?"

He turned to Tristan, who nodded as well.

"Good. I'll pick you up tomorrow at ten. Check out from the hotel, and then I'll take you to a different address under a different name. Won't be as posh as this place but on the plus side, you might come out of it alive."

"How long will I have to stay there?" Tristan asked.

"Until I say so," McCord snapped. Then, more gently, he added, "A week minimum, maybe two. You've been waiting so long; a few more days surely won't matter. Now, get to sleep and leave it all to me."

* * *

Emily waved at them from the door and took Tristan's arm as they went in.

Exhausted from the evening's events, McCord and Dharwan leant back in their seats.

"I hope you haven't promised them too much," Dharwan said to McCord.

"So do I," he replied. "Dessert?" He picked up the yoghurt bar and proudly held it out to her.

Dharwan wrinkled her nose.

"Thanks, if it's all the same to you, sir, I'll have the chocolate bar."

* * *

When Dharwan stopped outside his Portobello flat, McCord turned to her before getting out.

"Obviously, I must ask you to keep quiet about this, too. Don't speak to *anybody* at the station about this. As far as they're concerned, we've been checking the perimeter of the hospital and then you drove me home, which is not even a lie."

Dharwan nodded.

"Shall I pick you up in the morning?"

McCord slapped his forehead.

"Damn, I forgot all about the bloody car. No, thanks, I'll take the bus in and get a car from the station pool. And, PC Dharwan, you did well today. Thanks," he said, and meant it.

"No problem," she said, "any time."

* * *

After a quick shower and a shave, McCord sank into his pillow when he suddenly remembered he had not phoned DI Giles. He was tempted to make her wait just as she had made him but then he picked up his phone and sent her a text. He lowered his phone and was asleep before it hit the duvet.

Chapter 33

At nine o'clock the next morning, McCord was at the station, signing out a Skoda from the carpool. He admired the gleaming exterior, unblemished by rust, and the myriad of controls on the dashboard. He touched the locked steering wheel, and it did not move a millimetre. I really need to buy a car, he thought for the umpteenth time.

It was too early to get Tristan, so he called his garage in Portobello to arrange for them to pick up the Ford from the petrol station. Maybe somebody at the garage would give him a couple of hundred quid for the parts.

He had just called off when he got a text from Heather the Hacker.

Got something.

He ran up the stairs and arrived at her workstation, breathing heavily.

She did not comment on the speed of his response, but he thought he saw a glimmer of appreciation in her magnified eyes.

"Transfer of £10,000 from Kenneth McAdie's account into a bank account of somebody called Riley Wynn the day before the double murder and £10,000 the day after into a different account of the same name," she said. "Banks usually only flag up more than £10,000 a month."

McCord banged the partition separating DC Sutton from the rest of the world with his fist, making it sway dangerously.

"DC Sutton, I could kiss you," he blurted out and immediately regretted it.

She edged away from him with a horror-stricken face. He held up his hands.

"Sorry," he said. "So sorry, I just meant I am so pleased that you found this out."

He slowly backed out of her workspace, muttering apologies, and hurried over to the incident board. He banged the metal frame with a pen until he had everybody's attention.

"We're looking for a connection between Katz Kaminski and a Riley Wynn."

He stopped when Fraser entered the room, slightly out of breath.

"Sorry, I didn't realise there was a meeting."

McCord just nodded and scribbled the name Riley Wynn on the board.

"There is no doubt in my mind that they are one and the same person. I want everybody onto that until we've found him. Jeffries, get in touch with Organised Crime about this, they might have come across the name. You can get me on my mobile, I'll be back in an hour or two."

"Catching up on your sleep, sir?" DC Struthers called out, and there was a general snigger around the room.

McCord looked around the room, confused.

"What…"

He broke off when his eyes fastened on Surina Dharwan. She was staring at her desk, looking mortified.

McCord grew suddenly very still, and the others knew that this was not a good sign.

When he spoke, his voice was so quiet that nobody even dared to breathe.

"If I so much get an inkling of a hint of a trace of such a rumour again, the persons spreading them will find themselves on Saturday night duty with me for the rest of the year, and if there is ever a rubbish dump to rake through, they will be the first on that task because that is clearly something they enjoy. Have I made myself clear, DC Struthers?"

Struthers swallowed.

"Yes, sir. It was only a joke, sir."

"Do I look as if I have a sense of humour?" McCord shot back, secretly enjoying the dilemma DC Struthers was now in.

"No, sir, eh, yes, sir," he stammered while a silent wave of mirth went through the room.

DC Struthers was always stirring and his frequent salacious remarks had not made him popular.

McCord put his pen down.

"Now enough of this nonsense. I want this Riley Wynn found by the time I get back."

* * *

McCord picked Tristan up from his hotel and drove him to Marchmont where he parked the Skoda in front of a neat bungalow.

"This is where you'll be staying for the time being," he said and, grabbing a ring binder from the backseat, marched ahead of Tristan along the meticulously weeded garden path lined by grinning gnomes.

Tristan snorted.

"Great design. Any intruder is going to fall over laughing."

"Don't be fooled by appearances," McCord warned him. "This is Gertrude Westwater's front garden, and judging by her past modus operandi, there may well be hidden booby traps, so mind where you go. She used to be in Special Forces. Word is, she stabbed a known serial killer through the heart with her hairpin. Retired now but helps us out occasionally."

He rang the bell.

A tall, broad-shouldered woman of an indefinable age opened the door after a few seconds. Her hair was pleated and pinned up at the back with a long, vicious-looking spike. Tristan wondered if that was *the* hairpin and shuddered.

"DI McCord, lovely to see you," she said with a tinge of irony, "do come in. And you must be Tristan."

She turned and led the way into a lounge overcrowded with heavy mahogany furniture, china figures and plant pots. Tristan guessed she had moved from a large house into this snug bungalow and not been able to part with any of her things.

She motioned them to sit on the flowery settee.

"Tea? Coffee?" she asked Tristan.

"Coffee would be great, thanks, Mrs Westwater," he answered politely.

She clearly was not a woman you would want to be on the wrong side of.

"Call me Gertrude," she commanded, and Tristan nodded, looking uncomfortable.

When she had disappeared into the kitchen, Tristan whispered, "She didn't ask you what you want."

"She knows what I want," McCord replied and sank deep into the cushions.

"By the way, for the time being, you'll be paying the bill. Eighty quid a night for dinner, bed and breakfast. I take it you can afford that?"

Tristan shrugged in agreement and wondered what to put on the receipt for his solicitor who had granted him a generous allowance until his mother's estate had legally been transferred to him. 'Holiday accommodation' might do.

"Can she cook?" he mumbled.

"Whether she can or not, you'd better eat it all with a grateful smile," McCord advised. "I'll speak to Superintendent Gilchrist this afternoon about expenses

191

and protection but don't get your hopes up. He's an awkward sod."

Tristan sniggered.

Gertrude suddenly appeared from nowhere with a tray. She set it down noiselessly, poured coffee and handed a plate of cookies round. When everybody was served, she sat down.

"Let's talk house rules, then, Tristan. One: you will not leave the house without my knowledge and permission."

She waited for his agreement before continuing.

"Two: you will not reveal your location to anybody apart from DI McCord or persons he expressly allows you to tell. Give me your phone."

Tristan hesitated. Since he was ten, he had never been for more than a few hours without a phone, and he remembered those hours with dread.

"Your phone?"

There was more than a little impatience in Gertrude's tone, and with an unhappy glance at McCord, he handed it over. Gertrude checked his settings and disabled Bluetooth and the location service.

"You kids are so naïve," she sighed and handed it back to him.

"Can I get in touch with Emily?" he asked McCord.

The detective looked at their host.

"Emily Fullerton," he explained to Gertrude, "her details are in the file."

He pointed to the ring binder.

Gertrude nodded.

"Rule number three: no smoking, no alcohol."

Tristan agreed.

"Four: quiet time between 11pm and 6am. Five: breakfast order in by 5pm every night."

She handed him a sheet with a list of breakfast items he was to tick.

"There are weights, a rowing machine and an exercise bike in the garage you can use. Access is through the utility room. Do *not* go outside. Let me know if you don't know what you're doing with the equipment, and I'll show you. At least one hour a day is recommended."

It sounded like an order, and Tristan was not going to argue.

McCord had finished his coffee and heaved himself out of the sofa with some difficulty.

"Well, I'll be off then. Thanks, Gertrude, for stepping in at such short notice. I hope he won't be any trouble."

"He won't be," she answered with a disconcerting smile.

McCord patted him on the shoulder.

"Bye, Tristan, I'll be in touch soon."

"Yes, please," he said, pleadingly. "Thanks."

As McCord was walking through the row of ghastly gnomes, his phone buzzed. Emily was on the London train.

The engine started first time, and he smiled. Two out of three at least were safe.

Chapter 34

McCord drove due north along Bruntsfield Place and Lothian Road and parked his car right in front of the *Forth Write* offices. It was one of the great perks of being a detective that he could park anywhere he liked in a city whose streets had clearly been designed by an angry god. Inside, he was greeted by a man dressed in what seemed to be a peacock costume and led to John Campbell's office where he found the owner and Amy discussing her fashion feature. John greeted him warmly, but there was an awkward pause before Amy eventually shook his hand. Both were aware that McCord had caused Amy a very unpleasant evening at home.

"Have you come to check on Amy? How kind of you," John said in his plummy accent that would have got on McCord's nerves, had John not made such good coffee, which he now offered again.

There was another uncomfortable silence when John had left the office to make the coffee.

"I'm sorry about the other day," McCord began, "I didn't realise–"

"No need to apologise," Amy cut in. "It was my own fault. And, to be honest, it was quite a relief not having to lie anymore. I didn't like it," she said simply.

There was a more congenial silence after that, which McCord broke again.

"It's unusual for a boss to make the coffee himself," McCord remarked. "Very decent of him."

"Oh, John is very modest, actually," Amy said. "Quite remarkable, considering his background, especially his mama."

She stressed the last syllable long enough to convey her feelings for Mrs Campbell.

"On the other hand, I don't think anybody apart from him and Martin can actually work the coffee machine."

McCord smiled.

"Do you trust the people working here?" he asked, and a little chill crept down Amy's spine.

"Of course," she said at once.

Right on cue, John entered with the coffee.

"There has been a development," McCord explained, "and I think you should both know. I can't emphasize enough, though, how important it is going to be in the next few days to be discreet and vigilant."

John and Amy hung on his lips.

"Last night, Tristan, Lord Foveran's son, attempted to kill Magnus, or Angus. But," he added hastily as Amy covered her mouth with her hands to stifle a scream, "he never went through with it. I don't believe that he poses a danger to anybody now. He has admitted to writing the letters and the graffiti on the pub wall but denies throwing the petrol bomb and killing the cat, and I believe him."

"That is good news, isn't it?" John said. "It means we can relax now?"

"Not really," McCord said. "My worry is that Magnus's – sorry – Angus's father is on the warpath and prepared to harm anybody who poses a real or imagined threat to his son."

"But how could he think that of me?" Amy protested. "I would never–"

"You have been snooping around in Angus's private life, blown his cover and talked to the police. I'm afraid that is quite enough."

Amy shook her head.

"Maybe if I talked to him, I could convince him–"

"Like you could convince an enraged bull," McCord interrupted her. "Listen, Amy, I know now why Tristan was after Angus, and believe me, he had good reason. But for justice to be done, I need your help. I need you–"

"I don't believe you!" Her voice was shrill. "You always had it in for Angus, right from the start."

Tears welled up in her eyes.

McCord felt his stomach tighten. He would have preferred to keep her in the dark because he feared her honesty would make it impossible for her to deceive Angus. But his whole plan depended on Amy's cooperation, and while she was harbouring any illusions with regard to Angus, he would not get it.

"Right," he said, "come with me. I hope that's okay?" he asked John perfunctorily.

"Of course," John agreed. "Amy, please go with DI McCord and listen to what he has to say."

"You don't need to listen to *me*," the detective said to Amy. "Somebody else will be much better placed to explain."

As Amy went ahead to fetch her bag, McCord turned to John.

"One way or the other, Amy has to speak to Angus tonight or tomorrow and then I need her to leave Edinburgh until I'm ready. Is there anywhere you can take her, where she would be out of harm's way?"

"I don't know," John said, desperately trying to think. Then his face lit up. "I have an idea. Leave it with me. She'll be safely out of the city for as long as you see fit. Just text me the dates."

"Thank you," McCord said, regarding John with renewed respect, "the timing is going to be crucial."

"Where are we going then?" Amy stood in the doorway, every inch a strop. "I'm telling you, this is a total waste of time."

"We'll see."

McCord ushered her outside and while she was sliding into the passenger seat of the Skoda, he sent a text. Then, for the second time that day, he headed out to Gertrude Westwater's bungalow in Marchmont.

* * *

A couple of hours later they were on their way back into town. Amy had been weeping next to McCord for the last ten minutes, and he realised that he had never comforted a crying woman before. In his private life, he had always done his very best to keep the women he had spent a night with happily satisfied and always left before they could start imagining that they had embarked on a relationship. Only with Louise had he stayed for long enough to create deeper emotions but when she left, she had not cried either. In his professional life, he had seen many tears but thankfully the force had trained family liaison officers who put their arms around shoulders and said the right things. He now wished he had taken PC Dharwan with him. He gripped the steering wheel tight and looked straight ahead, pretending that he had to concentrate on the road.

Slowly, the pitch and quality of the noises emanating from Amy changed. The high-frequency wail turned into a deep growl, and the limp arms, up to now helplessly lying in her lap and only occasionally wiping tears and snot from her face, started banging the dashboard in a fury. When he had to stop at a traffic light at the Meadows, passers-by suspiciously eyed the car in which a woman shouted obscenities and seemed to be trying to demolish the interior. McCord shrugged apologetically and yet again was relieved not to be identifiable as a police officer. As they approached South Bridge, Amy's emotional energy was spent. She slumped back into her seat and looked out of the window.

"Why are you taking me home?" she asked. "I should be at the office."

McCord glanced across at her swollen eyes and flushed face.

"I don't think you are in a fit state, do you? And you seem to have a very understanding boss."

He parked the car halfway up the pavement and placed his CID parking permit on the dashboard.

"Come on, I'll see you inside."

Amy had lost all strength in her legs, so they climbed the rusty metal stairs to the flat very slowly.

It was quiet and cold inside. Amy pressed the switch on the central heating in the hall.

"Coffee?" she offered automatically although she felt unable to move.

"I'll get it," McCord offered, "or do you have one of these infernal machines as well?"

For the first time since they had left this morning, Amy smiled.

"No, we've just got a humble cafetière. The coffee is in the cupboard above."

McCord switched on the kettle and looked around for something to eat as his stomach was rumbling. While the coffee was brewing, he opened some cupboards looking for mugs.

"There's bread in the tin if you want to make some toast?" Amy's voice sounded hoarse from crying.

"Great," he shouted back.

A few minutes later, he came through with a tray, laden with two steaming mugs, a plate with buttered toast, some cheddar and a jar of raspberry jam.

"I wasn't sure what you wanted," he said.

"I couldn't eat a thing," Amy declared indignantly and sipped her coffee.

McCord sprinkled grated cheddar on a slice of toast and took a large bite, careful not to drop any shavings onto the carpet. Amy watched him for a while and then proceeded to demolish two slices of her own. Her face had returned to its usual tan colour, and her distress had morphed into deep thought. McCord remained silent, not through any psychological finesse but because he didn't know what to say. Instead, he spread jam on the last slice of toast and brought the cafetière and milk through to top up their mugs.

Amy turned to him. He could see she was resigned to the facts and gathering strength for what needed to be done now.

"Do you think you're up to it?" McCord asked. "It might be better to leave it until tomorrow when you've had a chance to get over the shock."

"I'll do it tonight," she said. "The sooner this is over, the better."

* * *

As soon as McCord returned to the station, the officer at reception told him with a sympathetic voice, normally reserved for grieving members of the public, that he was to see the boss asap. The Super's handsome face was an unhealthy shade of purple, and as he was shouting at his junior officer, his spittle sprayed across the mahogany desk.

"And where the hell have you been, McCord? I hear you've hardly been at the station these past two days and have been gallivanting around town with female officers. And then an unauthorised large-scale operation at the Infirmary? Like a bull in a china shop, so I heard. I had the press here this morning and didn't know what to say! I looked like a right idiot, thanks to you!"

McCord swallowed the obvious reply that sat on his tongue.

"I had reason to believe that there would be an attempt on the life of a patient at the Infirmary. I thought my priority should be to prevent a murder."

"And was there an attempted murder, McCord, was there?" The Super was beginning to enjoy himself.

McCord thought of Tristan sitting on the grass in the light of the torch, crying, swaying back and forth.

"No, sir," McCord said through clenched teeth.

"And instead of coming straight back to the station to write your report, you disappear with PC Dharwan for the rest of the evening! The whole station is talking about it!"

"PC Dharwan assisted me in securing the perimeter of the hospital. On my orders, she then drove me home because my car had broken down, and from there, she immediately returned to the station."

Gilchrist eyed him furiously.

"It's about time you bought yourself a new car. A bloody disgrace this banger of yours! It's the laughing stock of the station."

Distracted from his rant, the Super tried to recapture the thread of his interrogation.

"And this morning? The officers tell me you just ran off on an errand nobody knows anything about?"

McCord's mind raced. If he were to ask Gilchrist to provide protection for Tristan and Amy, he would have to reveal Tristan's attempt to kill Magnus, and judging by the mood his boss was in, he would probably insist on arresting Tristan instead.

"I was interviewing witnesses. As of this morning, we have a strong lead in the double murder at Musselburgh Lagoons. We have the name of a potential suspect we are trying to locate. Maybe this is something you could mention to the press?"

The Super's dark face brightened up as suddenly as a Scottish April sky.

"Well, that is at least something."

His eyes took on a dreamy quality as he prepared the statement in his mind.

McCord sat quietly, waiting for the pleasant daydream to take its effect.

"Would that be all, sir? There is much to do."

"Yes, yes, off you go. And I want a progress report on my desk asap."

"Yes, sir," McCord said brightly and wondered what the hell he was going to write in that.

Chapter 35

When McCord had left, Amy tried to rehearse her performance for the evening, but her mind was swirling with pictures and sounds from events four years ago. A boy falling in slow motion from a roof, screams, a dead body in a summerhouse, and all the horror interspersed with memories of Angus's lips on hers and his pleading eyes.

She looked out of the window where a fresh breeze played with the litter on the pavement. A brisk walk usually cleared her head. But then she thought of Tristan, guarded by Gertrude Westwater, and Emily, safe with her parents in London. McCord had made her promise not to go out alone until this was over. So how was she going to sort out the mess in her head? Then she remembered who she was. Not just a silly cow taken for a fool. She was a journalist, after all. She went to her room and opened her laptop. The file marked 'Mystery Man' stared at her, mocking her naïvety. She deleted the random list of notes and thoughts and with it her girlish dreams. She opened a new document and started at the very beginning.

* * *

At three o'clock she printed out a sheet with notes and snapped shut the laptop. Following DI McCord's instructions, she wrote the Marchmont address and a date on a piece of paper and slipped it into her coat pocket.

Past and recent events had all found their place in her mind, and what she had to do was clear. It was also clear to her that it would be the hardest thing she had ever done in her life. Whenever a doubt tried to surface, she pushed it resolutely away. Failing was not an option.

A taxi had been booked for five o'clock. Clutching the paper, she went into the living room and rehearsed for an hour. Then she went to the bathroom and looked in the mirror. Her face betrayed the tears she had cried, her hair was dull and lank, and the smell of fear seemed to exude from her body. She switched on the shower and fetched a fresh towel while the water was heating up. She shampooed her hair, soaped her body and stood under the hot stream until she felt calm. She dressed in fresh clothes, carefully applied her make-up and dried her hair. Wearing it pinned up made her look older, more grown-up somehow, and she chose the broad silver clip with the Celtic design her mother had given her for her birthday. It reminded her of the happy evening she had spent with her mother and she felt protected by her symbolic presence.

She dabbed some perfume on her wrists and behind her ears and, so armed, waited for the taxi to arrive.

* * *

The bright sun in a rare cloudless sky seemed to be mocking the dark thoughts swirling inside Amy's mind. Only when her fingers began to hurt did she realise that she had been clutching her seatbelt for most of the journey. She opened and closed her palm to get some circulation back into her hand and tried to breathe slowly in and out.

The driver beamed when she handed him the fare with a generous tip.

"Have a great day, miss."

Amy only managed a weak smile that instantly disappeared as she walked towards the hospital entrance and into the HDU.

The ward was quiet, but Cathy was not.

"Have you heard what happened yesterday?" she welcomed Amy breathlessly. "The police came and–"

"Yes, I know," Amy rudely interrupted her, unable to bear any delay. "Thankfully, it was a false alarm."

"He'll be so glad to see you," Cathy said.

Some machine beeped in the next room, and she hurried off.

Amy gathered all her inner strength and pulled aside the curtain. The sunlight streaming in from the window played on Angus's face, illuminating his handsome features as if trying to weaken her resolve. Quickly, she shut the curtain behind her. Angus had heard her coming and was sitting up expectantly.

"Hi," he said. "I've been waiting all day for you."

"I was at work, remember?" she said and bent down to kiss him on the cheek, but he turned his head and opened her lips with his, his tongue looking for hers. She felt herself gag but held out for long enough not to seem too reluctant.

"How are you?" she enquired casually.

"How do you think?" he said incredulously. "I hardly slept a wink last night."

"I thought it was a false alarm?" she asked innocently.

"Of course, it was," he said hastily, "but that odious detective insinuated that it wasn't. I do believe he was threatening me."

"Oh, I doubt that," Amy said lightly. "He never believed me in the past when I told him you were in danger."

She immediately knew it was a mistake to remind him of her visits to the police.

His eyes narrowed.

"How did you know about last night, anyway? It's not been in the papers yet, has it?"

Her palms broke out in sweat.

"I saw Cathy on my way in. She told me."

He seemed satisfied, and it was time to launch the attack.

"Oh," she said, "by the way, I've got great news."

"A-ha?" He still seemed preoccupied with the police visit the night before.

"You know how my boss had promised I could move away from the fashion desk and cover more human-interest stories?"

Angus shook his head. He did not seem particularly interested.

"Well," she continued with what she hoped came across as enthusiasm, "my boss wants me to do a huge feature over several weeks about the long-term effect of drugs on the families of the victims. The topic is all the rage just now, so I've looked at famous drug deaths over the past few years, and guess who I've managed to get an interview with?"

"Who?" he asked.

Amy prattled on, trying to get it all out before losing her nerve.

"Tristan, the son of Lord Foveran, you know, the one whose whole family died after his brother took drugs and jumped off the roof? You must have heard about it at the time, it was all over the newspapers. He is in Edinburgh. Would you believe it? And he agreed to talk to me! On Wednesday evening! At eight! Because his girlfriend is coming up then as well, Emily she's called, and he hinted that they might have a big story for me. Imagine! I might become famous and get a job at *The Scotsman* and be able to afford my own place!"

His smile froze, just for a fraction of a second, but long enough for Amy to notice.

"That sounds like a real scoop, congratulations!"

Amy bounced up and down with excitement.

"I must get home and tell my mum – she'll be so thrilled!"

She threw her arms in the air, knocking over the cup that stood on his bedside table.

"Oh, I'm so sorry, I don't know where to put myself!"

She pulled a tissue out of her pocket and dabbed at the spilled water.

"Oh, and I won't see you until next week because my mum is taking me to Lisbon. Isn't it incredible? Although I'd rather go to Paris. Paris is so romantic. Will you take me there one day?" she asked, pleadingly.

He smiled ruefully.

"That would be great."

She kissed him forcefully on the lips and waved goodbye as she left. Outside, she turned around and peeked through a gap in the curtains.

Angus leaned out of the bed to pick up the piece of paper that she had dropped when she had pulled out the tissue. His face contorted when he read what was written on it: the address in Marchmont. He sank back onto his pillow, turning the note nervously in his hand. Then he picked up his phone.

Quietly, Amy slunk away.

Chapter 36

McCord was on his second coffee, flicking through the *What Car?* guide. Having always had a car that he was attached to for sentimental reasons, he found it difficult to make up his mind now that the only restriction on choice was his salary. He was not one of these men for whom the car is a status symbol or an imaginary reflection of their sexual prowess. This car just had to get him from A to B without breaking down. Clear about his first priority, reliability, he settled on the next: economy, i.e. low fuel consumption. After that, comfort and design. He started making a list of models in his price range that scored top marks on the first two points.

In the Mazda section, he came across the racy little number he had been a passenger in last week. He looked at the picture and data next to it for a long time until the sadness that had gripped him turned into anger.

He picked up his phone.

"DI Marshall," said a grumpy voice.

"McCord, here."

"I'm off duty, McCord. I'm trying to get three children ready for the pool. The wife is out shopping. What's the matter?"

"Sorry," said McCord apologetically. If he was honest, he could not understand what could ever be more important or interesting than a case. "Did you get the duty rota I sent you yesterday? You didn't get back to me."

He heard a door banging repeatedly in the background.

"Mia, please don't do that... I did. We were busy trying to find out when and where Turnbull's next consignment of girls arrives but since he busted our man's cover last month, we don't have anybody on the inside. Mia, *stop* that!"

The banging continued unabated, while a persistent whining sound McCord interpreted as 'Daddy, Daddy' emanated from closer quarters. Probably a smaller child attached to his colleague's lower leg.

"If our little plan works, you might not need that anymore," McCord reminded him. "Have you set up the bait?"

"The 'bait' is one of my best officers, and yes, she's been wasting her time for three nights now. If nothing happens today, I'll have to pull her, McCord. We're stretched to the limit as it is, and I don't have the resources to tie up officers just on the off chance. Mia! STOP!"

McCord jerked the receiver away from his ringing ear.

"I'm sure we're on the right track. Just get her there tonight. Enjoy your swim!" he shouted.

Marshall gave a desperate moan and put the phone down. McCord had no doubt that at this moment DI Marshall would much prefer to be at work.

* * *

Amy had not slept well. In disjointed tatters of dreams, she had been chased by a car, had tried to catch a boy flying away through the night air, stroked a tabby cat rubbing its cheek against her leg and had woken up gasping after being strangled with some of her mum's fabric. Covered in sweat, she kicked off the duvet and stretched out on the mattress. She blinked in the spring sunshine that sneaked through the gap in the heavy blue curtains and bounced off the metal frame of her bed. When her heartbeat had slowed and goose pimples erupted on her skin, she jumped up and opened the curtains. Harsh morning light flooded the room, and the sight of the Saturday morning traffic brought her slowly back to reality. She had done well, she kept telling herself, echoing McCord's words from last night. He had gone as far as saying she would make a decent investigative journalist or even detective one day.

She was startled by a loud knock on the door.

"Coffee is ready", she heard her mother say, "come and have breakfast with us."

Still only half awake, she wondered about the 'us' but then remembered. After her call explaining why she had not come back to work, John had insisted on staying overnight in the spare bedroom, 'for protection'. The time when she had plotted to get John and her mum together seemed a lifetime away; a time when love and crime had just been a game she played to relieve her boredom with frills and pleats.

"Coming," she shouted, slipping into her velvety bathrobe.

* * *

The kitchen table was laden with croissants, toast, jam and honey, and on the stove, bacon sizzled in the pan.

"Good morning," John greeted her cheerfully, giving her a sideways glance as he got up and turned to the cooker.

"Poached egg?"

"Yes, please," Amy said, suddenly hungry, and watched as John cracked two eggs into a small black dish and popped them into the microwave.

"One of John's little gadgets," Valerie said, seeing Amy's questioning look, and poured her a coffee.

Amy took a large gulp and devoured half a croissant smothered in jam while still standing next to the table.

"Sit down while you're eating," Valerie said irritably. "John's friend Phoebe Smythe-Tennyson will think I brought you up in a stable. It is very kind of her to let us stay on her estate for a few days."

John turned round.

"Did I tell you? Phoebe has planned a hike up Glencorse View for tomorrow."

"Good God," said Valerie, aghast. "I think I'd rather stay here and get myself assassinated."

John shook his head.

"No need to worry. With Phoebe you are never further than two miles from the nearest café or pub. It is beautiful up on her estate; you will love it. Just take some warm clothes and boots. You do have boots?" he asked cautiously.

Valerie shrugged. "I do have boots," she said defensively, "but they are made from calf leather and have two-inch heels. I definitely won't be traipsing up a mountain with them."

John looked incredulous.

"Well," he thought aloud, "I am sure you can borrow a pair from Phoebe."

Valerie's eyes fell on the clock.

"Is that the time?" she exclaimed. "I still have to pack!"

She got up and rushed across the hall.

The microwave pinged, and John spooned the poached eggs carefully onto a piece of toast.

Amy looked up from her mug.

"I haven't really thanked you for everything you do for Mum and me," she said quietly.

He put the eggs in front of her, looking embarrassed.

"You should thank Phoebe. She is a great friend. I am just being entirely selfish."

Amy smiled.

"Just make sure Mum doesn't slip on a cowpat."

* * *

McCord was spending Saturday evening with his father, who was delighted with the Nissan Juke.

"Three years old, and only five thousand on the clock," McCord explained proudly. "As good as new, and half the price."

"Well done, Russell. At least you won't get stuck again at a petrol station, needing to be rescued by a young policewoman. Mind you," – he winked at his son – "you did say she was very attractive."

"Don't start, Dad," McCord said in mock frustration. "I called her because she was there. And she is a bloody good officer."

"Good for her," Keith said, unconvinced. "Why don't you ask her out sometime?"

"Dad!"

After their usual ritual of curry and chess, as always watched over by the smiling picture of his mum who had died giving birth to him, McCord was helping to tidy up the kitchen when his mobile buzzed.

"Not work, surely," Keith said disapprovingly. "You are working ridiculous hours as it is."

McCord read the message, ignoring his father's comments. He quickly typed a couple of sentences then phoned DI Marshall, who answered with a groan.

"Sorry to interrupt your marital bliss," McCord said insincerely. "Our friend is on the move. Trajectory perfect. Roughly seven minutes away."

A sceptical grunt with a question mark at the end was all he got in reply.

"This time I had a little help. Explain later. Make your calls."

He hung up and gave his dad a hug.

"Must dash. Bad guys to catch."

"Be careful, son," Keith shouted after him with a mixture of pride and worry as McCord sped away in the Juke.

Chapter 37

DC Gill Morton was fed up. This was her fourth time out on Clarence Street, and she had lost faith in her boss's judgement. The first night had been great. She had been like a coiled spring, ready to pounce. It had given her a thrill wearing her disguise. It was oddly empowering to be moving about without anybody recognising you, as if you could say and do what you wanted with impunity.

She would never have worn such an outfit in real life although during the hours sitting in the grubby café across the road, she had wondered how her boyfriend would react to that. Probably he would have been appalled. He was certainly not impressed when she had told him what her assignment was. She wasn't supposed to say, of course, but he was the jealous type, and being away half the night without explanation would have triggered a major bust-up.

She was thinking about the man whose bait she was. A thousand times she had gone over how she would break his nose, hit his solar plexus to wind him and put handcuffs on him. After reading him his rights, she would deliver him to her boss.

On the second night, she had tried to while away the time speaking to the Albanian girls. Maybe she could find out something that would nail Turnbull? That would certainly help her career prospects. She had been warned, though, because many prostitutes are very protective of their patch and do not take kindly to someone else invading their territory. This had not turned out to be the main problem, however, when she tried to strike up a conversation over a fag. The problem was that the girls barely spoke English. They had been ferried here in lorries, dumped in a room, screamed at that they owed ten thousand pounds and then they had been beaten and raped until their resistance was broken. They had been taught the ten phrases they needed to procure the money and been given drugs to see them through the process. Once they had outlived their usefulness, they ended up in a stinking toilet or a dark alley, another number in a sad statistic.

Anything had to be worthwhile to find and punish the men who were behind this filthy business, but she was convinced that she was wasting her time. She prowled hopelessly along the street, her calves aching from the five-inch heels, her legs itching but still cold underneath the stockings and the white skin on her painfully pushed up breasts puckering against the bitter night air. She made up a guessing game how long each girl had been here for; how slick the soliciting, how thin the bare arms, how empty the look in their eyes.

With a ruckus erupting outside one of the takeaway places, she almost missed the alert on her phone.

A few minutes, probably coming in from the west. Good luck.

Suddenly, she did not feel the cold anymore, only a huge adrenaline rush. She walked as quickly as her heels allowed westward along the road, keeping close to the kerb. She was just about thirty yards from the corner when a red car came into sight and crawled along the pavement. She slid her skimpy leather jacket off her shoulders and waved it with what she hoped was a seductive move. Twenty yards. "Come on", she coaxed, "come to mummy..."

The car slowed down even more. Gotcha, she thought, when suddenly, out of nowhere, shot the skeletal figure of a girl who bent through the open window, exchanged a few words with the driver, tripped round the car and slipped into the passenger seat. Muttering obscenities, Gill watched the car pass her, turn left into the next side street and disappear from sight. Trembling, she pressed the call button on her phone.

"Suspect driven off with girl, turned into Clarence Lane, in pursuit."

Clutching her phone, she hurried across the road but looking ahead, she missed a drain. One of her heels went into it, throwing her off balance. Instinctively protecting her phone, she did not have time to break the fall and crashed face down onto the pavement. She shouted out as a searing pain shot through her right ankle that was stuck between the metal bars of the drain. Her arms were scraped raw by the asphalt on the pavement, and her right elbow was bleeding. Crying with fury, she pulled her foot out of the drain, slipped off her shoes and tried to stand up.

This side of the street was dark and deserted. Most of the shops were shut or derelict, and nobody from across the street made a move to help. The pain in her ankle was excruciating but the thought of what was happening to the girl in the car pushed her on. Leaving her jacket behind, she gritted her teeth and hobbled along the lane, stones and shards of broken glass piercing the sole of her weight-bearing foot. The report said that he did not drive far from where he picked up the women, usually to a dark, deserted spot. After about fifty agonising yards, the lane opened into an industrial retail park, only sparsely lit by the few streetlights that had not been smashed.

There was no car in sight. Choking away tears, she was about to collapse and wait for backup to arrive, when she heard a muted scream close by. She stood still and listened but could hear nothing. She thought the cries had come from the left, which seemed impossible. There was only a wooden fence, and behind the fence a large warehouse.

Not knowing where else to turn, she hobbled on, and her heart leapt when she saw that between the fence and the warehouse there was a drive, and the car stood there, looking black in the darkness. Hoping he would not see her too soon, she sneaked up to the driver's door, positioned her phone, set it on record and yanked open the door.

"Stop!" she yelled. "Let go of her!"

The man, lying with his trousers pulled down on top of the whimpering girl, lifted off almost vertically with fright and hit his head on the low ceiling of the car. He took his hands off her throat, leaving her gasping for air, and did not seem to know what to do next.

"Get out of the car, slowly!" Gill commanded, sliding her phone down her waistband.

Automatically, she reached for her handcuffs but suddenly realised they were in the pockets of the jacket she had abandoned by the drain.

The man edged himself backwards out of the car and stumbled over the trouser legs that were twisted round his ankles. He hastily pulled them up and turned round, seeing now who it was that had so rudely interrupted him: a cheap whore with mascara running down her face, scraped arms and something that looked like a club foot.

"Nice try." He smirked. "Desperate to do some business, eh, or are you worried about your chum? How touching," he sneered. "Now piss off, or you'll get the same treatment."

He lifted his arms to push her away from the open door when Gill's dream came true after all. In one fluid movement, practised for many hours in the police gym, she kneed him in the groin and, as he doubled up in agony, hit his temple with locked hands. He fell to the ground like a sack of cement. She knelt on his back, bending his right arm at an angle until his moans became a pierced scream. She loosened her grip a tiny fraction just so that he could hear what she would say next.

"DS Gavin Fraser, I'm arresting you on suspicion of rape, attempted rape, aggravated assault and attempted murder, you bastard."

Before she could break his arm, three police cars with flashing blue lights tore up Clarence Lane and screeched to a halt behind the Mazda.

Chapter 38

McCord had arrived at the station just in time to see his onetime pal being locked up in a cell. The prostitute he had attacked was being seen by a police doctor, who documented the finger marks on her neck, her dislocated jaw and the bleeding scratches on her thighs. DC Gill Morton had her sprained ankle and injured elbow bandaged and had been duly praised for her fighting spirit.

McCord had been keen to interview Gavin Fraser straightaway, but DI Marshall insisted that he should stew in a cell overnight. He argued that criminals were a great deal more pliable after they had some time to think about the mess they were in. He also wanted to show Candy a picture of Gavin Fraser before the interview. McCord had a sneaking suspicion, however, that through this arrangement, DI Marshall had cunningly just avoided the weekly visit to his in-laws.

* * *

On Sunday morning, therefore, both DI Marshall and McCord found themselves in an interview room back at the station, waiting for Gavin Fraser to be brought in.

"By the way," DI Marshall asked, "why were you so sure he was going to Clarence Street this time? Or should I not ask?" he added when McCord did not immediately answer.

"Let's just say, a little bug on his car helped one of my officers with her tracking software."

"So, you've suspected him a while?"

"It started when he claimed there was no usable CCTV footage of a car chase, and then it turned out there was. That could just have been a lie covering up laziness, but that officer I mentioned had a wee look at Fraser's finances, and a lot of money went into an account of his, curiously coinciding with the dates when you conducted your failed raids at Turnbull's place. That car of his is not cheap either. I certainly couldn't afford it. Then, when you gave me the dates of the attacks, I found that he had always been off duty then. Turnbull must have turned a blind eye to Fraser's rapes because he was such a valuable asset. He is our mole all right. Now we have to use what we have on him in order to get Turnbull."

He went silent.

"You don't look very happy for someone who has just cracked a case that wasn't even yours," DI Marshall observed. "If I were in your shoes, I'd be unbearably smug."

McCord gave a bitter laugh.

"I've been working with him for five years, I thought he was a friend. That doesn't say much for my judgement, does it?"

"Do you want me to lead the interview?" DI Marshall asked.

"Probably better if you do it. I might just strangle him," McCord agreed.

The door opened and Gavin Fraser strode in, a very expensive-looking lawyer behind him.

After DI Marshall had switched on the recorder and named all the people present, the lawyer cleared his throat.

"I've advised my client not to make a statement," he declared, stroking his immaculately trimmed black beard, "until we have been presented with the evidence and witness statements. Considering my client is a long-serving police officer with an immaculate record, I have already applied for bail pending the arrival of the former."

He made a move to pick up his briefcase and leave.

DI Marshall smiled knowingly.

"I think your client has not given you the full picture. We don't need a statement; we just need him to listen. We have a video recording and an undercover police officer's witness report of him assaulting a prostitute. We have another victim who recognised him from a photograph and is prepared to swear in court that he assaulted and raped her on 15 March. We are confident that given time, further victims will come forward. What do we think he'll get for aggravated assault in several cases, rape and attempted rape?" he asked McCord.

McCord pretended to calculate figures in his head.

"Give or take ten years?" he suggested.

"Probably," DI Marshall agreed. "But sadly, that is not all. By tomorrow we will have a warrant to access all his accounts and communications, and we are confident, aren't we?" – he turned again to McCord as if needing confirmation – "that we will find a money trail proving that he passed on confidential police data to a certain Archie Turnbull alerting him to planned raids on his business premises."

DI Marshall leaned back to let this information sink in. He noted with great satisfaction that the lawyer had ceased to caress his facial hair and that Fraser had started to sweat.

"There are two options the way I see it," he continued eventually, this time addressing Fraser directly. "We can release you on bail, pending the forensic evidence and witness statements as your lawyer demanded. Then we'll invite Mr Turnbull for an interview and ask him about his dealings with you."

Fraser jumped up, his eyes dilated in horror.

"You can't do that, that would be my death sentence!"

DI Marshall grinned broadly.

"Surely not. Thanks to your communications with him, we have no evidence that suggests that Mr Turnbull is anything but a perfectly respectable businessman. But I take your comment as confirmation that you are familiar with Mr Turnbull's alleged business practices."

The lawyer looked at DI Marshall.

"You mentioned a second option?"

DI Marshall pretended to have forgotten.

"Of course, the second option." He locked eyes with Fraser. "We keep you in custody, deny you bail on the grounds that you are a violent serial offender and give you an opportunity to demonstrate your willingness to cooperate fully with the police investigation into Mr Turnbull. If your cooperation contributes to Mr Turnbull's subsequent conviction, I'm sure that the Crown will take that into account when deliberating your case."

Fraser exchanged pleading looks with his lawyer who stroked his beard thoughtfully.

"I think I would like some time to confer with my client."

"Please do," DI Marshall said cheerfully. "Interview suspended at 10.15am."

* * *

When they had left the room, DI Marshall punched the air.

"Yes! Did you see his face when I suggested letting him go?"

McCord did not say anything.

"What's the matter with you? He's going to give us Turnbull!"

DI Marshall was pacing up and down with excitement.

"Yes, he'll go into a witness programme and end up with a laughable sentence, maybe even suspended. Great." The sarcasm in McCord's voice was dripping onto the shiny linoleum of the interview room.

"I know you're feeling betrayed, and I don't like that aspect one bit myself, but we have to look at the bigger picture. Taking out Turnbull and his network is going to save so many people from abject misery."

Chapter 39

On Monday morning, DI McCord knocked on the door of Superintendent Gilchrist's office. After DS Fraser's arrest and the prospect of bringing Turnbull down, he for once looked pleased to see McCord.

"What can I do for you?" he asked.

McCord put his superior in the picture about the planned operation on Wednesday evening.

Gilchrist was apoplectic.

"You are setting a trap using three civilians as bait in order to catch this Kaminski?" he asked, incredulously. "Do you think you're in some kind of cowboy film?"

McCord had expected as much.

"I am convinced that all three witnesses are in danger. At least this way I can keep them safe until we are ready. The opportunity to dispose of all of them at once will be too tempting. And please remember, it is not just about Kaminski, an assassin sought by Europol, but also about the person who hired him. I believe it is the same person who ordered the Musselburgh Lagoons murders. If this goes according to plan, it'll be quite a scoop that the press will love."

Even at that, the Super's frown did not disappear.

"What if it goes belly-up? He might not turn up, and we'll be ridiculed in the papers. Or, even worse, he does turn up, and we have dead bodies and an official inquiry on our hands."

McCord had thought about little else for the past few days, but there was no way back now.

"We'll just have to make sure nothing goes wrong."

Gilchrist leant forward.

"Oh no, McCord, not we. *You* have to make sure nothing goes wrong, or you'll have to find yourself a new job."

* * *

McCord went back to the open-plan office and called a staff meeting to share updates and prepare for Wednesday night. Sunshine was streaming through the large windows, prompting some of the men to discard their jackets and roll up their shirtsleeves. The relaxed, summery scene was in stark contrast to the dark mood among the officers. The room was humming with subdued conversation. Some just sat there, quietly in shock.

"Good morning," McCord said, standing up on front of the incident board still showing the grisly scene at Musselburgh Lagoons. He had chosen this spot deliberately to focus their minds back on the still unsolved murders. There was an immediate hush.

"You will all have heard about DS Fraser's arrest on Saturday evening. He has been charged with rape, attempted rape and assault as well as corruption. For those of you still in doubt, I can assure you that there is plenty of evidence for all these charges. He has signed a written confession."

His words had fallen like lead into the room. His colleagues sat hunched, weighed down by a sense of despair and utter betrayal. DS Fraser had been popular, and many still struggled to believe McCord.

"He is cooperating with Vice as regards the crimes committed by Archie Turnbull and in all likelihood will become a Crown witness should Turnbull go on trial, which we all hope will happen, of course," McCord ploughed on.

Normally, such a statement would have elicited whoops and cheers but not today.

"I understand your shock and disgust," he said quietly.

He did not need to add that nobody in the room had been more reluctant to believe it and more disappointed than he himself.

"A bent policeman is like a cancer in our very core. It needs to be uncovered and cut out completely. If anybody has any information on DS Fraser that might be helpful, please come forward. At the moment, we are assuming that Turnbull was the only criminal who had Fraser in his pocket, but we don't know. The press will be all over us as well, of course. You'll have received an email suggesting phrases you can use when the hacks approach you. Needless to say, you *never* comment on any case, this or others. We leave that to our well-briefed superintendent."

A tentative giggle went through the room.

PC Turner's angry voice cut through the mirth.

"Why did he do it? How could he?"

McCord's first instinct was to remind him that he was not a psychoanalyst, but he saw that the young constable was genuinely shaken. These officers often put their health and lives on the line, and the idea that one of their own could be a traitor was incomprehensible.

"He comes from a deprived area," he began.

"So do you," PC Turner interjected, "and you would never sell us down the river – would you?"

The slight hesitation and intonation at the end told McCord just how much damage Fraser had done. It would probably take years to restore trust and the reputation of this unit.

"No," he said calmly. "I wouldn't. I think he was stuck in a life that he felt wasn't going anywhere. The temptation of retiring in the sun and living a life of luxury was too great for him." He felt that was more than enough explanation and added a heartfelt, "He is just a weak, pathetic scumbag."

He straightened up.

"Enough of the long faces. We've still got a double murder to solve and an operation to prepare that is complex and very dangerous. The Super has just given his approval but very reluctantly. I've put my job on the line promising him that nothing will go wrong."

As he said it, the hair on the back of his neck rose. 'Don't tempt fate,' his father would have said, 'pride comes before the fall.'

"Are we any further on linking Kaminski with Wynn or knowing where they are?"

He scanned the room and noticed Heather the Hacker looking uncomfortable. He nodded encouragingly.

"Have you got something for us, DS Sutton?"

She fixed her eyes on the screen.

"Credit cards first used by Kaminski and then Wynn at the same service station on the M6. Killington Lake. Fairly regular intervals, about once a month."

McCord's face lit up.

"Have you got dates, times?"

"Yes. Last transaction yesterday."

"Brilliant, thank you. Turner, get onto that. Check if there is CCTV. They've probably wiped it but it's worth a try. Tell them to make sure the CCTV is running and call us the second he turns up. I want a picture of him."

"Yes, sir." Turner beamed and immediately bent over his keyboard to find the number of the service station manager.

"Right, all of you, keep looking. Remember, all hands on deck until Thursday. No sickies, no repeatedly dying grannies, please. Now I need to speak to the team involved in Wednesday's operation. Conference room 3 in five minutes, but grab a coffee first."

* * *

When they were all assembled around the table, McCord projected a picture of the cottage in Marchmont on the screen.

"Gertrude and Tristan are currently at the cottage. I had a text from Tristan this morning, so she hasn't yet killed him with her cooking. Amy Thornton and Emily Fullerton are arriving separately by taxis driven by our guys as close to 8pm as possible. We want to keep the window of opportunity for the killer or killers as narrow as possible."

Jeffries hesitantly lifted his hand.

"Do we have any confirmation that an attempt on their life is, eh, actually planned?"

"Magnus McAdie phoned his father immediately after Miss Thornton's visit. That's it," McCord admitted. "But we have established a link between McAdie senior and Wynn, who I'm sure is Kaminski. DC Sutton has tracked payments from McAdie to Wynn's account which coincide with the double murder. I am convinced that McAdie is prepared to dispatch anybody who poses a threat to his son. And Tristan is the biggest threat."

Jeffries nodded reluctantly.

"Now to the important part. The cottage has two exits, front and back. The front will be covered by four officers; two stationed in the house opposite and two in the cottage next door on the right. We can't use the property on the left, the couple there are compulsive gossips, Gertrude tells me."

He clicked on two slides showing the properties.

"The other neighbours are on board. Officers arrive during the course of the afternoon posing as visiting family, in case Kaminski or Wynn is watching the house. McAdie could have hired a different assassin, of course, but I think he is more likely to stick with someone he knows."

He took a sip of coffee.

"Gertrude Westwater is armed, as you know, and trained in combat."

He noticed Jeffries' sceptical look.

"Even if is she's getting on a bit, I wouldn't fancy my chances against her. The others will be given defensive weapons, just in case. If it goes according to plan, Kaminski never gets into the house at all. And *if* there is an almighty cock-up and he gets in before we catch him, Gertrude will hold him off until we get there."

He clicked on a slide showing the back of the cottage.

"As you see, there is a patio door leading to the back garden. The garden shed has been fitted with spyholes and all mod cons. Two officers will be spending a happy evening in there. It is surrounded by a solid but not very high wall with a door out into the back lane. Covering that without being spotted is going to be the trickiest part. Two groups of two are covering the entrances to the lane."

Jeffries was still frowning. "That is ten officers for most of the day, not counting Gertrude. Is that not a bit of an overkill? Excuse the pun."

McCord had anticipated scepticism, but Jeffries' negativity was beginning to grate on his nerves.

"We have three innocent civilians in there who have agreed to be sitting ducks for an assassin who is wanted by Europol. The least we can do is ensure they come out of this still in one piece, would you not agree?"

Jeffries nodded reluctantly.

"I've been thinking how I would go about killing four people inside a house. Breaking in and shooting them is risky, especially if he is on his own. Once he starts shooting, the others will run and if even one escapes, he is in big trouble. So, I thought he might use fire; block the doors and pour petrol through the letterbox. Risky at this time of night but there are mainly retired people living on the street, and it is very quiet after dark. I've alerted the fire brigade to that possibility, and they said unless there is a big call-out, they'll position one in the retail park just two streets away."

He looked round the table.

"Any thoughts? Anything I might have missed?"

They shook their heads.

"Good. Jeffries, allocate the positions and let me know."

He looked closely at every member of his team.

"I know you want this as badly as I do. But remember, top priority is the safety of the witnesses and all the officers involved. Even" – he raised his voice – "if it means letting Kaminski escape. Understood?"

They all murmured assent.

"Right, we'll meet again Wednesday morning for a final run-through. Time for lunch."

* * *

McCord had only just returned from lunch when PC Turner turned up in his office with a strange mixture of elation and frustration.

"The service station does have CCTV in the shop, and they keep footage for three days, but their machine broke yesterday, so they can't play the tapes."

McCord rested his head in his hand. It suddenly seemed very heavy. After a couple of seconds, he pulled himself up.

"Get them to send the whole lot up by courier today. Then call the techies and tell them it's coming. I need a picture tomorrow."

PC Turner had brightened up.

"Consider it done, sir."

* * *

On Tuesday afternoon McCord called PC Turner into his office.

"Where are we with the CCTV?"

"The courier only arrived this morning. I took it straight over, but the guys said it is completely bust. It's an ancient machine and they don't know if they can find another one."

McCord felt his blood pressure rise and fumbled for his nicotine gum.

"I need that footage. By tomorrow morning, even if you have to sift through tons of junk all day in second-hand shops and recycling centres, so be it. Take Dharwan with you."

PC Turner was barely out of the door when McCord's phone rang. It was DI Marshall.

"I thought you should be the first to know. After you'd left on Sunday, Fraser gave us the time and place for Turnbull's latest consignment. Arrived last night. Quite a scramble to put the op together but we did it. A lorry full of illegals from Albania again, mainly girls around sixteen. Some of them half-dead from the journey. Social services are taking care of them, and we're bringing in the others from his various establishments. Two of Turnbull's lieutenants are behind bars and singing like canaries. Got their phones with messages from Turnbull, the boys are bringing him in as we speak."

"Congratulations," McCord said, sincerely pleased. "Did you ask them about the Musselburgh Lagoons victims?"

"Yes, Tait and Murales were working for Turnbull, trying to put the frighteners on young McAdie who wanted a piece of the Edinburgh drug trade and was running a little sideline in drugs himself. Stupid boy, he had no idea who he was messing with. Probably thought he could be a big bad guy like his father. Tait and Murales were responsible for vandalising the pub in the weeks before the accident. On the day of the accident, they met him pretending to be after a drug deal and went for him. He just about made it into his car, so they chased him. When McAdie had them killed, Turnbull held Magnus responsible, and it was open warfare. He sent in a couple of his men to firebomb the pub. If the manager had not put the fire out, the flat would have gone up in flames as well. Magnus McAdie was lucky to be in hospital all this time, or sure as hell he would be dead by now."

"That would have been a great loss indeed," McCord commented drily. "Thanks, well done. Send me a copy of your files and I'll add them to mine regarding Tait and Murales."

"How is it going your end?" DI Marshall asked. "Getting anywhere with them?"

"Maybe," McCord said. "Fingers crossed. Any chance you could let me have your plucky DC Gill Morton tomorrow evening?"

DI Marshall chuckled.

"No chance, she's mine."

* * *

By Wednesday lunchtime, McCord's nerves were in shreds. He had spent all night going over scenarios that without exception ended in disaster and humiliation and him looking for another job.

"Where is that bloody CCTV?" he shouted at PC Turner, whose bloodshot eyes had dark shadows underneath. Clearly, he had not slept much either.

"We found a second-hand electronics dealer last night who said he knew somebody who might have one. By the time we got there, he was shut, and nobody was answering the phone. I've been calling him all morning, but he was out on deliveries. He says he has a machine, but it's been sitting here for a decade and he's not sure if it works. I'm going there now and will deliver it to Tech."

"Good man," McCord said, mollified. "Keep me posted. And use the siren."

Chapter 40

It was two minutes past eight. McCord was hanging around the corner shop a couple of streets away and decided that his cover warranted him smoking a cigarette. Inhaling deeply, he felt the hit. Only now did he realise how much he had missed it. The gum just wasn't the same. Despite the sleepless nights, he felt sharp as a blade. Emily and Amy had arrived in their separate taxis. Gertrude had put on a great show of welcoming them in case Kaminski was watching. Two officers were ensconced in Gertrude's garden shed and all the others had checked in from their various locations. A fire engine had slowly driven past and disappeared from sight. Everything was in place.

"Any sign of him?" he asked into his radio.

"Negative," came the answer from all the hiding places.

McCord phoned the station again.

"Turner, have we got a picture, for crying out loud?"

"Well, I, the thing is," Turner stammered, "he is not there."

"What do you mean, *he's not there*? Haven't you got the exact time of the credit card transaction Sutton gave you?"

"Yes, but–"

McCord's radio bleeped. "Hang on," he interrupted Turner. "Have to go. Just send me the footage on my phone. I'll have a look myself, for God's sake."

The call was from the officer in the house opposite the cottage.

"Young female approaching front door of cottage. Her clothes are torn, she is limping and crying. She's ringing the bell now."

McCord uttered a dreadful curse, sending a little old lady scurrying across the road to safety.

Gertrude had already spotted the young woman through the camera covering the doors.

"What shall I do with her?" her voice whispered into his earpiece.

"Ignore her," McCord barked.

"The lights are on, and if he watches, it'll look suspicious if we don't open the door to help or at least see what's going on."

"True," McCord grunted, "but for Christ's sake, get rid of her asap. And don't let her call the bloody police!"

* * *

Gertrude opened just a narrow gap in the door to face a young woman who was obviously distraught. Her mascara was running down her cheeks in black rivulets and the area around one of her eyes was bruised. Her trembling fingers were clutching the folds of a silky blouse that was torn above her breast.

"Please," she sobbed, "let me in before he sees me, or he'll kill me."

Gertrude decided that somebody else banging on her door was not desirable, so she invited the woman in and quickly shut the door behind her.

"Come into the living room where it's warm," she said, ushering in the woman who was shivering with cold and kept her arms folded around her chest as if giving herself a much-needed hug.

"Thank you," she sniffed. "Thank you so much."

"Who are you running away from?" Gertrude asked.

"My husband. He is insanely jealous. You won't let him in if he comes, will you?" she pleaded in a sudden panic.

"Of course not," Gertrude replied impatiently, willing her to shut up so that she could listen out for unfamiliar noises around the house. As they entered the sitting room, Gertrude quickly slipped past the unwelcome guest and slid her gun under the cushion on her armchair. Amy offered the visitor her seat by the fire and squeezed onto the floral sofa next to Emily.

"I'm Gertrude. Amy, Tristan and Emily," Gertrude said by way of introduction, pointing to them in turn.

"Hi," they said in unison, eyeing her with sympathetic curiosity.

The tension that had built up in the room as they were waiting for a deadly assault had eased with the unexpected new arrival. Amy, a new feature about domestic violence already forming in her head, spoke first.

"What's your name?"

* * *

McCord's phone alerted him to an incoming message with attachment. It was the ten-second CCTV footage of the time a credit card purchase was made by Riley Wynn. Watching it, he choked on the smoke of his cigarette, coughed and gasped for air. He dropped the half-finished fag and enlarged the grainy picture to just before it became blurred.

"God, no!" he whispered, wiping his hand that was slippery with cold sweat on his trousers. His fingers trembled as he picked up his device.

"Come in," he rasped into his radio, "Kaminski is a woman, and she's just entered the house."

* * *

Katz Kaminski pulled a gun from the folds of her blouse and pointed it at Amy. But before she could pull the trigger, she heard a familiar click. Gertrude was slowly getting up, pointing her gun at Kaminski's head.

"Put it down," she said matter-of-factly, "you pull that trigger, you're dead. The house is surrounded by police. The game's up."

Katz Kaminski's eyes flickered between the three young people, frozen in their movements on the sofa, and the old woman with the knitted cardigan and the cold eyes.

"You police?" she asked, surprised, keeping the barrel unflinchingly aimed at Amy's forehead.

"Special Branch, retired," Gertrude replied. "But not past putting a bullet into a killer's head. Put it down."

"We're at a bit of an impasse, aren't we," Kaminski observed, still not moving. "We women should stick together. It's not easy out there in a man's world."

"I'm about to cry," Gertrude said sarcastically. "You have a choice. Putting the gun down is by far the better one."

"I don't have any choice," Kaminski hissed. "I can only get out of here as long as my gun is in line with one of your brains. So, listen carefully, this is what we'll do: l am going to walk out of the front door with Amy and disappear. One false move from anybody, and she's dead."

She got up slowly and motioned Amy to do the same. Amy struggled to get onto her feet, her knees trembling.

Kaminski's gun now almost touched Amy's hair.

"Please," Tristan begged, "don't hurt her. Tell McAdie I won't say anything to the police or the press. Please…!"

Kaminski kept her eyes unwaveringly on Amy's head.

"Shut up!" she shouted, furiously. "I had a job to do, and Granny's interference has cost me a lot of money, blown my cover and damaged my reputation. So don't piss me off any more. Now move!"

Amy cast a pleading glance back at Gertrude, whose poised gun followed Kaminski as if it was attached to the killer by an invisible thread, and walked slowly towards the front door.

* * *

McCord sprinted towards the cottage. He had heard most of the conversation through Gertrude's wire.

"Stand back," he gasped his order to the troops. "Do not endanger the life of the hostage under any circumstances."

He had reached the side street two houses away from the cottage and peeked round the corner. He could see the front door from here, which was still shut. He wondered how Kaminski planned to get away. There were several cars parked along the road, any of them could be hers. Ambulances and backup were on their way, and the whole area was being closed off, but he wondered if the roadblocks would all be set up in time.

Then, the front door opened slowly, and Amy appeared on the threshold. Very stiffly, she stepped out onto the garden path and walked with slow, robotic movements towards the gate. Right behind her, Kaminski followed, her earlier vulnerability replaced by sheer menace.

* * *

Amy, terrified, felt the cold pressure of the gun barrel. One slow step at a time, she forced her body forward, each step further from the people who might protect her; each step closer to being alone with a homicidal psychopath. Without moving her head, she scanned the street in front of her. There must be police, maybe snipers who could take Kaminski out? But they would not dare while a gun was pointed at her head.

Amy remembered that the pros always tried to strike a rapport with the killer who threatened them. Eventually he or she would break down and decide to do the right thing after all. The main thing was to get them talking.

"You really got us there," Amy said, trying to keep the trembling out of her voice. "Nobody had the faintest idea you were a woman. What made you want to be an–"

"Shut up!" Kaminski's voice was vicious.

Amy fell silent. The garden gate was only a few steps away. Where was this madwoman going to take her?

Suddenly, she heard somebody sneeze, right next to her leg. Forgetting her determination not to move, she looked down, her heart leaping with hope. All in a split second, she saw that there was nobody there, felt the pressure of the barrel ease and heard two shots ring out at almost the same time. A warm, viscous mass drenched the back of her head, and her right leg was on fire.

Somebody screamed, and after a moment Amy realised they were her own screams. Seeing several police officers running towards her, she tried to reach the gate but collapsed on the path where the blood spurting from the wound in her lower leg mingled with the blood that had already turned the concrete crimson. Then everything went dark.

* * *

By the time Amy hobbled into the family waiting room, wearing sweatpants and a jumper far too big for her, McCord had phoned John and Valerie to fill them in on the events leading up to the shooting.

Valerie jumped up and hugged her daughter.

"How are you?"

"Fine," Amy said, smiling weakly, "the painkillers are kicking in. I'll be right as rain in a few days."

"Thank God for that," John said.

"Your hair is wet, and what has happened to your clothes?" Valerie asked.

"Forensics," McCord hastily intervened when he saw Amy turning a deathly green colour.

No need to explain to her mother that Amy had been covered in Katz Kaminski's blood and brains.

"What actually happened on that path?" John said.

"I don't know," Amy said. "It feels like a dream. I thought I heard a sneeze coming from the ground next to me, and then there were shots, but I must be imagining it."

"No, you didn't," McCord assured her. "Sneezy the Dwarf is one of Gertrude's little toys, bought in a joke shop, and remotely controlled. She used it to distract Kaminski. She saw her turn the gun instinctively towards the noise and she took her chance. Unfortunately, Kaminski still managed to shoot you in the leg before she, eh, went down."

"How dare this Gertrude endanger my girl's life like that! She could have been killed!" Valerie said accusingly to McCord.

McCord shrugged.

"Without Gertrude's presence of mind, the whole thing would have ended much worse. And Gertrude *really* didn't appreciate Kaminski calling her Granny."

Chapter 41

On Thursday morning, McCord got the message he had been waiting for from the hospital: 'Parents with him now.'

McCord locked his computer, ran down to the car park and jumped into the Juke. It took him less than twenty minutes to reach Little France Drive and another three for the ward where Magnus McAdie was sitting, fully dressed, on his bed and looking forward to being discharged. McCord pulled the curtain aside with a flourish.

"A very good morning to you, Mr McAdie, Mrs McAdie and Mr McAdie junior." He bowed slightly to them all, who had abruptly stopped their conversation. "I could never get used to the Angus Adamson name. It was just a mask to hide behind, after all, wasn't it?"

"Have you come to harass my son again?" McAdie blustered. "Because if you are–"

"Actually, I've come to arrest *you*," McCord said cheerfully, "for hiring Katz Kaminski alias Riley Wynn to murder Lord Foveran's son Tristan, Emily Fullerton and Amy Thornton."

Mrs McAdie covered her mouth with her hand. Magnus looked at McCord, aghast.

Kenneth McAdie jumped from his seat.

"Don't be ridiculous, I've never heard of that woman."

"That's interesting," McCord said. "You see, we all had assumed, even Europol, that Kaminski was a man, but her names can be used for both sexes, of course. What makes it even more interesting," he continued, seeing with gratification that McAdie was rattled, "is that we've got a message from you on her phone congratulating her on a job well done and promising the rest of the money today. Have you transferred the money yet? Because if you have, she has no use for it anymore."

McAdie straightened up, his face a well-practised blank but McCord could see his mind racing behind the calm façade.

"Ken, what is going on?" his wife demanded. "What is this man talking about?"

"I have no idea." He turned to McCord. "If you persist in spouting nonsense, I want to see my solicitor."

"Oh, I *am* going to persist. You see, Kaminski had her head blown off last night after taking Amy Thornton hostage, but thankfully her fingers were intact and allowed me to access her phone. I took the liberty of sending a message on her behalf, and you most obligingly replied. We have also established that payments from you to Kaminski coincide beautifully with the timing of the hit on Tait and Murales, where she did a much better job than yesterday. Bit of a shambles, really. I'm sure the papers will make a meal of it. Don't worry, you'll have twenty years at least to read all about it."

McAdie's eyes flashed, and McCord thought he might try to make a run for it.

"There is no point," he said. "Police everywhere. And when you call your solicitor, tell him that we did have a warrant for all our searches – in case he wants to try the same tactics that were so successful in getting you off in the London trial."

"So, what are we waiting for?" McAdie snarled. "We'll see who comes out on top in the end."

"We will," McCord agreed, "but first I have some business with your son."

Mrs McAdie, now panic-stricken, looked from the detective to her son, who had blanched.

"What do you want with him?" Kenneth McAdie demanded, and for the first time anxiety crept into his voice. "He has nothing to do with anything."

"Oh, he has everything to do with everything," McCord stated. "After all, everything you did, you did for him, isn't that right? You could have had such a nice retirement, and then Magnus goes and meddles with the local crime lord. Tried to step into Daddy's shoes, did we?" he said to Magnus. "But not quite up to it, were we?"

Magnus's face flushed in anger.

"And then you got unlucky because you almost knocked down a young woman, and instead of getting on with her life, she snoops around and digs up a nasty secret of yours, one you tried to escape from by changing your identity and moving to Edinburgh."

McAdie's face turned purple, while his son's turned as white as the sheets he was sitting on.

"Don't say anything," McAdie warned Magnus. "They have nothing on you. It's just that disturbed boy who has been persecuting you for years. They'll laugh him out of court if he tries it on."

"It actually doesn't matter what Magnus says. Maybe you're not quite aware of the latest developments, Mr McAdie," McCord interjected gleefully. "It so happens that Tristan only recently found the inner strength to go through his father's things, and what did he discover?"

McCord pulled out his phone and pressed a few buttons. "A receipt for a CCTV camera that his father had installed in the summerhouse a couple of days before that school-leaving party. I think Lord Foveran

237

was worried about hosting a party for forty or so young adults and suspected that it would be used for all sorts of shenanigans. The camera recorded Magnus handing Daniel Littlejohn a glass of vodka laced with enough speed to induce a heart attack, then writing a suicide note and leaving him there to die."

Mrs McAdie collapsed onto the chair, holding on to the edge of the bed to steady herself.

McCord played the recording and turned to Magnus, whose eyes flicked between the figures moving on the screen and his tormentor. His lips were trembling.

"Daniel panicked, didn't he, when he saw Fabian's shattered body on the ground?" McCord went on, mercilessly. "He threatened to tell the police that *you* had supplied the drugs; you just used him as a go-between. So, you called big Daddy to bail you out, as always, and he–"

"I *didn't*," Magnus said. "He would've gone mental and there was no time–"

"Shut up, you fool!" McAdie roared. He had leaned in to look more closely at the video. "The recording shows nothing but a hooded figure. It could be anybody!"

McCord put his phone away.

"Not quite," he said. "Forensics can determine the height of a person with only the slightest margin of error and I'm sure Magnus will turn out to be a perfect match. That alone might not have been enough for a conviction, but Magnus has kindly obliged us with a confession that I have just recorded in front of three witnesses."

He unbuttoned his shirt to reveal a wire and pushed back the curtain where the three police officers had been standing. "And," he added, "next time you write somebody else's suicide note, Magnus, check your spelling. Daniel was on a scholarship and would never have mixed up 'bear' and 'bare', which Emily, his girlfriend, spotted immediately. Sadly, nobody believed her at the time."

He turned to the two male officers. "Read them their rights and take them to the station."

Magnus's mother reached out to McCord, tears streaming down her face.

"Please, it can't be... not my boy as well!"

McCord nodded to the PC, who gently prised Mrs McAdie's fingers off McCord's hands and helped her to stand up.

"Mrs McAdie, please go with the officer. We also need a statement from you."

* * *

In the family room, he was greeted by five anxious faces.

"And?" Amy asked when he did not speak immediately.

"We've got them," McCord said. "Magnus was so keen to prove that he was not Daddy's little boy anymore that he gave himself away. He'll go down for a long time, as will his father."

He turned to Tristan and Emily.

"I hope you find peace now. It'll still be months or even years until the trials are over but at least you can get on with your lives."

Tristan shook his hand.

"Thank you," he said simply, but in those two words McCord heard all Tristan wanted to say.

Emily insisted on a hug that McCord awkwardly returned.

"Good luck with your degree. Well, Miss Thornton," McCord continued, turning to Amy. "It seems you've got yourself a story."

Amy nodded with her biggest smile.

"Tristan and Emily have agreed to give the *Forth Write* exclusive in-depth interviews about the whole affair."

"That should keep your magazine going for a while," McCord said to John, who also shook his hand.

"Thank you for everything."

Valerie stood there quietly and rather stiffly. She was still angry that McCord had used her daughter as bait and got her injured but felt a grudging gratitude that he had brought this whole business to such a satisfactory conclusion. McCord read the conflict in her face.

"I'm sorry that Amy was hurt. If you could keep your daughter out of my hair for the next few months or so, I'd be most grateful."

* * *

McCord politely declined the invitation to a celebratory brunch with them as the Super had left several messages urging him to hand in his preliminary report in time for the press briefing later that morning. On the way to the car park, he noticed a message alerting him to the sighting of a rose-coloured starling at St Abb's Head but that would have to wait until the next day. He texted his dad, telling him to watch the lunchtime news and suggesting a curry and a game of chess in the evening. Turning the key in the ignition and listening to the contented hum of the Juke's engine as if it were music, he drove towards St Leonard's.

List of characters

Police

Detective Inspector Russell McCord
Detective Sergeant Gavin Fraser
DI Stuart Marshall – Vice
DC Alan Struthers
Superintendent Gilchrist
DC Heather 'The Hacker' Sutton
PC Mike Turner
PC Surina Dharwan
DC Jeffries
DC Gillespie
DC Collins
DC Beveridge
DC Gill Morton – Vice
DI Giles – Met officer
Gertrude Westwater – retired Special Branch

Others

Amy Thornton – fashion journalist at the *Forth Write* magazine
Valerie Thornton – Amy's mother
Martin Eden – Amy's colleague
John Campbell – owner of *Forth Write*
Edith Campbell – John's mother
Lady Phoebe Smythe-Tennyson – John's friend

Dolly – madam at The Orchard
Candy – worker at The Orchard
Angus Adamson – pub owner
Norman (Norrie) Mitchell – pub manager
Fiona – nurse
Cathy – nurse
Professor Singh – doctor
Kenneth McAdie – member of London high society
Colleen McAdie – Kenneth's wife
Magnus McAdie – Kenneth's son
Mr Phillips – former associate of Kenneth McAdie
James Kilpatrick – Kingdom Country Club manager
Stephanie – receptionist
Miroslav – waiter
Archie Turnbull – sex trafficking criminal
Fergus Tait and Josh Murales – victims
Katz Kaminski – hired assassin
Fabian – victim
Tristan – Fabian's brother
Lord Foveran – Fabian's father
Lady Foveran – Fabian's mother
Mrs Pomfreys – the Foverans' neighbour
Mrs Linton – the Foverans' housekeeper
Daniel (Danny) Littlejohn – victim
Emily Fullerton – Daniel's girlfriend

If you enjoyed this book, please let others know by leaving a quick review on Amazon. Also, if you spot anything untoward in the paperback, get in touch. We strive for the best quality and appreciate reader feedback.

editor@thebookfolks.com

Also in this series

HIGH HAND (book 2)

When a man is killed after a shooting party on a Scottish country estate, DI McCord gets nowhere interviewing the arrogant landowners. He'll have to rely on information passed on by journalist Amy Thornton, who is more accustomed to high society. But will his class resentment colour his judgement when it comes to putting the murderer behind bars?

LAST TRAIN FOR MURDER (book 3)

An investigative journalist who made a career out of sticking it to the man dies on a train to Edinburgh, having been poisoned. DI Russell McCord struggles in the investigation after getting banned from contacting helpful but self-serving reporter Amy Thornton. But the latter is ready to go in, all guns blazing. After the smoke has cleared, what will remain standing?

SHIFTING ICE (book 4)

After a jewellery thief meets a bitter end, DI McCord tries to make sense of his dying words. Are they a clue to his killer? He'll find out. Meanwhile journalist Amy Thornton is forbidden from taking on dangerous investigations, and sent on a fool's errand. Hmmm. She'll wiggle out of just about anything. Except perhaps the place she might hold in the cop's heart.

BRIGHT SPARKS (book 5)

The death of a local businesswoman in a house fire has grumpy detective Russell McCord running around in circles looking for the culprit. Sassy journalist Amy Thornton has some ideas of her own. But when the smoke has cleared, can the two crime-solvers put their differences aside and their heads together to work out the truth?

All FREE with Kindle Unlimited and available in paperback and hardback from Amazon.

Other titles of interest

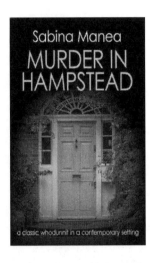

MURDER IN HAMPSTEAD by Sabina Manea

After ex-lawyer, now interior designer, Lucia Steer
accepts a job renovating a large London house, she has
no idea she'll discover the owner dead. Lucia is
determined to unlock the secret of this closed room
mystery, no matter the trouble she'll inevitably land in.

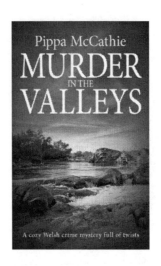

MURDER IN THE VALLEYS by Pippa McCathie

Having left the police following a corruption
investigation, ex-superintendent Fabia Havard is
struggling with civilian life. When a girl is murdered in
her town, she can't help trying to find the killer. Will her
former colleague Matt Lambert stop her, or realize the
value of his former boss to the floundering inquiry?

Made in the USA
Columbia, SC
22 November 2023

26956656R00152